TIME

MIKE DAVIS
Dark Raptures: A Consumers' Guide to the Destruction of Los Angeles
6

LUIS BUÑUEL
Why I Don't Wear a Watch
18

CHARLES RAY
1953... (PORTFOLIO)
23

JAMES TATE
Restless Leg Syndrome
35

JOHN KING
The Football Factory
38

JOSEPH LEASE
Two Poems
54

SPAIN
Libidinous Boulevards (PORTFOLIO)
57

TIMOTHY LIU
Two Poems
68

WILLIAM S. BURROUGHS / BRION GYSIN
Ports of Entry
70

ART CHARTS: TIMELINES BY ARTISTS
80

GRAND STREET   TIME

CPLY
The Evil I or The Story of My Life (PORTFOLIO)
89

ADAM LEFEVRE
Two Poems
99

JOHN SZARKOWSKI / HILTON ALS
Looking at Pictures
102

LYNN DAVIS
Stealing Time (PORTFOLIO)
122

GIORGIO MANGANELLI
From Centuria
132

CLAYTON ESHLEMAN
De Kooning's Woman I
144

ILYA KABAKOV
The Boat of My Life (PORTFOLIO)
147

KENNETH ROSEN
Death in March
155

NAGUIB MAHFOUZ
From Echoes of an Autobiography
156

ADONIS
The Time
166

ÉTIENNE-JULES MAREY
Chronophotographs (PORTFOLIO)
174

ANGELA KRAUSS
Currents
181

RICHARD MISRACH
Bravo 20 Bombing Range, Nevada (PORTFOLIO)
194

ERIN BELIEU
Nocturne: My Sister Life
204

GYÖRGY LIGETI
Le Grand Macabre, introduced by PETER SELLARS
206

NINA BERBEROVA
Roquenval (Chronicle of a Château)
215

CONTRIBUTORS
251

ILLUSTRATIONS
260

FRONT COVER AND TITLE PAGE Charles Ray, *Clock Man*, 1978. Wood, paint, and artist as clockworks, 30 x 30 x 54 in. Charles Ray on *Clock Man*, one of the large-scale representations of architectural references he worked on while at Rutgers University in the 1970s: "There were great blocks of time when I was bored . . . which led to this piece called *Clock Man*. There was a huge hall with a big clock that people looked at all the time. I built my own clock and took the other one down. I had these little controls in there that I could turn; so I tried to become a clock. I got in there in the morning and was going to get out at six in the evening. I didn't like it, I was miserable. And I made the mistake of lighting up a cigarette in there. It was excruciatingly boring. And during the day I became three hours fast, so what I thought was six was three in the afternoon."

BACK COVER Richard Misrach, *Unexploded Ordnance #3*, 1986.

"From *Centuria*" by Giorgio Manganelli. Copyright © 1995, Adelphi Edizioni.

"Currents" by Angela Krauss. Copyright © 1988, Aufbau Verlag Berlin und Weimar. Alle Rechte vorbehalten durch Suhrkamp Verlag, Frankfurt am Main.

"From *Echoes of an Autobiography*" by Naguib Mahfouz. Copyright © 1994, Naguib Mahfouz. English copyright © 1997 by American University in Cairo Press. To be published by Doubleday, New York.

"The Football Factory" by John King. Copyright © 1996, John King. Published by Jonathan Cape Ltd., London.

"Le Grand Macabre" by György Ligeti. Copyright © 1997, Schott Musik International, Mainz. All rights reserved. Used by permission of European American Music Distributors Corporation, sole U.S. and Canadian agent for Schott Musik International, Mainz.

"Roquenval (Chronicle of a Château)" by Nina Berberova is a translation of *Rokanval*. Copyright © 1991, Actes Sud.

Grand Street (ISSN 0734-5496; ISBN 1-885490-10-0) is published quarterly by Grand Street Press (a project of the New York Foundation for the Arts, Inc., a not-for-profit corporation), 131 Varick Street, Room 906, New York, NY 10013. Tel: (212) 807-6548, Fax: (212) 807-6544. Contributions and gifts to Grand Street Press are tax-deductible to the extent allowed by law. This publication is made possible, in part, by a grant from the New York State Council on the Arts.

Volume Fifteen, Number Three (*Grand Street* 59—Winter 1997). Copyright © 1996 by the New York Foundation for the Arts, Inc., Grand Street Press. All rights reserved. Reproduction, whether in whole or in part, without permission is strictly prohibited. Second-class postage paid at New York, NY and additional mailing offices. Postmaster: Please send address changes to Grand Street Subscription Service, Dept. GRS, P.O. Box 3000, Denville, NJ 07834. Subscriptions are $40 a year (four issues). Foreign subscriptions (including Canada) are $55 a year, payable in U.S. funds. Single-copy price is $12.95 ($18 in Canada). For subscription inquiries, please call (800) 807-6548.

Grand Street is printed by Hull Printing in Meriden, CT. It is distributed to the trade by D.A.P./Distributed Art Publishers, 155 Avenue of the Americas, New York, NY 10013, Tel: (212) 627-1999, Fax: (212) 627-9484, and to newsstands only by B. DeBoer, Inc., 113 E. Centre Street, Nutley, NJ 07110 and Fine Print Distributors, 6448 Highway 290 E., Austin, TX 78723. *Grand Street* is distributed in Australia and New Zealand by Peribo Pty, Ltd., 58 Beaumont Road, Mount Kuring-Gai, NSW 2080, Australia, Tel: (2) 457-0011, and in the United Kingdom by Central Books, 99 Wallis Road, London E9 5LN, Tel: (181) 986-4854.

GRAND STREET

EDITOR
Jean Stein

MANAGING EDITOR
Deborah Treisman

ART EDITOR
Walter Hopps

POETRY EDITOR
William Corbett

DESIGN
J. Abbott Miller, Luke Hayman, Paul Carlos
DESIGN/WRITING/RESEARCH, NEW YORK

ASSISTANT EDITOR
Julie A. Tate

ASSISTANT ART EDITOR
Anne Doran

ADMINISTRATIVE ASSISTANT
Lisa Brodus

INTERNS
Layla Hearth, Christina Persico

ADVISORY EDITORS
Hilton Als, Edward W. Said

CONTRIBUTING EDITORS
Dominique Bourgois, Colin de Land, Mike Davis
Raymond Foye, Jonathan Galassi, Stephen Graham
Dennis Hopper, Hudson, Jane Kramer
Erik Rieselbach, Jeremy Treglown, Katrina vanden Heuvel
Wendy vanden Heuvel, John Waters, Drenka Willen

FOUNDING CONTRIBUTING EDITOR
Andrew Kopkind (1935–1994)

PUBLISHERS
Jean Stein & Torsten Wiesel

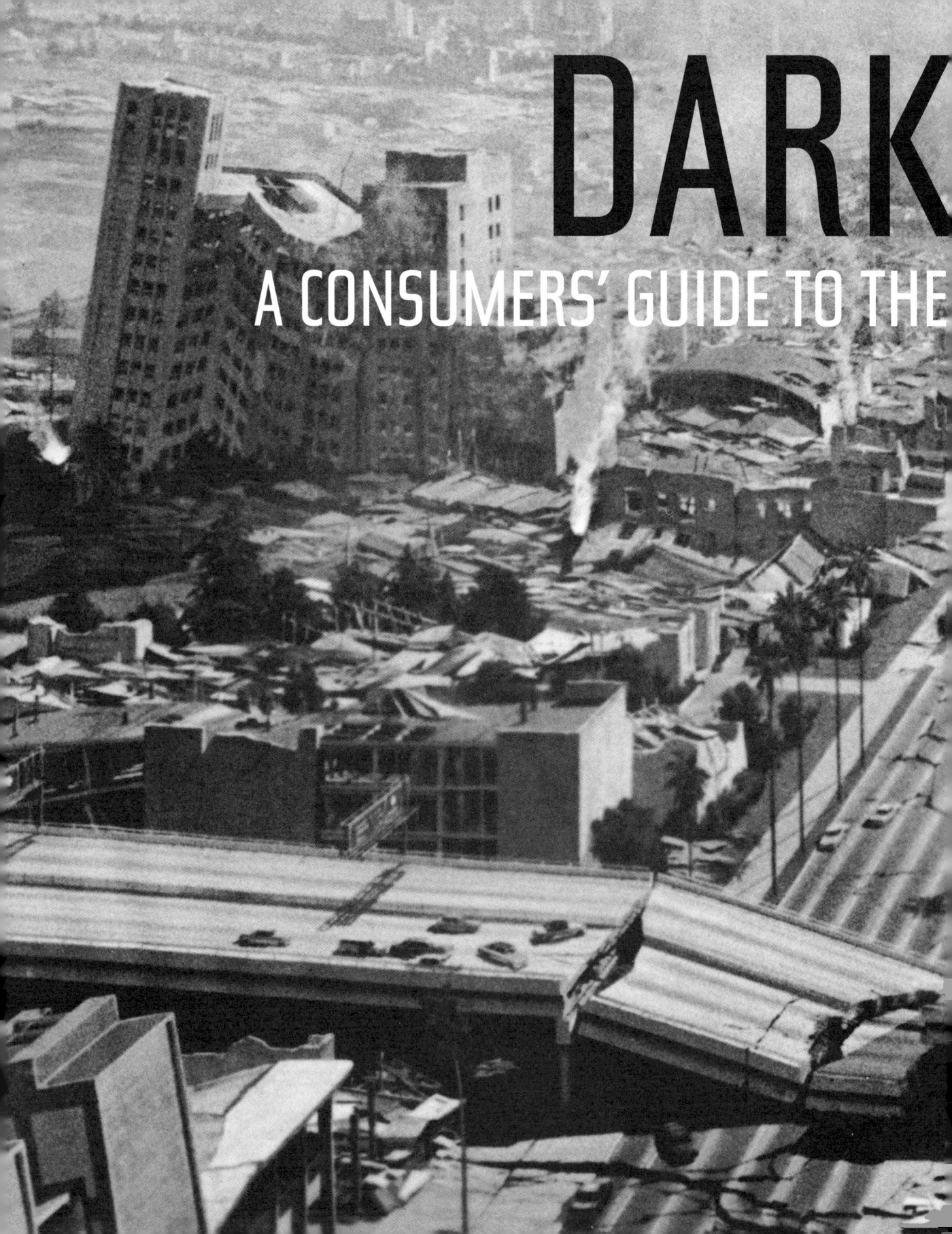

DARK
A CONSUMERS' GUIDE TO THE

RAPTURES
DESTRUCTION OF LOS ANGELES
BY MIKE DAVIS

> "City of Angels trembling with Lust. City of Angels destined to dust."
> Clarence Winchester, *Earthquake in Los Angeles and Other Poems* (1938)

A swelteringly hot day in Los Angeles, 1962. A pretty girl ("she reminded him of well water and farm breakfasts") is absentmindedly taking off her clothes at a bus stop. The corner newsboy gawks delightedly, but most passersby simply glance nervously and continue on their way. A nerdish mathematician named Potiphar Breen finally comes to the rescue. As he wraps his coat around her, he explains that she is the victim of a strange epidemic of involuntary nudism known as the "Gypsy Rose Syndrome."

It is a small omen of the approaching chaos. Breen has discovered that Los Angeles is the global epicenter of a sinister convergence of pathological trends. All the warning lights have started to flash in unison: the mercury soars, skies darken, dams creak, faults strain, and politicians wave rockets. Then, despite an epic drought, suburbanites are gripped by the death wish to water their lawns: "The Metropolitan Water district commissioners tried to stop it. It fell between the stools of the police powers of fifty 'sovereign cities.' The taps remained open, trickling away the lifeblood of the desert paradise."

The drought is quickly followed by flood, earthquake, nuclear war, plague, a Communist invasion, and the reemergence of Atlantis. Breen hides out in the San Gabriel Mountains with his new girlfriend, amusing himself by shooting the odd Soviet paratrooper or two. Then, just when the worst seems to be over, he notices an unusually large sunspot. The sun has begun to die....

So ends Robert Heinlein's tongue-in-cheek story, *The Year of the Jackpot* (1952). In crowning Los Angeles doom capital of the universe, Heinlein cannily anticipated the cornucopia of disaster to follow. The destruction of Los Angeles has been the central theme or dominating image in more than a hundred and fifty novels, short stories, and films. Moreover, since 1960, the city and its suburbs have been punctually destroyed an average of three times per year, with the rate dramatically accelerating in the 1990s.

> "As we drove down the empty streets, I saw ruins and dust where houses were and, among the powdery debris of stucco all in mounds, the rusted antennae of television sets like the bones of awful beasts whose vague but terrible proportions will alone survive to attract the unborn stranger's eye."
> Gore Vidal, *Messiah* (1954)

Since last summer, for example, Los Angeles has been parboiled by aliens (*Independence Day*), reduced to barbarism by mega-earthquakes (*Escape from L.A.* and *The Crow: City of Angels*), and transformed into a postmodern Pompeii (*Volcano*)—all to the sheer delight of millions of viewers. No other city seems to excite such dark rapture. The entire world seems to be rooting for

Los Angeles to slide into the Pacific or be swallowed up by the San Andreas.

Some of these conflagrations are just doom-laden slapstick; others are obvious expressions of racial hysteria. For true connoisseurs I offer the following guide to some of the stranger L.A. apocalypses.

"Do you realize that Los Angeles stands zero chance of surviving as the Elysian Park Fault fissures up the whole city, dropping entire blocks miles down into the ground, never to be seen again?"
Arthur C. Clarke and Mike McQuay, *Richter 10* (1996)

THE VALOR OF IGNORANCE
BY HOMER LEA (1909)

L.A. disaster fiction is inaugurated, not with an earthquake or flood, but with this lurid account of the Japanese invasion of Southern California. Lea, a Chinese-speaking adventurer who commanded a ragtag army during the Boxer Rebellion, was obsessed with the Japanese threat to the West Coast. Los Angeles, he argued, was utterly defenseless. "One regiment can occupy the city with impunity."

In his fictional account, the Japanese armada, having already conquered Hawaii and the Pacific Northwest, feints at the "worthless" fortifications in San Pedro, then lands unopposed in Santa Monica. Los Angeles falls the next day, precipitating a chain of events that leads to Japanese world supremacy and a military monarchy in the eastern United States.

INVASION!
BY WHITMAN CHAMBERS (1943)

Shortly after Pearl Harbor, when invasion hysteria was at its height, Lea's book was reissued (with a new introduction by Clare Booth Luce), stimulating a hack writer named Whitman Chambers to fill in the grisly details. In his version, a Japanese airborne landing in Santa Monica is accompanied by incendiary and poison-gas bombardment that reduces much of L.A. to stucco rubble.

A small group of civilian and military survivors, hiding in a Westlake storm drain, are transformed into guerrilla warriors by Happy McGonigle, a middle-aged "newsboy" who delights in killing the Japanese (who are portrayed as apes or insects) with his bare hands.

McGonigle's band find their ultimate revenge at the battle-scarred corner of Alvarado Street and Glendale Boulevard, where they surprise a platoon of Japanese soldiers eating oranges (a particularly obscene image to Chambers). Happy delegates the slaughter of the prisoners to a Jewish GI named Abe, while the rest of the band debates the tactics of total race war against the invaders.

"On the beaches corpses were being tossed by the waves, corpses that had come drifting down from the foothills..."

Rupert Hughes, *City of Angels* (1941)

THE SECRET POWER: A ROMANCE OF THE TIME
BY MARIE CORRELLI (1921)

Long before the Manhattan Project, romance novelist Marie Correlli used an atomic explosion (first conceived by H. G. Wells in 1912) to decimate Los Angeles. In her incomparably strange story, Roger Seaton, the world's foremost physicist and a self-proclaimed Nietzschean superman, lives reclusively in a cabin in the San Gabriel Mountains, where he tinkers with his homemade atomic bomb and nurses a broken heart.

He has been jilted by Morgana Royal, "a modern Cleopatra," who, aside from being the richest woman in the world, is also the "second most brilliant theorist of the future development of radioactivity." When not engaged in telepathic conversations with the inhabitants of a mysterious desert city, she tools around the world in her great airship, the White Eagle, which is powered by "throbbing atomic disks."

On one of these jaunts, she visits Roger and meets Manella Sorisa, a dark-eyed Spanish beauty who is smoldering with unrequited passion for Roger. The women immediately develop a sisterly solidarity. A few weeks later, Manella surprises Roger in his cave laboratory while he is playing with atomic toys. He drops the bomb.

The resulting explosion sets off a gigantic earthquake that devastates the Los Angeles area, killing most of its inhabitants. Morgana, however, flies over Sicily (where she cohabits a castle with a flirtatious priest) and retrieves the bodies of Roger and Manella. Radioactivity restores Manella to miraculous health, but Roger is left as a helpless infant, confined to bed and incessantly muttering, "I am the master of the world."

Both Manella and Morgana are delighted with the scope this situation affords their maternal instincts. Manella marries Roger, while Morgana flies off to her Brazen City in the Sahara. In her last telepathic message, she declares: "'Masters of the World' are poor creatures at best... but the secret makers of the New Race are the gods of the Future!"

THE FLUTTER OF AN EYELID
BY MYRON BRINIG (1933)

Kooky religious cults and (un)natural disasters are pea and pod in L.A. fiction. The original equation was made by Brinig in this savage satire of Southern California's cultural and religious peripheries.

Caslon Roanoke, Harvard man and esteemed historical novelist, is suffering from an acute case of Puritan gloom when his doctor orders him out to Los Angeles for sunshine and recreation. He is instantly seduced by the fluttering eyelids of Sylvia Prowse whom he meets at a cocktail party in the libertine beach colony of Alta Vista.

"'And you?' he dared to address her at last, 'What do you do?'

"'I give and receive pain,' she said.

"'Ah, that's interesting,' said Caslon, already in pain."

After this typically L.A. introduction and a skinny-dip in the Pacific with Sylvia (where he marvels at his first erection in years), Caslon becomes a full-fledged member of a Bohemian clique that includes the famous revivalist Angela Flower—a thinly disguised Aimee Semple McPherson. When Angela is not healing the blind and lame at her Ten Million Dollar Heavenly Temple, she is prowling Alta Vista for 'love mean' to feed her voracious sexual appetite.

On one of these expeditions, she beds a handsome but dim-witted sailor (Milton) who is a dead ringer for a Nordic Jesus. Grooming him to respond on demand with Christ-like injunctions, Angela goes on radio to announce the Second Coming in downtown Los Angeles.

For a while, Jesus (who becomes a fervent L.A. booster and movie fan) is more popular than Valentino or Lindbergh, but gradually the novelty fades, and jaded listeners begin to turn their dials "to a different station, a dance orchestra, a comedy sketch, a talk on beauty preparations."

In a desperate attempt to revive Christ's flagging popularity, Angela convinces him to walk on the waves at Venice Beach. Milton defies gravity for a few moments until he sees Sylvia swimming by in the nude. Her fluttering eyelids break the trance and he sinks like a stone.

Thousands of his disconsolate followers then drown themselves in the sea, severely reducing the advertising revenue for Angela's radio show.

Milton's death opens the door to further tragedies and occult occurences, all of which are prefigured as self-fulfilling prophecy in the novel Caslon is writing about Alta Vista. Recognizing that the end is nigh, he retreats to Boston on the eve of a cataclysmic earthquake. For the first time in pulp fiction, all of the Southland "slides swiftly, relentlessly, into the Pacific Ocean."

"Los Angeles tobogganed with almost one continuous movement into the water, the shore cities going first, followed by the inland communities; the business streets, the buildings, the motion-picture studios in Hollywood where actors became stark and pallid under their mustard-colored makeup."

"Take any boulevard and in the fourth bungalow on the right they'll be busy raising the dead or talking things over with Dante and Shakespeare."
J. B. Priestley, *The Doomsday Men* (1938)

GREENER THAN YOU THINK
BY WARD MOORE (1947)

This is about the lawn that ate Hollywood.

Albert Weener is a huckster, down on his luck,

but convinced that he possesses messianic sales ability. An obscure want ad introduces him to Josephine Spencer Francis, the inventor of "Metamorphizer," a super-fertilizer that allows plants to metabolize virtually anything.

Francis wants to end hunger by turning wastelands into grainbelts, but Weener is only interested in his commission. Ignoring her complaint about "imbeciles [who] grow grass in a desert," he peddles her formula door-to-door as a miracle cure for tired lawns.

His first and only customers, in a dowdy section of Hollywood, are the Dinkmans. Once Meta stimulates an insatiable appetite in their Bermuda grass, Los Angeles, and eventually the world, are doomed. In the futile war against the Dinkmans' lawn, mowers are replaced by sickles, then by flamethrowers and tanks, and eventually by atomic bombs.

But all the explosive energy expended against the devil grass merely increases the fervor with which its green tentacles engorge the city: "Out through Cahuenga Pass it flowed, toward the fertile San Fernando Valley. Steadily it climbed to the hilltops, masticating sage, greasewood, oak, sycamore, and manzanita with the same ease that it bolted down houses and pavements. Into Griffith Park it swaggered, mumbling the planetarium, Mount Hollywood, and Fern Dell in successive mouthfuls, and swarmed down to the concrete-lined bed of the Los Angeles River. Here ineffectual shallow pools had preserved illusion and given tourists something to laugh at in the dry season; the weed licked them up like a thirsty cow at wallow."

It is left to *Time* magazine to announce the official obituary: "Death, as it must to all, came last week to Los Angeles. The metropolis of the Southwest died gracelessly, undignifiedly . . . swallowed up, Jonah-wise, by the advance of the terrifying Bermuda grass."

THE DAY THEY H-BOMBED LOS ANGELES
BY ROBERT MOORE WILLIAMS (1961)
AND MIRACLE MILE
A FILM BY STEVE DE JARNATT (1988)

Atomic bombs fell like rain on Los Angeles during the Cold War decades. Of the thirty-six novels and films that depict the nuclear destruction of the land of Sunshine, two stand out for their sheer eccentricity.

In Robert Moore Williams's 1961 novel, stunned survivors emerge from a San Pedro bomb shelter to discover that it is not the "dirty commies," but the Pentagon that has nuked Los Angeles. The reason: to destroy the giant mutant protein molecules (the result of American H-bomb testing in the South Pacific) that are turning the population into flesh-eating zombies. The patriotic survivalists, led by an FBI agent and a tough ex-Marine, exterminate vast multitudes of the undead in heroic hand-to-hand combat.

The novel's most poignant scene occurs when a "bullet knocks a molecule out of control" [sic] and allows a dying zombie to briefly regain his humanity. "This is the human part of me talking," Eric Bloor's whisper came again. "This is the kid you once knew; the kid who was scared of a pet poodle, the kid who had to whistle to find the courage to pass a cemetery at night...."

Miracle Mile finds both black humor and true love at ground zero. Until the ICBMs come arching over the Hollywood sign, it is not clear whether nuclear war is really imminent or Los Angeles has simply been unhinged by rumor. The city is so close to its ultimate boiling point that the nukes are almost superfluous. Yet, even on the last shopping day in the history of the world, romance manages to brighten the face of extinction. As the doomed lovers, Harry and Julie, slowly sink into the La Brea Tarpits, they find consolation in the prospect that "we will metamorphosize together."

"The saga of the Donner Party was well remembered as bits and pieces of news filtered in from the Palmdale/Lancaster area. The reports shocked and astounded all those who heard them. The people—maddened by hunger, determined to survive at any cost—had been driven to cannibalism."
Thom Racina, *The Great Los Angeles Blizzard* (1977)

THE TURNER DIARIES
BY ANDREW MacDONALD (1978)

This piece of neo-Nazi excrement, which Timothy McVeigh and other Aryan warriors call their bible, focuses on the ethnic cleansing of Los Angeles. After a federal crackdown on gun owners, the Organization launches a guerrilla war to rid the earth of Jews and non-whites. Taking advantage of the chaos created by terrorist bombings and race riots, the militias conquer Los Angeles and exterminate or drive out all people of color. They also hang 60,000 suspected white "race traitors." In retaliation, "Jews plot the nuclear destruction of California...."

The Turner Diaries invert the terms of the traditional racist apocalypse: instead of Los Angeles being the WASP sanctum threatened by yellow, brown, or red hordes, it is now a largely non-white "cancer" that the new Nazis must annihilate. MacDonald says out loud what many survivalist novels and *Terminator*-type movies imply: the destruction of post-Anglo Los Angeles would be no great loss to the Aryan Nation.

> "No need for rockets to wreck it, or another ice age to freeze it, or a huge earthquake to crack it off and dump it in the Pacific. It will die of overextension. It will die because its taproots have dried up the brashness and greed which have been its only strength."
>
> Christopher Isherwood, *A Single Man* (1964)

THE END OF THE AGE
BY PAT ROBERTSON (1995)

In Rev. Robertson's novel, God more or less flushes Los Angeles down the toilet with a mile-high tsunami generated by the impact of a "giant meteor." (Robertson apparently doesn't know the difference between a meteor and an asteroid.) The sole survivors of this holocaust are a family of Chicano fundamentalists hiding in trenches on the top of Mt. Wilson. This opening scenario is directly purloined from the 1977 potboiler, *Lucifer's Hammer*, by Larry Niven and Jerry Pournelle, but Robertson adds a few Old Testament touches of his own, like blazing crude oil on the top of the tsunami. (Niven and Pournelle, on the other hand, include more local color, like the stoked surfer who rides the doomsday wave inland until he—splat!—collides with the upper floor of a Westside skyscraper.)

In the end, divine genocide against Southern California is simply a neat way to clear the decks for the real action: righteous Texas Protestants battling Satan (now President of the United States) and his minions (a billion Indians, Pakistanis, Persians, and Arabs) in a wide-screen version of the Book of Revelations.

Ultimately, one of Robertson's square-jawed heroes, former Defense Secretary Al Augustus, gets to dis the Devil in person: "'Listen to me, you snake-headed freak,' he shouted.... 'You've been a loser from the very beginning. Jesus Christ is the winner, and I'm on His team. And, just for the record, I have eighteen Poseidon missiles aimed at the heart of Babylon at this minute....'"

APE AND ESSENCE
BY ALDOUS HUXLEY (1948)

"Catastrophes? Armaggedon? Last Days? My brother-in-law in the Valley can get them for you wholesale." The real imaginative challenge is what remains after the waves have swallowed Santa Monica, and the flames have reduced City Hall to its ferro-concrete skeleton.

Ape and Essence was conceived, according to a biographer, "at the end of a long, dark corridor" in Huxley's life, marked by his growing nausea with Hollywood, the death of his hero Gandhi, and the inception of the nuclear dark age.

Huxley caricatures himself as the once idealistic, now jaded screenwriter who becomes obsessed with a mysterious script that falls off the back of a studio garbage truck. The screenplay opens in February 2108, several generations after World War Three has scourged the planet, with the sole exceptions of central Africa and the antipodes.

Scientists from the New Zealand Re-Discovery Expedition to North America make landfall at a desolate beach once called Santa Monica. Los Angeles ("more brassieres than Buffalo, more deodorants than Denver, more oranges than anywhere") is a vast concrete ruin besieged by desert winds and shifting sand dunes. The few thousand survivors of all-out atomic and bacteriological war face slow but inevitable extinction from genetic damage and birth defects. Rather logically, they have accepted that history is fundamentally evil and now worship Belial, the Lord of the Flies.

The Biltmore Hotel's coffee shops and bars have become busy workshops where women weave on primitive looms and men craft human bones into drinking cups and flutes. Pitiful mothers with monster babies wait in the main lobby. On Belial Day, the babies will be sacrificed in the Coliseum as prologue to the annual two-week-long public mating season. (For the rest of the year, women wear handsewn NO!s across their chests and thighs.)

"The mayor stared a moment at the banks of TV screens. ... 'Look, boys, this is a pretty fritzy city to begin with. It wouldn't take much to panic the whole number right off its nut. *Firestorm?* Why not tell them the San Andy Fault just decided to split its gut?'"
Edward Stewart, *The Great Los Angeles Fire* (1980)

One of the New Zealanders, the shy but handsome botanist Poole, is captured and brought to Hollywood Cemetery where survivors are preoccupied with digging up graves for jewels and clothes. ("Except for a greenish discoloration around the toes, the stockings are in perfect condition.") He is eventually granted an audience with "His Eminence, the Arch Vicar of Belial, Lord of the Earth, Primate of California, Servant of the Proletariat and Bishop of Hollywood," who reigns in Pershing Square—"still the hub and center of the city's cultural life."

As the Bishop of Hollywood explains to the good Anglican Poole, none of this is deliberate cruelty, only the desperate eugenics of a genetically doomed society. Impressed by Poole's botanical expertise and, especially, his knowledge of irrigation (the L.A. Aqueduct was blown up during the war), the Bishop offers him the honor of castration and membership in the ruling priesthood.

Poole, of course, abdicates his larger social responsibility, and, instead, absconds with a beautiful girl (one of the small minority whose hormones still operate 365 days per year). On a clear moonlit night they leave behind the "cozy bourgeois ruins" of Los Angeles and begin a long journey over the rugged San Gabriel Mountains, stopping only to peel a hard-boiled egg over the grave of William Tallis (the mysterious author of *Ape and Essence*). They are the first of many to escape from L.A.

"With incredible speed, the city of Los Angeles virtually disintegrates. The earth tilts and is torn apart, creating crevasses that swallow hundreds of screaming men and women. High buildings crumble into rubble and dust. Elevated freeways collapse, dropping cars and trucks to destruction below."

from the *Earthquake* screenplay (1975)

Why I Don't

LUIS BUÑUEL

Wear a Watch

I was writing a letter of no importance, so what I am about to relate was not a suggestion produced by an altered state of consciousness, nor need it have been a dream, since a few moments earlier I had been hunting down an impertinent fly that was bothering me incessantly by speaking into my ear—like those old deaf people who whisper, low and laboriously, insufferable things—and on the day after my adventure I found its corpse in a coffin formed by the lid of the inkwell.

So, there I was, writing. Suddenly I heard nearby a ticktock louder than the others, announced by the only object worthy of attention; to my amazement, I found myself face to face with a being more strange than imagination could create.

It had two legs, one of lead and the other a quill; the body took the shape of a rusty steel rod, and the head was nothing more than a gilded brass disk with an uneven mustache in the form of two arrows and two minuscule crowns for eyes, like the kind used to wind wristwatches. Everything about him demonstrated a truly intolerable air of affectation and vanity.

Astonished, but no less offended, I questioned him: "Would you mind telling me why you have entered my room without having had the decency to knock?"

The extravagant mannequin wasn't flustered by my gruffness, and replied very casually: "You've been hanging around with me since the day you were born, Mr. Upstart, and until now you've never deigned to ask me such questions."

Irritated by his contemptuous tone, I said, "Mind your tongue, and don't call me Mr. Upstart, since I have other titles that are much more honorific"—and to prove it I was about to take documents that authorize them from my desk.

"Calm yourself, young man," he told me. "I am older than you could possibly dream, and my age permits me to speak to you in this authoritarian tone."

"Well, then, who are you?"

"I am Time."

A perfect Oh! of stupefaction drew a circle on my mouth. But he hastened to continue: "Don't be frightened. After all, I only materialized in this form out of pure sympathy for you. More important, I wish to make revelations that perhaps might interest you."

At that, he settled comfortably onto a cushion. In further astonishment, I saw the alarm clock and the clock on the wall remove themselves from their places and hightail it down to tick at his feet. Then there wasn't room for the slightest doubt that this was indeed Time himself to whom I was talking. Now I will transcribe his story in its entirety.

Here is what he said: "My friend, tonight I have undertaken a bold gesture. I myself have annulled several hours of my Eternity.

"No one but you will know that nothing will have aged while it remained here, and that all else that exists will have disappeared. But I am going to speak to you about my life. Everything about me can be divided into two periods: before the invention of clocks, and from then until now. My first era glided along in joyful frolicking with my brother Space everywhere we ruled in the Universe. We had a great time, upon my soul! and only one tiny cloud ruffled our existence. It was something of a gastronomic nature. Believe me, there wasn't a single kitchen, not one restaurant, not even a pasture. A complete lack of nourishment is what drove me to devour my children as soon as they were born. Later I saw myself portrayed as a monstrous and ferocious old man, driven by egotism and evil instincts. Moreover, I solemnly swear"—as he said this, his pendulum swung gracefully across his stomach—"that all of these so-called crimes were committed only to satisfy my appetite. On the other hand, eating one's children belongs to a code of ethics that was very fashionable some five or six thousand years ago."

He said five or six thousand years like someone might say three or four days.

"But, my friend, ever since the first clock appeared"—and his rather erect and martial mustaches now marked 7 and 25—"there hasn't been a moment's rest for me. I must multiply myself, raise myself to the nth power to be able to run every clock in existence. You yourself will have observed that I can't always keep up with so much work, and when that happens my enemies are in the habit of falling silent. The agitation has been excessive for at least a few centuries, despite which you will sometimes hear and even read, 'Time passes tranquilly . . .' 'Time quietly promises. . . .' But believe me, these are nothing more than lies and foolishness, to which you should pay no attention."

At this point, a slight throat irritation struck

him, and he coughed 8:00. Scarcely able to ticktock amidst the jubilant barking of my two clocks, which were also chiming 8:00, he went on: "I see here you have a portrait of that half-wit Einstein. Experience has armored me against insults, but the offense of relativity has grieved me above all others. As if the falsehoods raised against me weren't already enough, it turns out I'm the gossip of the whole world, thanks to this depraved person."

Suddenly his body began to lengthen inordinately. I swung around anxiously in my chair upon seeing a new prodigy in that phantasmagorical night. Time had stretched himself out of all proportion.

"Don't worry," he told me, already completely calm, "in a moment I'll finish and be gone. But I'm not leaving without first helping you in the best way possible. In a moment, when age moves to catch you with his trembling claws, it is I who will stop him and keep you eternally young."

"Thanks, but no thanks," I replied quickly. "I want my time to come like everyone else."

"You're a sensible man," he answered. "If you refuse this, then I will count you among my beloved children, and favor you as I do them."

"I would like to know who my brothers are going to be."

"Well, by God! Your brothers will be watch thieves and swindlers, because they do a lot to lighten my task by making those little instruments that for me are the most bothersome because they exist in the largest quantity, disappear from pockets. Lazy people are also my children, for they use me in moderation. My children are—"

"Don't go on," I said abruptly. "You want to throw me in with swindlers, with idlers? Under no circumstances will I accept your favors."

"You're an inexperienced young man, far too ingenuous. Open your eyes to the fact that they are the ones who have lived best, along with the many others I was about to cite. If you were an artist, you would love, for example, just a few hours of tedium, my favorite son."

"I'm beginning to see that your most beloved children are the traits most discredited among men. You're proving to me to be a vagrant, unscrupulous, selfish being."

Time was threatening to storm. His minute and hour hands became angry. He struck 8:30 in such a menacing way that I began to feel genuine fear.

"Enough, young man. Since you disdain my favors, you will suffer my disfavor. In the meantime, within two days you will be left without clocks." Having said this, he suddenly disappeared.

And his curse was fulfilled, for not two days had passed after my adventure, when I found myself without a dime and had to pawn my two dear clocks.

What's more, I was to suffer a constant obsession. Every clock I ran into glared at me threateningly, their hands bristled with wrath. Others, when I wanted to apprise myself of the hour, were out of order, spinning mockingly.

Because of this, I bought myself an hourglass and placed it on the table. But then the vengefulness of Time was bloodier still. I don't know what he did with it, but the fact is, its slender waist, a waist as thin as a needle, widened little by little until it allowed the sand to pass in thick streams.

Then I came to detest that poor, plump hourglass, which after all was not responsible for its disgrace, and one day I threw it out the window, like those intolerant masters of the house who cast out a maid who slips up.

Since then, I have resigned myself to getting by without a watch, which has caused me to lose some very good friends by missing our meetings.

Translated from the Spanish by Garrett White

I THOUGHT ABOUT THE SLIGHT AGING OF MY BODY BETWEEN SELF-PORTRAITS AND WORK THAT USED MY BODY AS A SCULPTURAL ELEMENT AS A DELICATE WAY OF GAUGING TIME. THE THREE SCULPTURES I HAVE INCLUDED WITHOUT MY IMAGE, I THINK, AGE OR PASS THROUGH TIME MIRRORING THE VARYING STATES OF MIND AND BODY OF THESE PORTRAITS.

CHARLES RAY
1953....

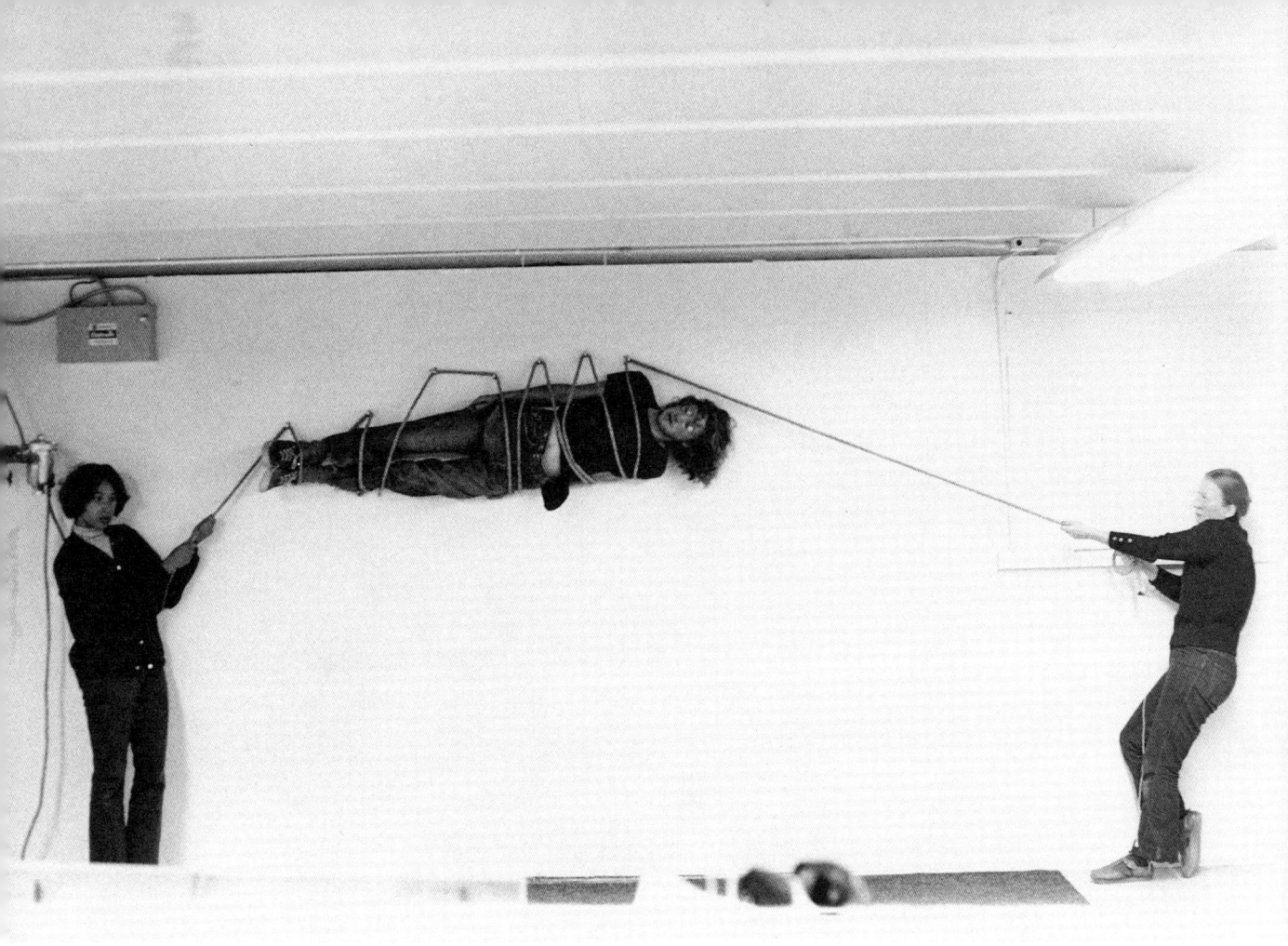

ABOVE *Untitled*, 1973. Artist, rope, wall, dimensions variable.
RIGHT *Shelf*, 1981. Artist, steel shelf, found objects, gray enamel, 71 x 78 x 10 in.

ABOVE *Ink Line*, 1987. Free-flowing printer's ink, circulating pump, dimensions variable.

RIGHT *Self-Portrait Mannequin*, 1990. Standard fiberglass mannequin body with cast of artist's head, 73 x 24 x 22 in.

PAGE 28   *7 1/2 Ton Cube*, 1990. Solid-steel cube, white automotive lacquer, 36 x 36 x 36 in.
PAGE 29   *Yes*, 1990. Convex framed portrait on convex wall, dimensions variable.
LEFT   *Fall '91*, 1991. Enlarged fabricated mannequin, clothing, accoutrements, 96 x 36 x 28 in.
ABOVE   *Puzzle Bottle*, 1995. Glass bottle, assembled wood figure, paint, 13 1/2 x 4 x 4 in.

Poster, 1994. Color photo of the artist and his boat, 39 1/4 x 27 7/16 in.

AN INTERVIEW WITH
CHARLES RAY

DENNIS COOPER: Let's start with *Rotating Circle*, your inclusion in the 1989 Whitney Biennial. I don't know if it was your idea, but that little protective barrier that someone erected in front of it . . . well, first it annoyed me. If museum-goers' hair got tangled in the work, big deal. But then I realized that it gave the piece this weird pretentious quality which made it even more of a double agent. It seemed "friendly" to the elitist Biennial at first glance, but the longer you looked, the more it became the exhibition's total enemy, a bona fide art-world Antichrist. Did you ever see Herzog's film *Aguirre, the Wrath of God?*

CHARLES RAY: No, why?

COOPER: Well, it's not worth recounting the plot in detail, but eventually these explorers who've spent the movie searching the Peruvian jungle for treasure are trapped forever—that's the implication—on a raft in a whirlpool in the middle of the Amazon River. Weird as it may sound, your disk suggests a similar narrative, but with conceptual artists in place of explorers. Warholian fame and power in place of treasure, and a museum—or a gallery—in place of the Amazon River.

RAY: Hmm. Well, sure. Why not? If the piece produces hallucinations, great.

COOPER: Well, it is shaped like a pill. Actually, it's more like a placebo, I guess.

RAY: Placebos are physically identical to the pills they're substituting for. That's their beauty.

COOPER: In any case, I really felt like I was on downers looking at it, the disk. It seemed so . . . nothing, so simplistically hypnotic. Still it must have lodged in my unconscious because about an hour later I started picturing all these round white things—ice rinks, Baldessari's dot paintings, wedding cakes, eyeballs, all in a kind of rush. Peculiar. I had to lie down. Am I way off base?

RAY: What drugs do is redesign the world a little. Not too much, just enough to make you realize how fascinating your surroundings could be if you really paid attention. And drugs never let you forget for a moment how much preexisting information you have to ignore in order to believe your life is significant.

COOPER: You could be describing your work.

RAY: Hmm. Let me tell you a little story, Dennis. When I was a kid, I was hit on the head by a falling timber at this construction site where I was playing. It made me lose my memory and I wandered off aimlessly into the city. I didn't mind not knowing who I was, and the fact that everything looked as vaguely familiar as everything else fascinated me. I walked for, oh, about two days, begging for money, eating garbage, shitting in bushes. Eventually I came to a small marina. The ocean looked so beautiful that I asked this rich old couple if I could be their cabin boy. They said, "Sure." I don't know why, except that I was supposedly an angelic child. At my insistence, we set off for the Arctic, a place that has always fascinated me. They were a nice couple but really boring. Since I had no history or ideas of my own, I was obliged to listen to tales of theirs all day every day. And having no value system, I thought all their stories of cocktail parties and backaches and summer homes were just fantastic. I couldn't get enough. The second week at sea the yacht developed engine trouble and we had to be rescued by the Coast Guard. That night in a hotel room somewhere in Canada I woke up in a sweat and remembered everything about my life up to the moment I was struck on the head, but nothing after. I couldn't figure out who these naked old people were on either side of me. So I got dressed and tiptoed downstairs to the lobby and asked someone to phone my parents, who flew out to get me. Years later I was standing naked in a gallery doing one of my shelf/body pieces when I heard a very familiar voice and opened my eyes a crack. It was the woman. Somehow she'd found me, and, after gallery hours were over, we met at a nearby restaurant. Over dinner she happily filled in that two-week-long blank in my memory with tales of our time at sea.

COOPER: Wow, so that explains your interest in duplicity, hidden agendas, incompletion, etc. So is the story true?

RAY: What's the difference? Yeah, it's true.

COOPER: I wasn't going to do this, I don't know why. Politeness, nerves . . . but I have these young friends who listen to bands like, uh, Christian Death, Haunted Garage, My Life With the Thrill Kill Kult. They love your work with this incredible passion, because they think it's art that could only come about at the end of the world. They think it's this nihilistic wink from humanity's deathbed, or pieces from Satan's toy chest . . . something like that. And they besieged me to ask you some questions for them. Maybe I could finish the interview with their questions. Is that okay?

RAY: Definitely.

COOPER: Okay, first: "If you were going to kill yourself, how would you do it?"

RAY: Hmm. Well, I understand there's a book available from some small publishing house in, I think, Seattle that explains how a human head can be kept alive *sans* body. Maybe I'd like to have my head cut off and kept alive for a while, assuming, that is, that the head could still think and see and speak and so on. When that state of affairs got boring, if it ever did, I don't know . . . I'd let those death-rock kids decide what to do with it.

COOPER: Another: "You have to kill somebody. Who?"

RAY: You don't know him. He's not famous.

COOPER: An artist? In the art world?

RAY: No. Yes.

COOPER: One last question from the kids: "You're in a white room with no doors or windows. It's completely empty and silent. You don't know how you got there. You don't know how to get out. So, how do you feel?"

RAY: I feel like I'm at one of my openings.

JAMES TATE

RESTLESS LEG SYNDROME

After the burial
we returned to our units
and assumed our poses.
Our posture was the new posture
and not the old sick posture.
When we left our stations
it was just to prove we could,
not a serious departure
or a search for yet another beginning.
We were done with all that.
We were settled in, as they say,
though it might have been otherwise.
What a story!
After the burial we returned to our units
and here is where I am experiencing
that leg-kicking syndrome thing.
My leg, for no apparent reason,
flies around the room kicking stuff,
well, whatever is in its way,
like a screen or a watering can.
Those are just two examples
and indeed I could give many more.

I could construct a catalogue
of the things it kicks,
perhaps I will do that later.
We'll just have to see if it's really wanted.
Or I could do a little now
and then return to listing later.
It kicked the scrimshaw collection,
yes it did. It kicked the ocelot,
which was rude and uncalled-for,
and yes hurtful. It kicked
the guacamole right out of its bowl,
which made for a grubby
and potentially dangerous workplace.
I was out testing the new speed bump
when it kicked the Viscountess,
which she probably deserved,
and I was happy, needless to say,
not to be a witness.
The kicking subsided for a while,
nobody was keeping track of time
at that time so it is impossible
to fill out the forms accurately.
Suffice it to say we remained
at our units on constant alert.
And then it kicked over the little cow town
we had set up for punching and that sort of thing,
a covered wagon filled with cover girls.
But now it was kicked over
and we had a moment of silence,
but it was clear to me
that many of our minions
were getting tetchy
and some of them were getting tetchier.
And then it kicked a particularly treasured snuffbox
which, legend has it, once belonged to somebody

named Bob Mackey, so we were understandably
saddened and returned to our units rather weary.
No one seemed to think I was in the least bit culpable.
It was my leg, of course, that was doing the actual kicking,
of that I am almost certain.
At any rate, we decided to bury it.
After the burial we returned to our units
and assumed our poses.
A little bit of time passed, not much,
and then John's leg started acting suspicious.
It looked like it wanted to kick the replica
of the White House we keep on hand
just for situations such as this.
And then, sure enough, it did.

JOHN KING

NORWICH AT HOME

Norwich always bring a lump to the throat. It's like some old fossil in power has decided to bring back hanging. That's what happens when you look back. You stitch yourself up. Get all emotional. Pensioners live off memories because they get nothing from the Government. Enough for light bulbs, but forget about the electricity to make them work. But I've got my own memories. None of those wartime stories of the Blitz. Chirpy cockney bollocks about sticking together in times of trouble. It doesn't work like that. Not these days. Not outside a few good mates. Not in Norwich.

We were kids at the time. Seventeen or eighteen and a bit slow. It was me and Rod after a game and we took the wrong turn outside Carrow Road. We were talking about nothing and not looking where we were going, like you do when you're a kid, and suddenly there's twenty Norwich fans in front of us. Just our dress sense must've told them we were Chelsea. They asked more for effect and I told them straight out because I knew we were going to get a kicking, but didn't realize how much it was going to hurt.

They didn't hang about. I dodged the kicks at first as they went for my balls, then looked to Rod, but he was on his knees in the street with his arms held out like he was being crucified and there were three or four farmers taking turns kicking him in the head. I went back and smacked one across the side of the face, then some cunt bundled me forward and my head hit a concrete post. I was on the ground and just remember being dazed. They were soon busy kicking seven shades of shit out of me and I must've been down for a good while.

Don't know how, but we managed to get up and stumble along an alley. It was a real panic job. My legs were fucked and Rod was swaying from side to side. Couldn't see much as we went. There were no pretty sights, just wood and bricks, though I remember the smell of rain on concrete. A strong, stale smell. We were on a slope which helped us along and we jumped over a fence and sat on the ground surrounded by stinging nettles, breathing heavy like we were old men choking to death.

The Norwich lads didn't follow us and we looked over the fence after a while and they'd fucked off. Melted away like they never existed. We just sat there. Didn't even get stung too bad which would have been the final insult. Rod was lying back against the fence saying fuck fuck fuck to himself like the needle was stuck. His eyes looked a bit mental. I thought his brain had gone, but was more bothered about myself. Must've sat there for half an hour and my body was beginning to ache and my head cracking in two. We were shitting ourselves because it was a fair walk to the station and we didn't fancy a second helping.

Eventually we got the bottle together and climbed over the fence. Walked up to the street and turned back along the side of the ground. There were people buying tickets for the next game. Young boys with Norwich souvenirs. Men, women, and kids. The great farmer support playing happy families. I wondered if they'd seen us get a kicking. They weren't giving anything away. Just living their lives. Maybe they watched the show, maybe not, I don't know. But nobody came to help us when Norwich were trying to inflict a bit of yokel tradition.

Can't blame them, of course. Scared people living shit lives aren't going to help a couple of teenage Chelsea boys. But they could've come down the alley and seen if we were still alive. They did fuck all. Left us to rot. Makes you think about all that decent citizen stuff. The public wants law and order and all the other stuff that goes with it, hanging and castration and short sharp shocks, but most of them are just small-minded cunts who don't want to get their hands dirty. They'll have their say as long as it doesn't go against what everyone else says, but they'll do fuck all when it comes to the crunch. They flow with the tide. A great tidal wave flowing through the sewers. Shit and used rubbers. Maybe they were just embarrassed, or reckoned we deserved it being young and away from home, but after Norwich we realized the score and grew up. A bit of an initiation really.

I had a headache for a week after and, being a kid and thinking too much about mights and maybes, started getting worried I could be brain-damaged. Imagined this blood clot spinning around my head waiting to kill me. None of it seemed worth the agony but once my head cleared I was fine and sense returned. Sometimes you need a bit of reason kicked into you and the whole thing raised the stakes. We realized there's more to life than being a cocky hooligan with a big mouth. If you're going to run the risk of getting a kicking it's better to get in first. Travel with a crew where you get maximum satisfaction and hopefully not too bad a hiding if things go wrong.

It's all about belonging and working together. Like in a war everything changes. Everyone pulls in the same direction and all the peacetime nonsense is knocked on the head. It's doing what's got to be done to survive the bad times, and when you're up against the wall you find all kinds of hidden strength. When he was still alive, my granddad called it war socialism. Said all the rich bastards bit their lips and reverted to a system they normally slagged off. It was different times and my granddad grew up with different notions, but the idea's the same, more or less. Makes sense that if you're going away looking for trouble you need a good mob that's going to get stuck in together. There's no point ten of you going somewhere like Leeds looking for a row because you'd last five minutes.

Flies around shit, those Norwich farmers saw us standing out and gave us a kicking like they were tenderizing some of their pigs. We were mugs and it hasn't happened that way since. It's all a bit of a laugh, because if you've got a good firm together you can turn a place over and generally walk away without too much damage. Of course, things can go wrong, especially against big clubs, or when it's an important game. The locals make an effort and you turn a corner and find yourself up against a thousand psyched-up Northerners determined to send you straight to Emergency. You shit yourself inside but the rush is so good you love it more than anything. You push yourself through the fear and you've done something that'll last you the rest of your life. They say it's adrenaline and that may be true, but all I know is that nothing compares. Not drugs, sex, money, nothing.

One day I'll be an old geezer pissed on a couple of pints and fuck knows what kind of world I'll be living in. I'll have some crippling disease and get mugged every time I walk out the door. There'll be no more pensions and I'll just be sitting around watching an endless stream of soap operas waiting to die. But at least I'll have lived a bit while I had the strength. And I won't be paying for my own funeral either. Dignity in death? Fuck off. I'll have stories to tell anyone bothered to listen and the kids will be surprised there was life in the good old days. They'll look at me a bit different.

I've done it myself. Listened to old geezers ramble on about their youth. But if you stop and listen it's not that at all. People are impatient and call a slow delivery rambling. The old people hanging around bus stops and libraries, the pub if they've got a bit of money spare, looking for something to do with their time, those are the ones who teach you about history. They can tell you about football riots. Or sex. Or drugs. Or anything you're into. Nothing's new. They just laugh and tell me we're nothing these days. That London's gone soft.

With football you make a choice. It's no easy option. You don't want to bottle out in front of your mates, and the more your reputation develops the more pressure there is to perform. Still, it's freedom of choice because I'm doing it for myself, not because the wankers in power tell me. That's what they don't like. When it really goes off the show's so far beyond their control it's unreal. The fat bastards who think they're in control realize how much power we have. Mob-handed we can do whatever we want. That's why they make a big noise about it all. Spend millions on cameras and police bills.

Look at a war and they kill millions, but how many deaths have you ever had through football? Funny thing is, people look at football fans and think they're scum. But your regular football supporter, right across the board, from young kid to old man, nutter to trainspotter, has seen the propaganda machine in action through the years. Firsthand knowledge. You can go to a game and see a bit of trouble and then when you get home and read the papers, or turn on the TV, you think it's happened somewhere else. The amount of time and effort they put into minor outbursts, the way they exaggerate, makes you think seriously about what's true and what's a lie. The great thing is, though, that it's us lot, the scum, especially the major firms, who understand it better than most. We know the truth because we've been there.

TOTTENHAM AWAY

Half-eleven on the dot and we're in King's Cross, standing at the bar in our North London local. The city's wide awake and there's a good mob packed into the pub. I'm sipping a pint of lager. Taking my time. Making it last. Mark's making do with orange juice and Rod holds a bottle of light ale. Harris is by the door watching people come in. Seeing who's who. He's got his usual firm on hand and there's small crews from all over West and South London. We're exclusive. There's no room for part-timers. The landlord must think it's Christmas because he's in the right place at the right time.

We usually use this pub before a game in North London, or when we've come back to King's Cross from up north. It always works like that. You find somewhere in a handy location where you can get together without the owner calling the old bill. You keep using it till it gets sussed. When there's a police van sitting across the road you know it's time to move. We just want to be left alone. Dress sensibly and leave the army fatigues and funny haircuts for school kids and sillies. You have to be casual and blend into the background.

Tottenham away is a cracker. There's always been a healthy hatred for Spurs. They're yids and wear skullcaps. They wave the Star of David and wind us up. We're Chelsea boys from the Anglo-Saxon estates of West London. Your average Chelsea fan coming up to Tottenham from Hayes and Hounslow is used to Pakis and niggers, but go up Seven Sisters Road and it's all bagels and kebab houses. Greeks, Turks, yids, Arabs. The Spurs mob like to get us going and it works both ways. Tottenham have always had a reputation for being flash. Silver Town yids. They're the rich spivs to West

Ham's poor dockers. At least that's how the story goes. You go through Stamford Hill and Tottenham and you wouldn't think you're in the same city as Hammersmith and Acton. We've got our Paddies down in West London, but none of these yid ghettos. I'm not Christian myself, but still Church of Fucking England.

Tottenham sent us down to the Second Division in the mid-Seventies and most of the Chelsea mob got locked out of White Hart Lane before kick-off. It went off inside and there were battles all over the pitch. Spurs had the numbers and though Chelsea put up a show they gave us a kicking. Tottenham won 2–0. Chelsea went down. They've been paying for it ever since. Talk to other clubs' supporters, whether they're from up north or London, and everyone hates Tottenham. But we're Chelsea and proud of the fact. Harris has had the old brain ticking over since last Saturday and we're working to a plan. Know where to find Tottenham before the match. There'll be a good turnout for this one because Chelsea always show up in force for Tottenham away.

Black Paul is next to us at the bar. A Chelsea nigger from Battersea. He lives in a tenth-floor flat looking over the river and sees the Stamford Bridge floodlights every morning when he gets out of bed. You can't get much better than that. He's no mug, Black Paul. Built like a concrete bunker and works on a building site. None of the lads wear colors because club shirts are the mark of a wanker, but Paul always has a kit top under his sweatshirt. Gets away with it because he's a mean cunt and nobody's going to say anything. He must be six foot four in his bare feet and his hands are full of scars. Building walls for the white man.

He makes up for this by shagging the white man's women, winding us up something chronic with stories of the blond birds flocking round his big black cock. It's always the same kind of birds. Blond hair stacked up on their heads listening to digital drum beats. Your typical ecstasy girls from the inner-city estates. Kids who won't touch a white bloke. They look us over like we can't compare with Black Paul and the niggers from Shepherd's Bush and Brixton. Like we're not up to scratch and it can cause bad feeling. Paul gives them a dose of jungle spunk but he's a Chelsea nigger first and foremost. Do the business for Chelsea and that's all that counts.

I fancy a decent drink but take my time. Last night was quiet. A hard week at the warehouse. It's a boring place to work but you've got to do something. Didn't want to shag myself out with Tottenham next day so had a couple of cans and watched this film about some smooth cunt who makes a fortune buying and selling property. Knobs everything in sight, jacks up on heroin to help him cope with his millions, but gets a bit careless and shares his works and then finds he's got AIDS. This makes him look up his old man who he's ignored for the last five years and they become the best of mates. The bloke dies and the old boy gets the cash. Rags-to-riches tale. Pile of shit basically, but there was nothing else on.

The lager tastes good but there's no point getting pissed and nicked for mouthing off along Tottenham High Road. You have to keep your wits about you when you're looking for a ruck. Get pissed and you're on for a kicking, not to mention a threatening behavior charge. Assault if the old bill are around to see you in action. The cream of every club knows the score and leaves the pissheads to make lots of noise, jump up and down, and generally create a show for the TV cameras. It's a mug's game. Like the older chaps dressing for action. Like they're out on parade with their boots and fatigues.

We call them sillies because it's all about melting into the background. You can be twice as tasty without the show. Just do the business and piss off before you're spotted. It's all about calculation. Think before you pile in. Use your brain. Don't rant and rave and give yourself a heart attack. Look after yourself and stay healthy. Find the opposition and batter them into the concrete. You don't have to march in with a brass band playing. Do it on the quiet and you get the same result with none of the comeback. It's basic politics. It's great though, because the papers and television always miss the point. There's no reporters down Kensington High Street when we pull scousers off the train and kick them into next week. The cunts are in the East Stand rubbing shoulders with the money men, hoping a politician will look their way. The commentators don't sit in a block of flats with their camera crew zooming in when we steam geordies at King's Cross. They're editing highlights and pocketing the wage packet. Suits us fine. Who needs the hassle?

One o'clock we start moving. It's a fair old walk along the Euston Road. We're out in the open then safe underground flooding the northbound platform of the Victoria Line, clockwork soldiers moving in time. Wind rushes down the tunnel and a Walthamstow train piles in. It's packed with Chelsea heading north. There's small mobs, kids, and decent citizens. Older geezers with lion tattoos and granddads who remember Bobby Tambling and Jimmy Greaves like it was yesterday. There's nothing aboard to compare with us though, and we get a few nervous looks. No colors. No sound. We wait for the next train a couple of minutes later, watched by London Underground lenses.

Video cameras see everything. You have to be sharp to achieve your ends because there's a market for Peeping Toms. Like this crime program on the box hunting a serial killer wiping out sadomasochistic queers. They took the cameras to a grubby flat in East London. Inside a bedroom with a body wrapped up on the bed. They were everywhere. Even went upstairs to talk with a granny who said she saw the victim and another bloke come home on the murder night. Said her eyesight wasn't too hot, but if the bloke's a nutter, which by rights he has to be, then he could well top the old girl as well.

They fucking loved it in the studio. Letting the country get off on the forensic team checking the flat. Pointing out old condom packets and an empty tube of KY. Then a camera at Waterloo picks up the killer with another bum bandit on their way to Putney and another murder. Cameras have a lot of power, but they won't stop anything. If you've got the urge to do something then it takes a special kind of strength to resist the desire. You don't have to get caught just because London's turning into a surveillance arcade. Not if you're clever.

The second train's half full and we spread out and take over. It's sauna conditions in the carriage with Mark and Rod pressed up against glass and Jim Barnes sweating last night's curry, moaning about some pig he shagged. Harris is in the next carriage down. I can see the back of his head through the door. Black Paul's against the wall, eyes to the ceiling. The train picks up speed. Curves through tunnels. There's a few women caught on the wrong train obviously worried, but we're Chelsea, not fucking Tottenham. We're not interested in bothering women. True, there are wankers about who'll get pissed up and give them a bad time, but they're nonces who wank their days away and spend their evenings telling everyone how hard they are.

We stop at Highbury & Islington and Finsbury Park. We check the platforms for Tottenham. If they're out looking for us and we get them underground that's their mistake. But the platforms are empty. Finsbury Park's Gooner territory, but Arsenal are away today, though there's a few memories of that particular area. The doors close and there's reflections in the windows. The next carriage starts singing "Spurs Are On Their Way To Auschwitz" and our lot joins in. A gang of kids in their late teens smells of too much drink. They start pulling at a seat. Flash a knife. One of them puts his hand on the emergency lever. Rod tells him to leave it out, we don't want the old bill fucking up our Saturday. Little hooligans showing off is okay when they do it away from us, but we don't need that kind of behavior. You have to have standards. Would have done the same when I was their age, but I'm not. Now is now. There's no room for nostalgia. The kid does the sensible thing. Puts the knife away. Rod's not a bloke to annoy.

When we arrive at Seven Sisters the platform is all Chelsea. There's jokes about what will be first on the menu. A launderette or kebab shop. Harris is ahead now and the rest of us filter through the crowd trying not to draw attention. Tottenham offers a bonus because the tube's so far from the ground. It's a long way down Tottenham High Road and the old bill can't police all the different routes properly. Gives us the chance we're looking for. The crowd spills through barriers into the street. There's a kebab house opposite and a queue forms at the counter. Fare dodgers get pulled at the barriers while we move onto the main road. Keeps the old bill busy. Makes them feel needed.

There's traffic clogging the street and men run for buses to save their legs. Harris is on the other side of the road with Black Paul and some of the Battersea lads behind him. There's Hammerhead, a fat cunt from Isleworth who never runs because he's too fucking heavy. He got a bad kicking at Leeds last season and reckons he didn't suffer permanent damage because of his weight. Sixteen stone of blubber. He's more a mascot than anything and heads for the kebab house saying he needs a feed. He's a funny bloke. Lot of humor about him. Not the kind of bloke who deserves a kicking. Leeds are scum doing him. Ten onto one. It's not the odds, just Hammerhead doesn't want to know when it comes to a fight, which is fair enough.

Tottenham's a dump. There's holes in the pavements and more fumes than Hammersmith. Pensioners sit on benches looking into space and an old black woman pushes a supermarket trolley packed with flattened cardboard and empty cans. There's a heavy smell of kebab meat and even the niggers look different. The streets are wider. Derelict flats boarded up against squatters. These are the areas kids from up north head for when they come to London. Cheap accommodation. But there's plenty of builders looking to do them up and make a few quid. Plenty of nutters around who'll carry out the eviction. You've got to look after yourself. Nothing comes free and you've got to do the other bloke before he does you. That's what the pensioners on the bench don't realize. They might be owed something but there's nobody left to cough up. It's a different world now. The war spirit is dead and gone, packaged and sold off to the highest bidder.

We cross over and follow Harris, the crowd from the tube stretching along the High Road. We're dedicated in our mission. Getting in tight behind the leader. Black Paul telling us he's going to have a Tottenham nigger. Makes the lads laugh. His mate Black John with him. A smaller bloke with a shinehead and a way of making you nervous. His eyes are always darting around and you know his mind's working overtime. Only turns up for big games. Usually the aways. Paul told me on the quiet John makes a packet flogging crack in South London. Five hundred quid for a couple of nights' work in Camberwell and Brixton. He's worth having along because you know he's always tooled up. There's enough full-time, would-be yardies around who don't like him hanging out with the white man. He has to watch his step. Loves going up to Tottenham and Arsenal. Gets to deal with his North London rivals, or at least their brothers.

There's a few yids hanging around further down the road. Half white, half black which means they're Spurs. They're scouting and move away all stroppy like. Look back and we're together now, spilling off the pavement into the road. They turn a corner and a wanker at the back disappears sharpish, as though he's running. They're trying to play it cool, at least till they're out of sight, but we're looking for their mob and they're off to give the warning. Harris moves a bit faster now, telling some of the younger lads to hang back, take it calm, don't spoil the party. We come to the corner and the yids have disappeared, a pub further down the street on another corner the target. We turn right and spread across the road. You can feel the tension and I'm buzzing. Been looking forward to this all week. Washes away all the boredom and slaving over hot cardboard boxes.

Some of the lads start kicking at a broken wall, breaking away chunks of brick and masonry. Harris is trying to keep things together. Black Paul's handing out half bricks. A professional who knows his trade. Makes me laugh. Rod and Mark's eyes shine. A chunk of concrete with wire sticking through the middle rests in my hand, and then we're running down the street and there's that noise that comes from somewhere deep down inside when you steam in. No words, just a roar like we're back in the fucking jungle or something and the bricks are flying through the pub windows and I can see shapes inside already heading for the door, vital seconds lost with indecision as the scouts got back and made their report. Tight cunts should try investing in a couple of mobile phones.

My hand's in the air and I see my lump of concrete among the bricks caving in windows, the sound of glass shattering a soft noise in the din of voices, and Tottenham are breaking through the doors but we're there to meet them and Harris is leading from the front with Black Paul and a load of other blokes, pulling the first yids into the street, weight of numbers piling out of the pub so we spill everywhere, Harris copying his mate from Camberwell, nutting a big cunt between the eyes, bridge of the nose job, no copper this one, and Black Paul kicks him in the bollocks, and as he stumbles forward a few of the blokes start kicking him in the head and gut, driving him under a parked car.

Rod's laying into some bloke with a Tottenham shirt on, silly cunt, and we're shoulder to shoulder, smacking a nigger in the mouth feeling the pain in my knuckles as I don't catch him right, try to kick him in the balls, but Mark's in first and we're in a position by the door of the pub, more yids inside trying to force their way out, but we've got the strategy and I do the geezer now, he falls back against the wall, Chelsea piling in and he sinks into the pavement, feet catching him in the head and for a split second I see his eyes glaze then he's fighting to survive, panicking in the crush, but they're piling into the street now because someone's lobbed tear gas into the pub, and we back off because it makes you choke and you feel like you're going to suffocate.

There's a split in the road and we're further back, those of us near the front rubbing our eyes, all the pub windows smashed, just long shards left, a pint glass flying through the air catching Mark on the side of the head sending blood down his shirt over his jeans, and the yids are getting it sorted out, a few of the cunts dazed on the pavement, others helping them away where they can half walk, half crawl, and we get ready to steam in again, the noise cranked up, car windows kicked in as the energy has to come out some way, held back by the gas, and there's a fucking giant Irish-looking geezer with red hair and pasty white skin coming through, and he's with a nigger with a machete and nobody's going to tangle with that cunt, the only weapons bricks which batter him and then Paul's saving face taking him out and the mob piles in kicking the bastard to fuck, paying him back for their fear, head on a stick, everyone reads the papers, and I'm in there feeling the sheer joy of kicking a deserving bastard in the bollocks, head, gut, anywhere we can get the cunt, in among the wrecked cars in this broken-down North London slum.

The two mobs clash again and this time it's less frantic, trouble flaring across the street, mostly punches and kicks, a couple of blades coming out, flashing in the early afternoon sunlight, sparks of silver fear which make you pull back and everyone mob together and do the offender. Martin Howe's in there, only got let out two weeks ago, did four months for smacking a bloke who cut him up at a set of traffic lights, and he's bleeding from his leg, pig stuck by Spurs, and it's slower now, picking our spot, and I'm after a mouthy cunt shouting insults and he goes for my head and misses and I do my kung fu impression because he's small enough and split his mouth open, Mark following through trying to do his knee like a kickboxer, Rod the man in the know using his karate to bruise his throat, sending the cunt spluttering into the crowd, choking on his words.

The battle moves along the street, the pub empty, scared faces watching from behind net curtains. A shitty street with broken walls and small run-down gardens. Piles of rotting rubbish left uncollected. Rusted bike frames on the pavement. Place smells of curry and decaying big ends. There's pale kids on doorsteps shitting themselves and you have to feel a bit bad for them, because when you're young you don't need this, not with your mum and dad at each other late into the night, but they'll get it from somewhere and we've all been through that shit ourselves anyway.

There's sirens screaming in the distance and one by one we take them in, know where they're heading. The sound sends us moving back toward the main road and there's a van flashing blue murder, just one of the cunts, and a brick sails through the windscreen, back door opening, and the old bill are looking for aggro. They're tooled up and Tottenham have scattered into the back streets. I turn round and Mark's holding his head together okay, Rod next to him, and I'm with Harris and his mob, looking further up the road. There's only the one van, and the old bill are sizing the situation up even as they pick on a young lad nearby and crack his head with their truncheons, one cunt with stripes smashing his head into the side of the van, another one kicking him, splitting his lip with the truncheon, screaming abuse, voice and siren together, fucking Chelsea scum. Somehow knows we're Chelsea.

The other coppers are lashing out and trying to nick some of the younger element, but they know they've fucked up and we're mobbing together and the cunts are on for a kicking. I want to laugh and shout because this is Tottenham. A fucking shit hole and the old bill don't put cameras down poor people's streets. They're only interested in protecting City wealth and the rich cunts in Hampstead and Kensington. Fuck the scum round here. There's no cameras this distance from the ground. No fucking chance. The old bill know they haven't got the numbers and there's no videotape deterrent. The road's jammed with traffic and we can see flashing lights further down the street blocked by buses. You couldn't ask for more.

There's a few seconds of quiet and everyone knows the score. We run toward the van and the coppers are shitting themselves. Even the sergeant leaves the kid alone. The boy murmurs to himself on the pavement. They've all got their numbers covered so there's no chance of identification and you know that any complaint you make against police brutality comes to nothing. They love football fans because they can do what they want. We're lower than niggers because there's no politician going to stand up for the rights of mainly white hooligans like us. And we don't want their help. We stand on our own feet. There's no easy place to hide. No Labor council protecting us because we're an ethnic minority stitched up by the system. No Tory minister to support our free-market right to kill or be killed. The old bill are the scum of the earth. They're the shit of creation. Lower than niggers, Pakis, yids, whatever, because at least they don't hide behind a uniform. You may take the piss out of the bastards occasionally, but you have some hidden respect somewhere.

But the old bill? Leave it out. We have the cunts in our sights. We pile in and the bastards don't have a chance. The sergeant takes the worst of it because he's all stripes and mouth and we've seen him batter the kid. Somehow he's worse because he's got a uniform and authority and we've been trained to respect uniforms and believe in the idea of justice. He shouts out as he sinks to the road, pulled to his feet by Black Paul, and a few of the Battersea mob take turns kicking him. His eyes are shut and bruised. Blood spews out of his nose. His head snaps back and opens up on broken glass. He's getting his reward and we're so frenzied we couldn't care less if he died.

The sirens are louder and police vans mount the pavement. We move off. Another train has arrived at Seven Sisters spilling more people onto the pavement, the vast majority of football fans who hate violence. Content to sing songs and have a few pints. We're evil bastards in their eyes and it gives us a special position. We split up and leave the battered coppers and the old bill unload their vans and block the road, a few coppers going over to check their mates, the rest piling into the crowd fresh off the train. They tug the nearest blokes and start laying into them. We look back and they've got some kids under a bus stop, kicking them black and blue, and a black woman's screaming at them to stop, that they haven't done anything wrong. A copper turns and lays her out with a single punch. Calls her a fucking slag.

The old bill are going mad and there's a couple of thousand people along the road now, and they lose it and start fighting back, defending themselves, and that's how you get a riot going. It only takes a few of you to start things off and the old bill are so fucking thick they whip everyone up. There's a helicopter above and more coppers piling down the road. They've got their shields out and try to form a barricade as Chelsea move forward, covering the area, kids and older blokes joining in. It's paradise this. A great way to spend your Saturday afternoon. There's a few bottles bouncing off shields and snatch squads running out to pick off young lads who look the business but are just caught up in the spectacle. We're ahead of the main lot now, nearing the ground, trying to suss out yids among the onlookers, but doing it from habit more than anything.

There's people in the street watching the battle. It's turned into a standoff with the crowd singing and smashing the odd car window. They've missed the nasty part and it's turning into a show. Something to put the shit up

Spurs. Mark and Rod catch up and we're on our own approaching the ground. I feel great inside. The rush is there and my body tingles. Sounds funny but it's true. It's better than shafting a bird. Better than speeding. Mark's head's a mess but the bleeding has stopped. My knuckles are bruised and Rod's eyes have gone a bit mental-looking. We join the crush trying to get in the ground. The crowd's already buzzing inside and we can hear the constant chant of CHELSEA. This is what life's all about. Tottenham away. Love it.

JOSEPH LEASE

ESSAY ON ADDICTION

A woman and a man
    stumble in the forest:
        she recognizes

the forest, knows
    the fairy tale in
        sunlight on wild roses,

in hot wind stopping
    and starting—
        she thinks,

We are looking
    for a house—
        there

will be an abandoned house,
    almost a mansion,
        cracking boards

with paint worn away.
    Do not let us
        be on these grounds,

exposed, when
    night comes on—
        we must not be

stumbling, running,
    falling in the brush—
        she gets furious with

her lover because
    he can't see what
        will happen, because he is

so nervous, so
    dependent on her.
        Then they get separated—

of course they
        get separated—there
                is no transition—

he is
        simply not there.
                She finds the house,

which looks almost exactly
        like her nightmare
                of a house,

almost a mansion, cracking
        boards with paint worn
                away—standing in

a vestibule, walking
        up a staircase with
                no banister, she knows he

is out there
        in the forest—
                she stays inside and waits—

standing in a vestibule,
        walking up a staircase—
                she thinks of him—

at the top
        of the stairs she waits
                until he appears

at the bottom of the stairs,
        and she thinks,
                He returned

as a ghost
to torment me—

THIEF

        Pressure of cotton against
            the back of a hand,
                paradise unbuttoned,

trumpet-flowers, night-
        blooming: she writes
            these answers on her hand,

on her eye.
        When the moon is down,
            what is dust under the bed?

Black plums in a plastic bag.
        When the moon rises
            black plums taste like whiskey.

Her answer on fire, echoes
        like nonsense in these promises.
            Summer-thunderstorm–colored light:

reach into flame but don't crash your bike.
        People sniff sex and a voice says,
            This has to be good.

Oh this would be
        perfect, was never
            perfect, will never be perfect.

Down. Unspeakable
        rituals become talk.
            Dawn becomes gossip.

It was always, Don't plan,
        so you planned all the ways
            not to plan . . .

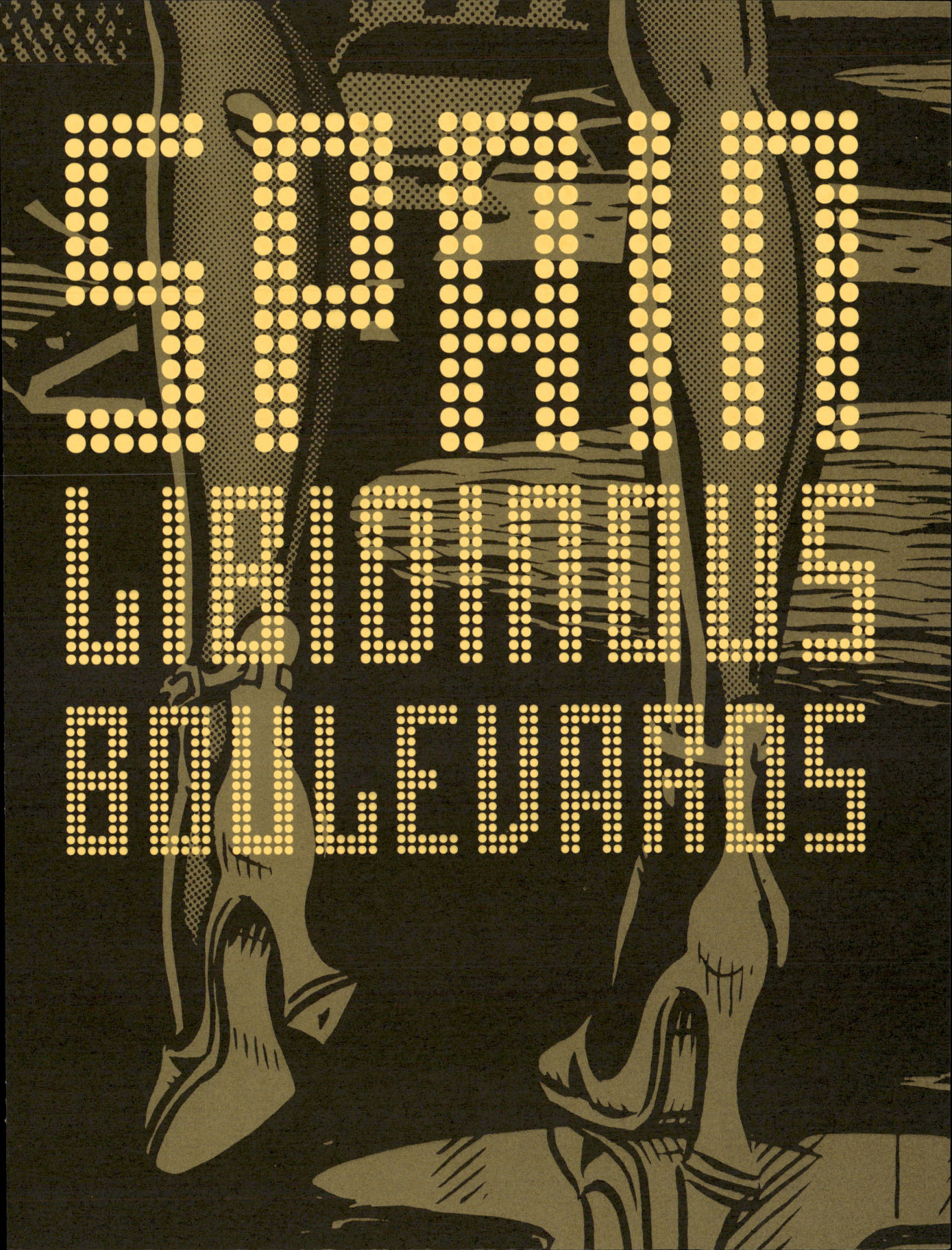

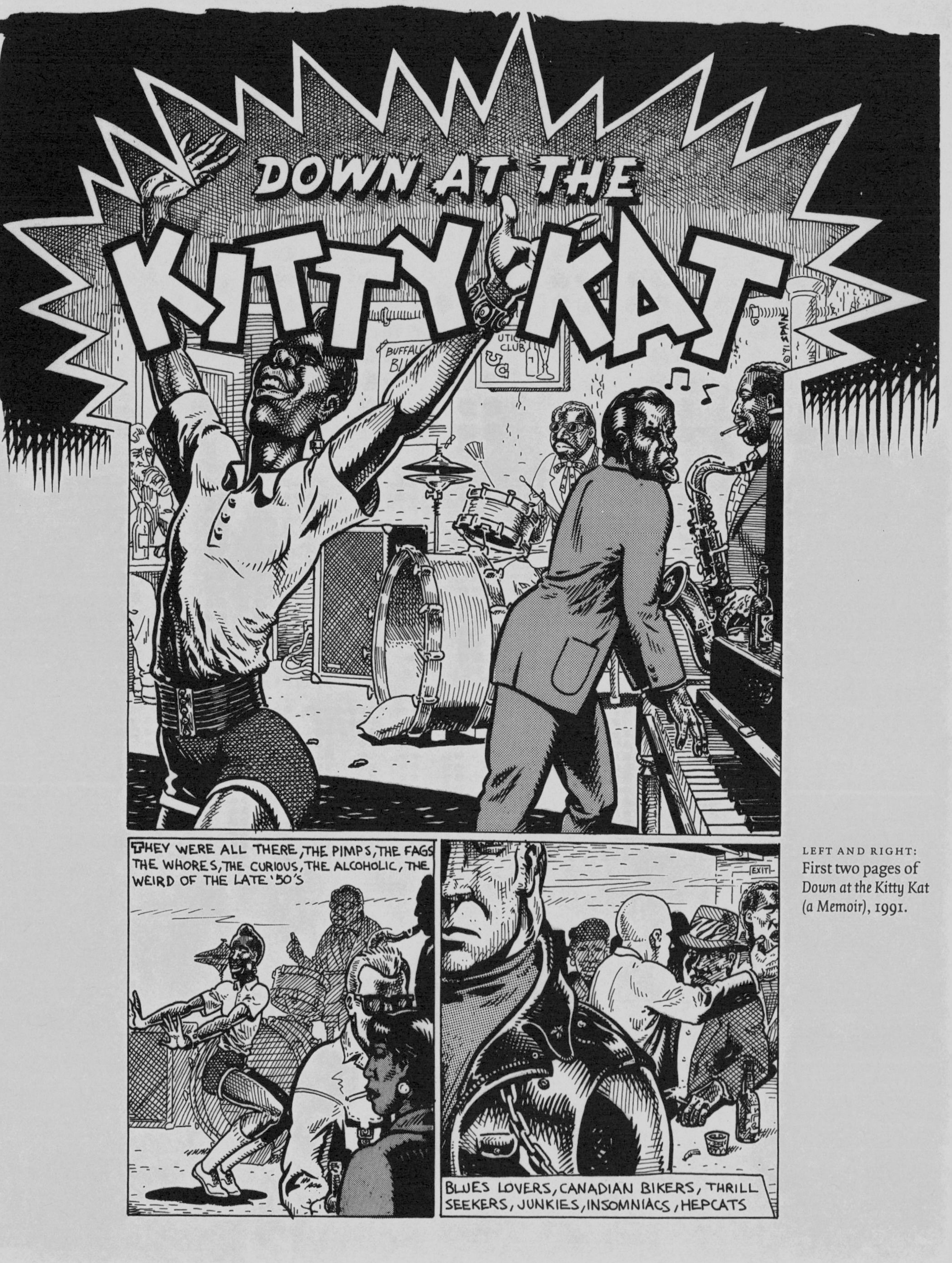

LEFT AND RIGHT: First two pages of *Down at the Kitty Kat (a Memoir)*, 1991.

LEFT
Free Other, 1966.

BELOW
Past on Parade:
The Demize of Psychedellia
1967.

ABOVE
Untitled, 1992.

BELOW
Welcome to Noctoum, 1983.

BELOW
Notebook page, October 1987.

RIGHT
Notebook page, February 1987.

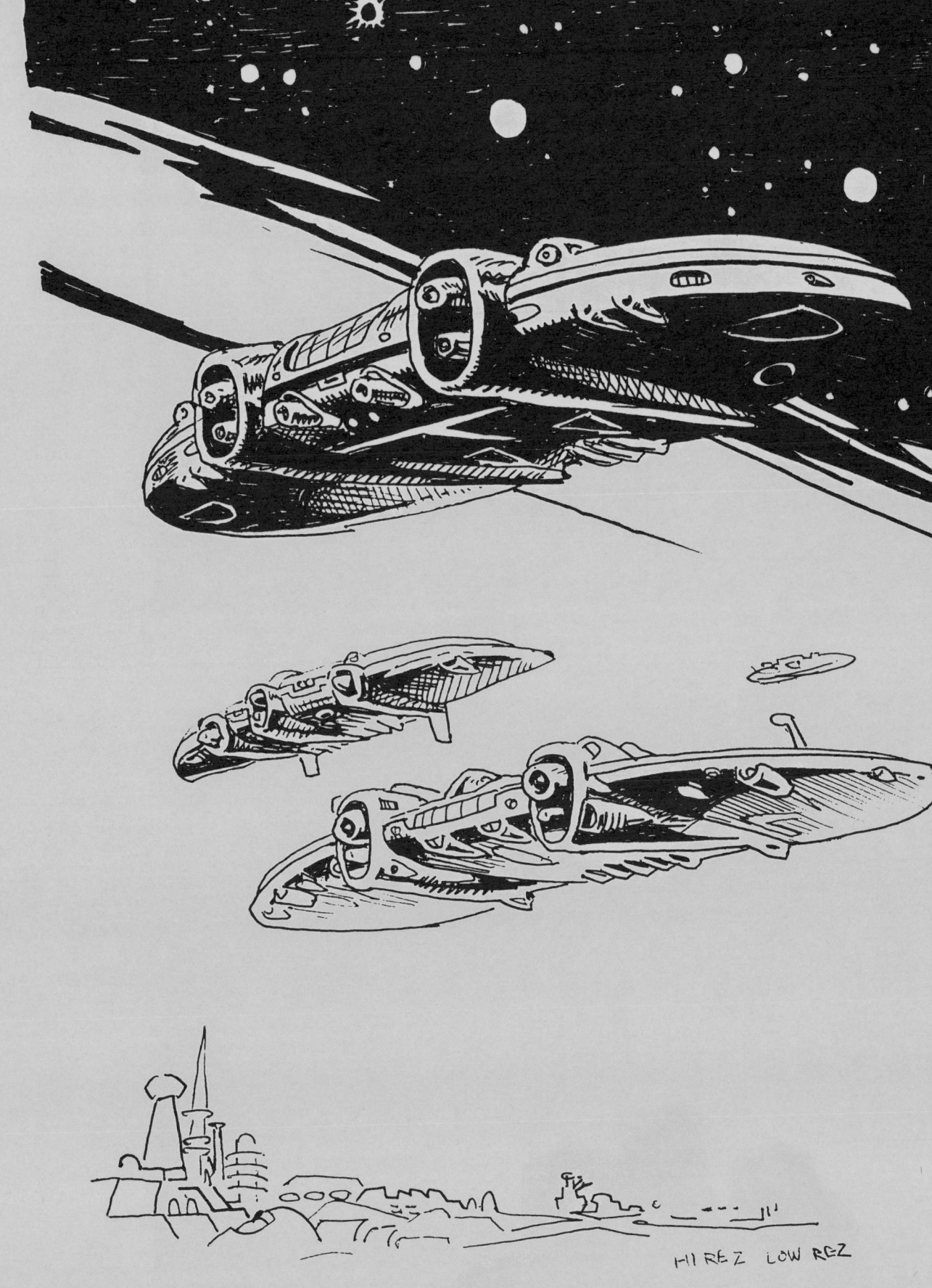

First page of
Nightmare Alley,
1995.

It's just a point in time that eventually makes a line. SPAIN

It's been thirty years since Spain Rodriguez first took pen to paper and began to distill a sharp and intoxicating brew of the gritty and phantasmagorical within the defiantly independent world of the counter-cultural '60s underground press. Although he signed his early strips for EVO as Rodriguez, it was as Spain that he gained an international cult following—becoming known and celebrated for his membership in the pantheon of underground comic greats as a contributor to R. Crumb's *Zap Comix*.

Although it is common to associate Spain with San Francisco—thanks to his work with *Zap* and the fact that he has made his home there—the genesis and heart of his work remain deeply embedded in his childhood memories of Buffalo and his youth in New York City.

As much as his artistic vision is predicated on personal experience, it remains neither a show of nostalgia nor a phobic reaction against the uncertainty of time embodied in our conception of the future. His persistent fascination with the motorcycle and street gangs of his East Coast past is as much remembrance as it is a dark shadow of asocial, outlaw, underground individuality and extremism, upon which he projects certain fantasies and truths about human nature. Memory here functions as both a creative process—an ongoing act of personal archaeology to reconstruct the past out of the miasma of forgetfulness and subjective distortion—and a device of history, a tribute to all the crazy outrageous characters with whom he hung around, shot the shit, and generally got into trouble.

All those who survive the ravages of a youth on the edge at some point feel compelled to record the lost voices and lives of those years. Not surprisingly, Spain's concept of the future is ultimately a projection of those myriad obsessions that constitute his art's autobiographical base. His future can be seen, in part, as a projection of eroticized fantasies, but it is ultimately imbued with the grisly urban realism engendered by his years in New York. As in his reworking of noir, the meat of the matter is less the presence of a grim nihilist viewpoint than the effect of *mise-en-scène*, a psyche of place defined by an abundance of finely articulated background detail.

For Spain, New York has always been a fantasy set, a tenement-laden old world "ripped open by different layers of modernity." If Rodriguez spent his childhood, like most kids of the '50s, dreaming of the future as sparkling cities of the perfectly new, it was Michael Anderson's 1955 British film classic, *1984*, that shocked him into the realization that any future is cluttered with vestiges of the past. Even when he ventures into more fantastical science fictions, it is not hard to see how they are in essence a twisted projection of the present, a visceral alternative to contemporary existence filled with the dreams and desires of the past—and the fears of a father, as Rodriguez imagines the world his seven-year-old daughter will someday inherit.

CARLO McCORMICK

TIMOTHY LIU

NOCTURNE: FIRE ISLAND

>   Shards of glass embedded
>   in the sand where the party
>
>   had broken up, only love's
>   detritus—embers faintly
>   glowing in a blackened hole,
>
>   condoms smeared with shit
>   discarded through the weeds.

TWO MEN ON A BENCH WATCHING THE LIGHT DIE DOWN

Rollerblades careening down concrete
as we face the ocean, the scent of star jasmine
stronger than dusk—our hands a trespass
against the stillness we embody. Must we
step out of modesty just to touch
the nipples of shirtless men bronzed by the sun
or follow trails of sweat streaking down
spandex shorts that lend desire shape?
To undress those men is to hasten
what stirs inside our bones—an ocean within
that spills into this world from dark to dark.

orts of entry

WILLIAM S. BURROUGHS / BRION GYSIN

Brion Gysin died of a heart attack on Sunday morning, July 13, 1986. He was the only man I have ever respected. I have admired many others, esteemed and valued others, but respected only him. His presence was regal without a trace of pretension. He was at all times impeccable.

Who was Brion Gysin? The only authentic heir to Hassan-i-Sabbah, the Old Man of the Mountain? Certainly that. Through his painting I caught glimpses of the Garden that the Old Man showed to his Assassins. The Garden cannot be faked. And Brion was incapable of fakery. He was Master of the Djoun forces, the Little People, who will never serve a faker or a coward.

Brion was suffering from emphysema and lung cancer. He knew he had only a few weeks to live. I was preparing to go to Paris when Brion died. I have this last glimpse through a letter from my friend Rosine Buhler, written in her own English:

"Brion asked to wear his Chevalier de l'Ordre des Arts et des Lettres medallion in a very elegant way and we started dinner with a wonderful

LEFT William Burroughs (left) and Brion Gysin in Geneva during the Tangier Conference, 1975.

Chinese soup. Brion finds the wine slightly *rapeux** to tease François de Palaminy, who has spent and concentrated to find a non-altered wine which is not so easy even in Paris. After occurs a dreamlike talk about having a large house by the sea in August, the shadowed room where all is burning hot outside. Brion said he knew he would sleep well and was really happy of that good day. He wanted no help to lift himself up from his green armchair, and went to his room. I was watching his tall, straight way to walk, his secure path . . . only kings and wild people have this way."

I don't think I had ever *seen* painting until I saw the painting of Brion Gysin. Here is a transcript of a tape we recorded while talking in front of some of these pictures during the time we both lived in the old Beat Hotel in Paris back in 1960, when I discovered I could really get into these paintings:

BRION GYSIN: How do you get into these paintings?

WILLIAM S. BURROUGHS: Usually I get in by a port of entry as I call it. It is often a face through whose eyes the picture opens into that landscape. Sometimes it is rather like an archway: any number of little details or a special spot of color make the port of entry and then the entire picture will suddenly become a three-dimensional frieze in plaster or jade or other precious material.

This picture in front of me (*Permutations*) is in four sections. The remarkable thing is the way in which the sections, when hung a few inches apart, seem literally to pull together. The substance of the paintings seems to bridge the gap. Something is streaming right across the void. Surely this is the first painting ever to be painted on the void itself. You can literally see the pull of one canvas on the other.

Now you suddenly see all sorts of things here. Beautiful jungle landscape. And then always bicycles. The whole bicycle world . . . scooters. All sorts of faces . . . monkey faces . . . typical withered monkey faces. Very archetypal in this world. And you do get whole worlds. Suddenly you get a whole violet world or a whole gray world which flashes all over the picture. The worlds are, as it were, illuminated by each individual color, made of that color. You think of them as the red world and then the blue world, for example. I was taking a color walk around Paris the other day, doing something I picked up from your pictures in which the colors shoot out all through the canvas like they do on the street. I was walking down the boulevard when I suddenly felt this cool wind on a warm day and when I looked out I was seeing all the blues in the street in front of me . . . blue on a foulard . . . blue on a young workman's ass . . . his blue jeans . . . a girl's blue sweater . . . blue neon . . . the sky . . . all the blues. When I looked again I saw nothing but all the reds of traffic lights . . . car lights . . . a café sign . . . a man's nose. Your paintings make me see the streets of Paris in a different way. And then there are deserts and the Mayan masks and the fantastic aerial architecture of your bridges and catwalks and Ferris wheels.

GYSIN: You mentioned once that you can't see all of these at the same time.

---

* Harsh.

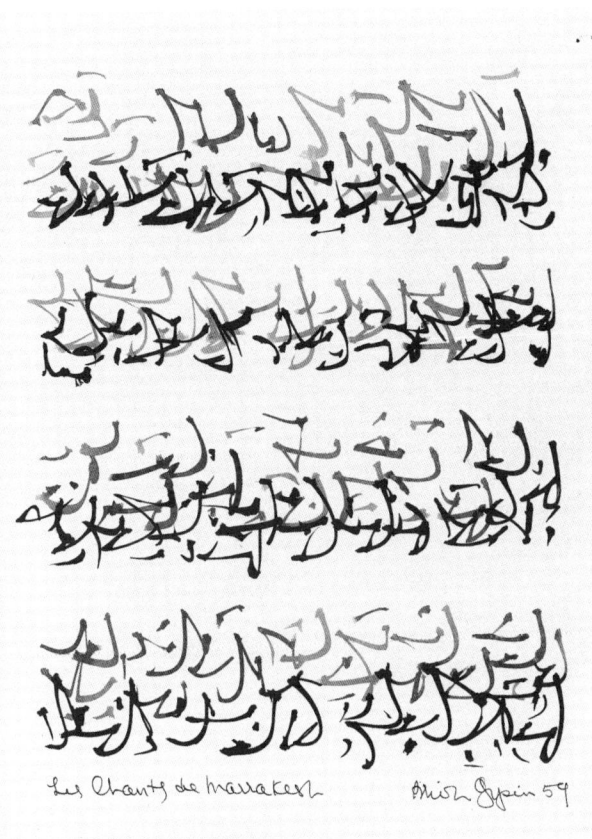

Brion Gysin, *Les Chants de Marrakesh*
(*The Songs of Marrakesh*), 1959.

BURROUGHS: No. This is the first real space-time painting in which there's a presentation of what is actually going on in front of the painter and the viewer—in a space-time sense, both through the forms and through the color, because the color makes the shifting forms. And then this is related to actual time sequences presented here. You see things in a sequence which is actually a time sequence. I know of no other example of the way in which time is represented here. I can't see all of these different levels at once because it is as if they existed independently only in their time sequence. Here is space-time painting. You can see way deep into all sorts of landscapes for instance and then you flash back to what appears on the surface. The substance of the painting exists with a double motion in and out.

When you see one layer of the picture then you suddenly see it all. The eye which I am using as a port of entry jerks me abruptly into a landscape I never saw before. It is a sort of toy world and one that is somehow alarming, populated with mechanical insects attacking each other and men in armor from other planets. Or they may be simply modern welders with bridges in the background.

GYSIN: Yes, people have objected.

BURROUGHS: I don't see why they should. It's a substance. Why, that's like jumping up from your microscope and screaming: "I won't look at *that anymore!* They're squirming around down there just carrying on so nasty!" Now I regard you, Brion, as being in my own line of work. Being strictly an experimenter, I say: *Science is pure science!* All of us are pure scientists exploring

Brion Gysin, Permutation I-II-III-IV, 1959.

different levels of fact and if we turn up something nasty we're not to blame. If someone finds a real nasty-looking microbe, is he going to stop because some idiot comes along and says: Pornographer! I must say that my whole family was nauseated by the sight of your slides! You and your filthy pictures! Now when they see things in your pictures that are obscene from their point of view, they don't dare say so. You painters can be as nasty and dirty as you like and people don't see it as quickly or they simply don't dare say so because it would be too much of a rare reflection on themselves. I'm seeing that in there so there's something dirty and nasty in me.

Oh, here [in this picture] are a lot of people on fire . . . streaming with gasoline on fire across the whole picture . . . people running and the upper corner of the picture seems to fold back over them. Why, it's the grasshopper world. Crystals. The Arab world. An Arab market. And there's my aunt encased in her electric motorcar covered with veils. She's caught in a glob of something or under a bowl. A laboratory with instrument panels and up above there is what looks like a city . . . a very strange drifting city that is moving through space-time at an incredible speed. There is something that swells up as this is happening. I see all sorts of faces . . . eyes opening into doors and windows . . . hundreds of them in the most amazing juxtapositions. From some, you can get into others and, from others, you cannot get anywhere and so on. Extremely intricate. There are some fish-men swimming down here looking as though they were made of waste-baskets from the waist down . . .

There are great flaring movements across the whole canvas . . . and then they turn into tubes . . . pulsing tubes. Some sort of energy is conducted through these tubes that run through the whole canvas which has become completely three-dimensional. You could look at this picture for months and see something new every time. Each time I look at this picture I see something I never saw before in the whole world. Sometimes you see familiar landmarks, but it is as if whole constellations change each time . . . like a street corner where you recognize the landmarks, but there are always new people to change the scene. It is inexplicable. Now there are all sorts of green men here made of that substance like shit from a cirrhotic liver. There are faces and there are cells in which people live in little pools of the stuff. The whole canvas is suddenly totally clear and accurate . . . a fantastic world of faces that are part house and all of it frozen over in a strange gelatinous pink substance . . . frozen hell there in that substance. The substance is moving all the time . . . shivering, moving, changing. You can see the canvas become self-sufficient by a switch of the image. Everything can and does become something else. I can hardly remember what that thing there was a minute ago. Oh yes, that was a head but now it has become a house flat on the ground. And this is a pink hill. When you relate to it, you can switch it back to the former image.

Now there is a point at which you can see both images simultaneously. It becomes rather uncomfortable. It gives you this tremendous feeling of vertigo, as if you had to breathe through your cock and you can only get it up to where the air is if you have a hard-on. Precarious position which is somehow related to the fear of falling from a great height. A basic fear of suffocation and a loss of support both being contained therein. That gives this picture a most disconcerting aura to say the least. Sometimes this seems to be pulsing with light and at other times it is all made out of stone . . . porous stone perhaps . . . an indeterminate substance between stone and flesh like coral. Then you get that strange vegetable substance as if these people I see in there were plants growing out of these tubes you have running through all the canvas.

Very strange! Just for a moment there I caught an absolutely clear photographic picture of Gregory Corso. It has gone now but I feel sure it really is in there and will come back again. It is queer how these photographic shocks of yours flash in and out. It is one of the most remarkable phenomena I have ever witnessed in my practice . . . in all my practice. These strangely familiar faces are all growing together bound up by vines and tendrils . . . monkeys' faces. At one point a very mean, ravished, seventeenth-century face with a ruff around his neck standing outside some sort of native hut.

LEFT Paul Bowles, Marrakesh, Djema el Fna, 1963.
ABOVE Brion Gysin, *A Blessing in Marrakesh*, 1967.

William Burroughs (left) and Brion Gysin
at the Beat Hotel, Paris, 1959.

GYSIN: Doesn't that look like some kind of writing?

BURROUGHS: It does. I can read it. *Wings tack quietly . . . not crying . . . kiss . . . noisy pissing Tex . . . Gysin not sin was not crying . . . fix Gysin . . . Brion . . .*

GYSIN: What I read is different: *My dear very yours . . . not crying . . .*

BURROUGHS: It looks like letters here, too, but they're harder to make out. I read: *Creeps . . .* Looking at these paintings of yours is often like focusing an optical instrument. I find that it takes about twenty seconds to focus at all. The viewer has to learn how to flicker back and forth between a telescopic and a microscopic point of view while his attention is centered on some small beautiful scene which may be no bigger than his index fingernail at one moment, and then his attention is suddenly jerked back to a clear long-range view of the picture or its all-over pattern. What you actually see at any given moment becomes only a part of a visual operation which includes an infinite series of images. This leads you along a certain path like a row or series of patterns . . . a series of neural patterns which already exist in the human brain.

★

It is to be remembered that all art is magical in origin—music, sculpture, writing, painting—and by magical I mean intended to produce very definite results. Writing and painting were one in cave paintings, which were formulae to ensure good hunting. Art is not an end in itself, any more than Einstein's matter-into-energy formula is an end in itself. Like all formulae, art was originally *functional*, intended to make things happen, the way an atom bomb happens from Einstein's formulae. Take a porcelain stove and disconnect it and put it in your living room with ivy growing over it: it may be a good-looking corpse but it isn't functional anymore. Or take a voodoo doll full of pins—authentic West Africa, $500 on 57th Street—and hang it on the wall of your duplex loft. It isn't killing enemies anymore, and the same goes for a $5,000 shrunk-down head, which a fashionable shrink bought for his consultation room.

The painting of Brion Gysin deals directly with the magical roots of art. . . . His paintings can be called space art. Time is seen spatially, that is, as series of images or fragments of images past, present, and future. . . . Here is a Gysin scene from Marrakesh—moving figures, phantom bicycles, cars . . . this is a literal representation of what actually happens in the human nervous system; a street reminds you of a car that went by yesterday, or a boy on a bicycle years ago, in fact everything that you have experienced on that street and other streets associated with it. The pictures constantly change because you are drawn into time travel on a network of associations. Brion Gysin paints from the viewpoint of timeless space.

WILLIAM S. BURROUGHS

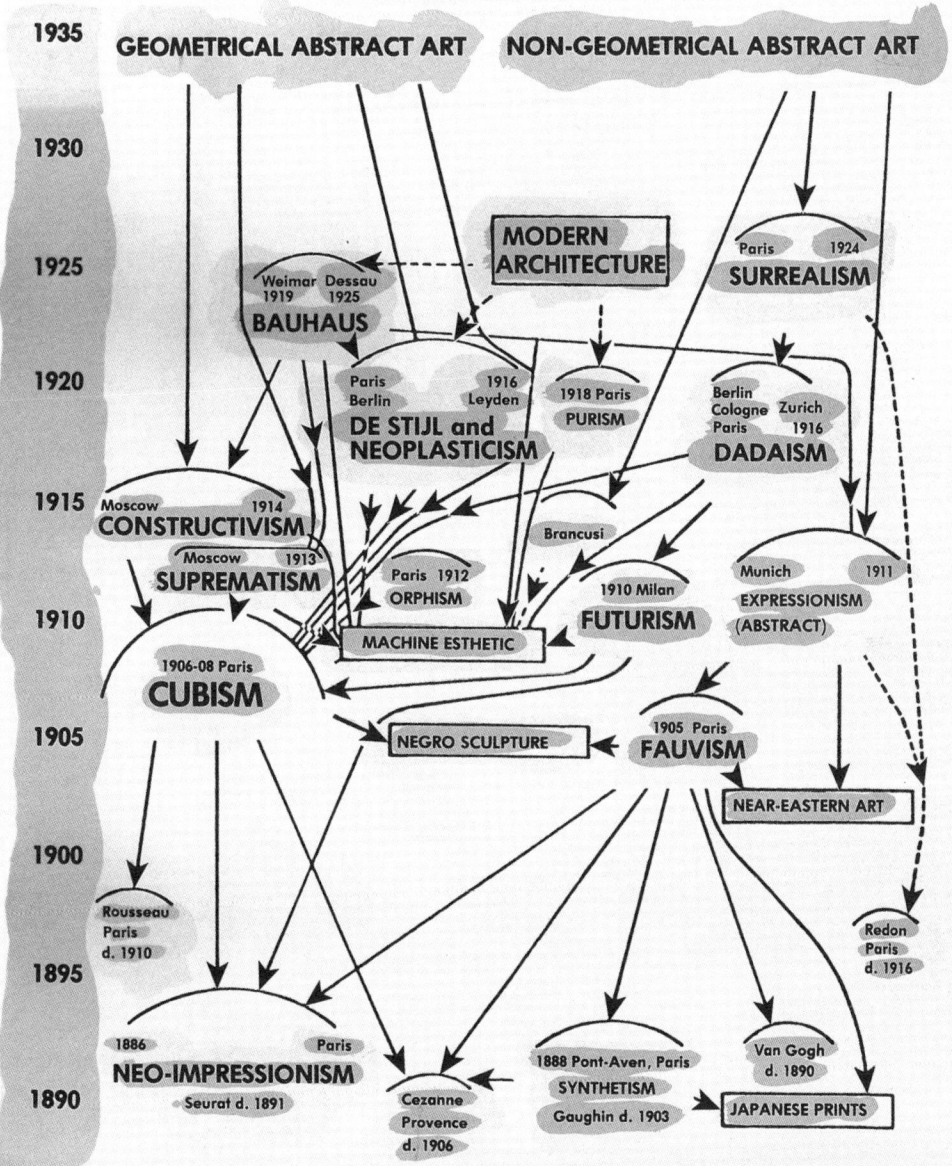

Michael Corris, *Decomposition (after Alfred Barr)*, 1983.

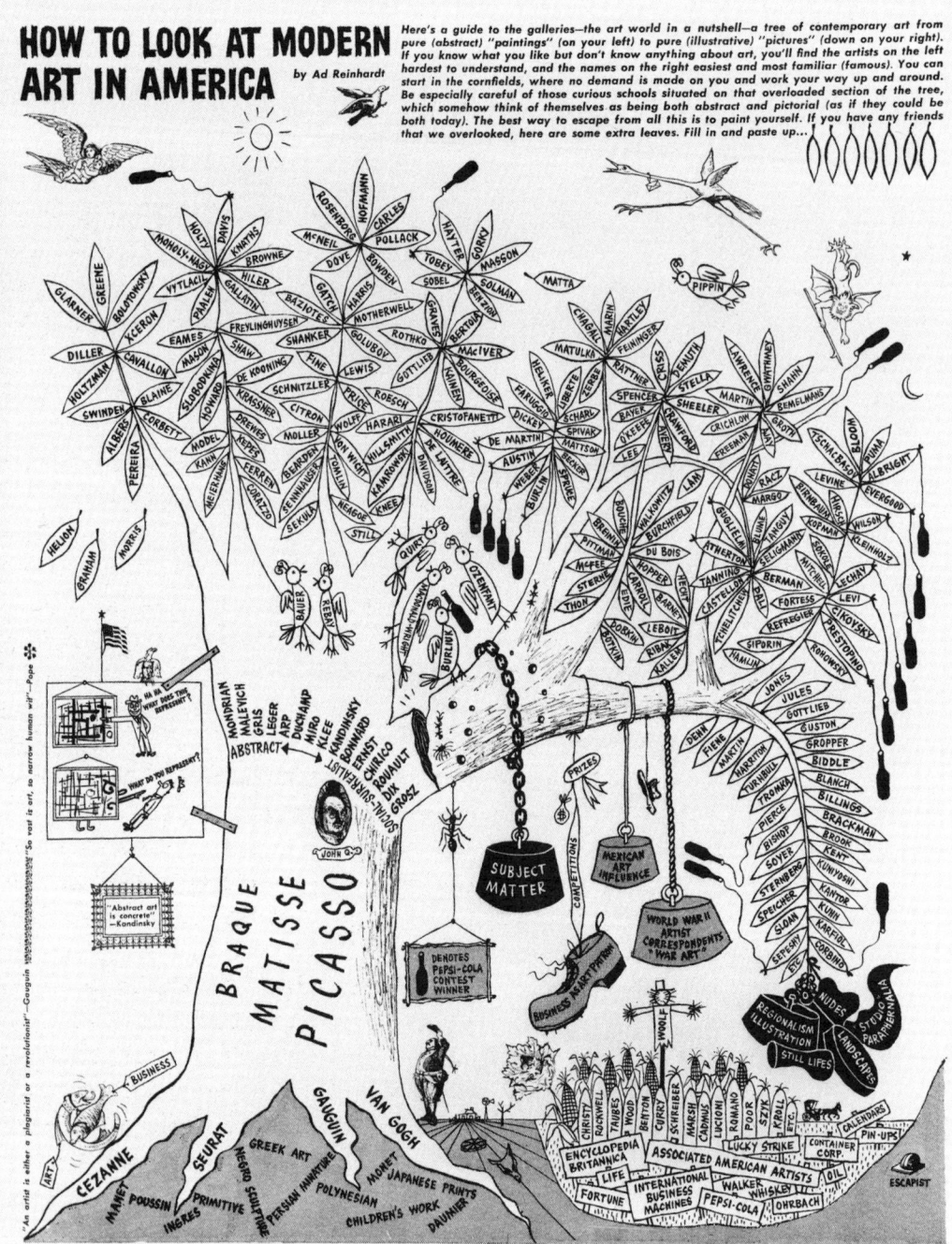

ABOVE Ad Reinhardt, *How to Look at Modern Art in America*, 1946.
RIGHT Jean-Michel Basquiat, *Untitled*, 1983.

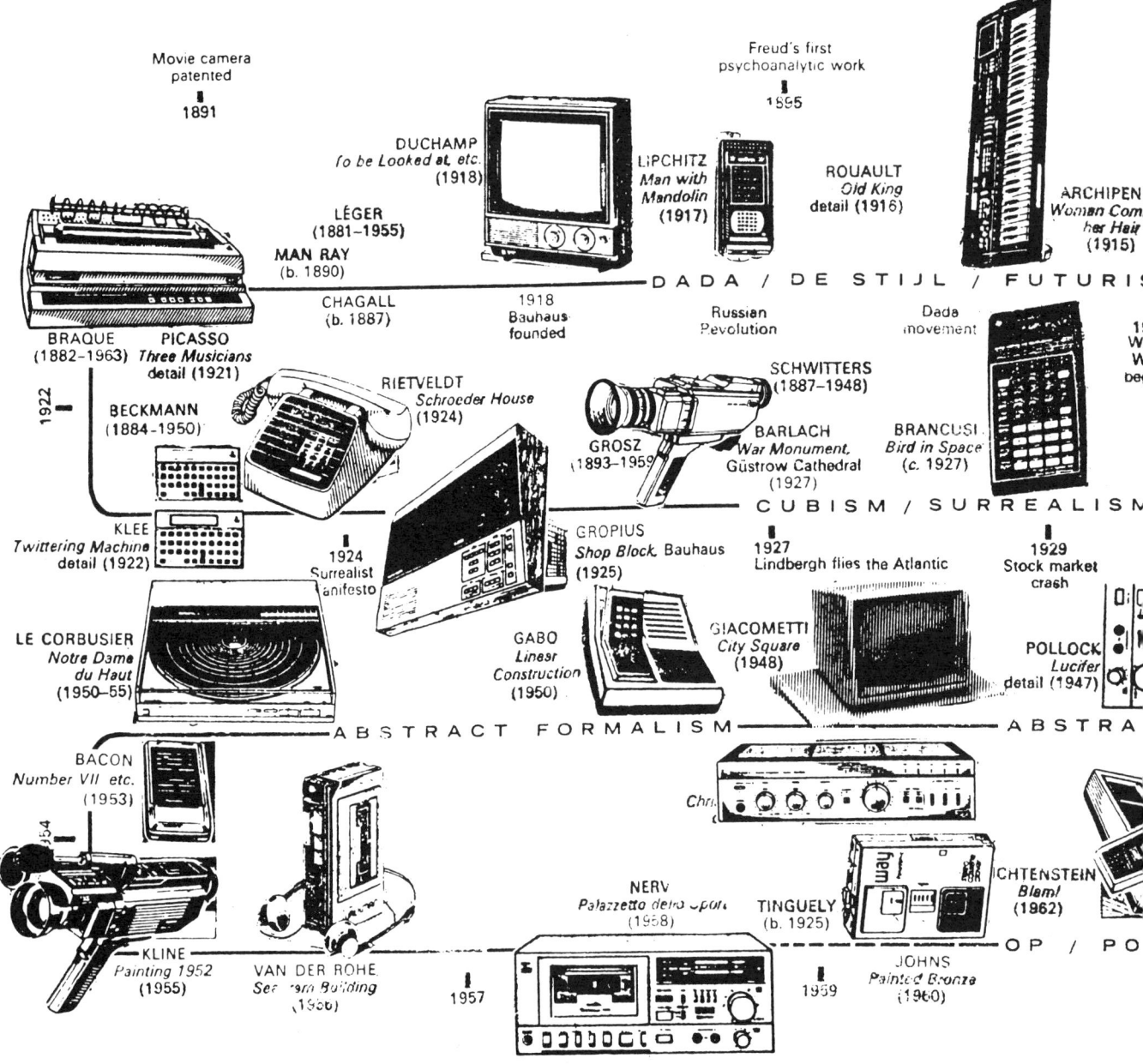

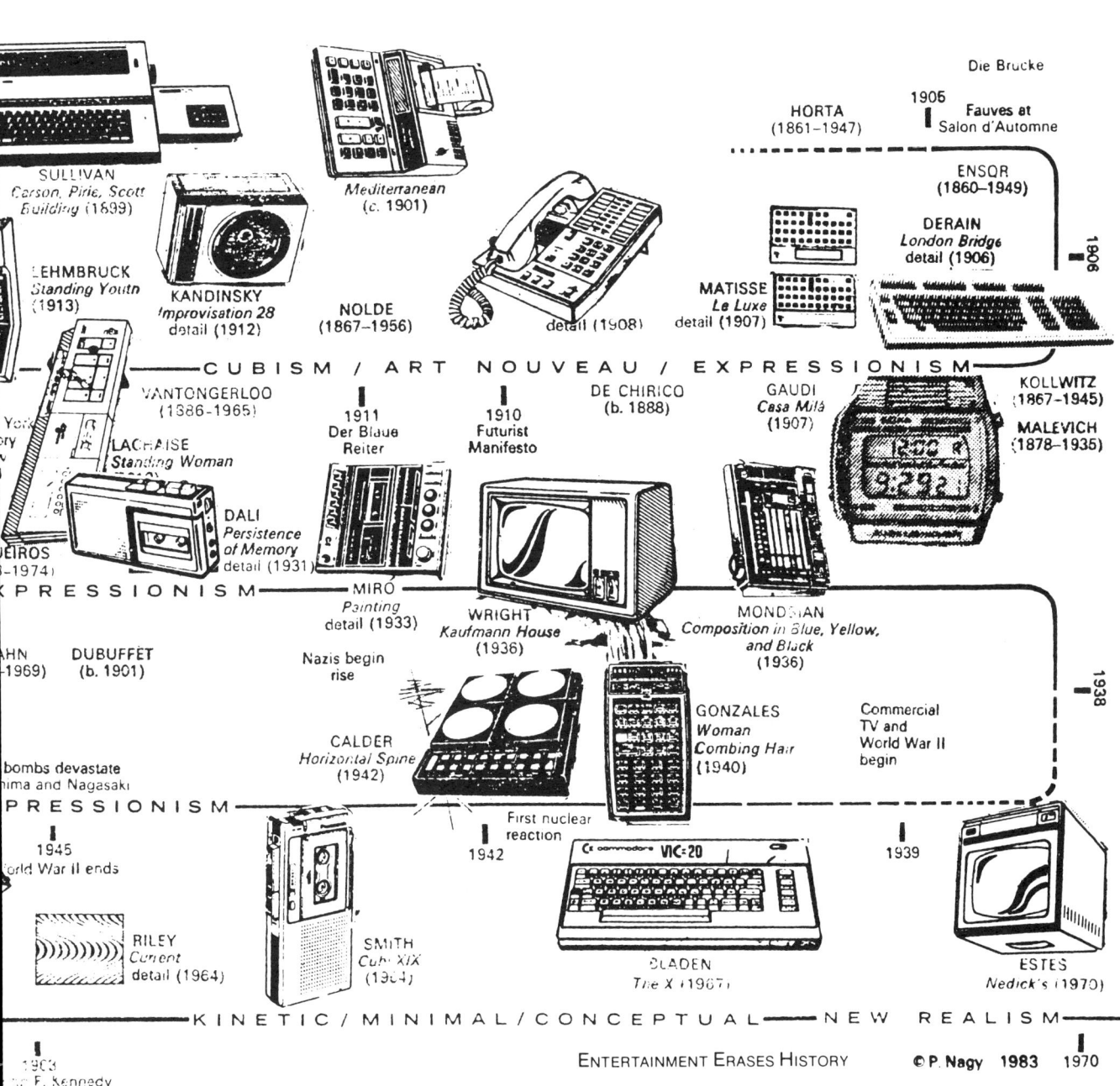

Entertainment Erases History © P. Nagy 1983

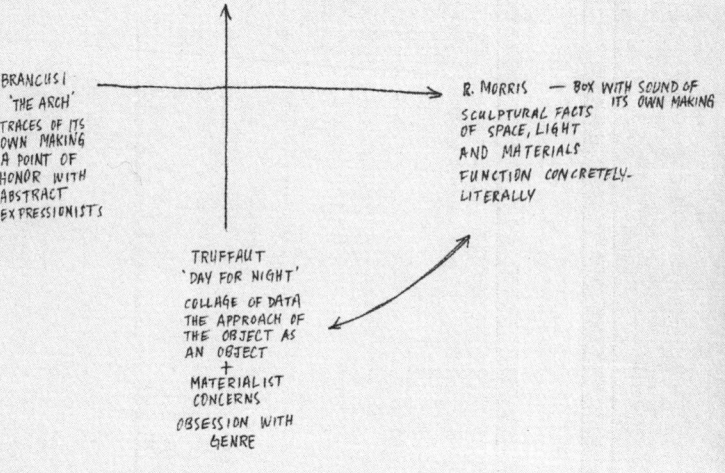
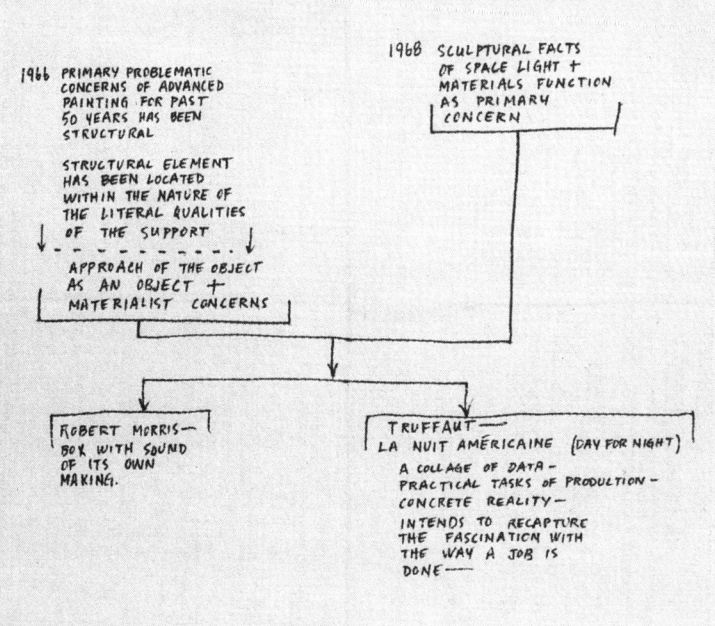

ABOVE   **Dennis Balk,** *Brancusi-Truffaut-Morris* **(detail), 1991.**
RIGHT   **Group Material,** *AIDS Timeline,* **1991.**

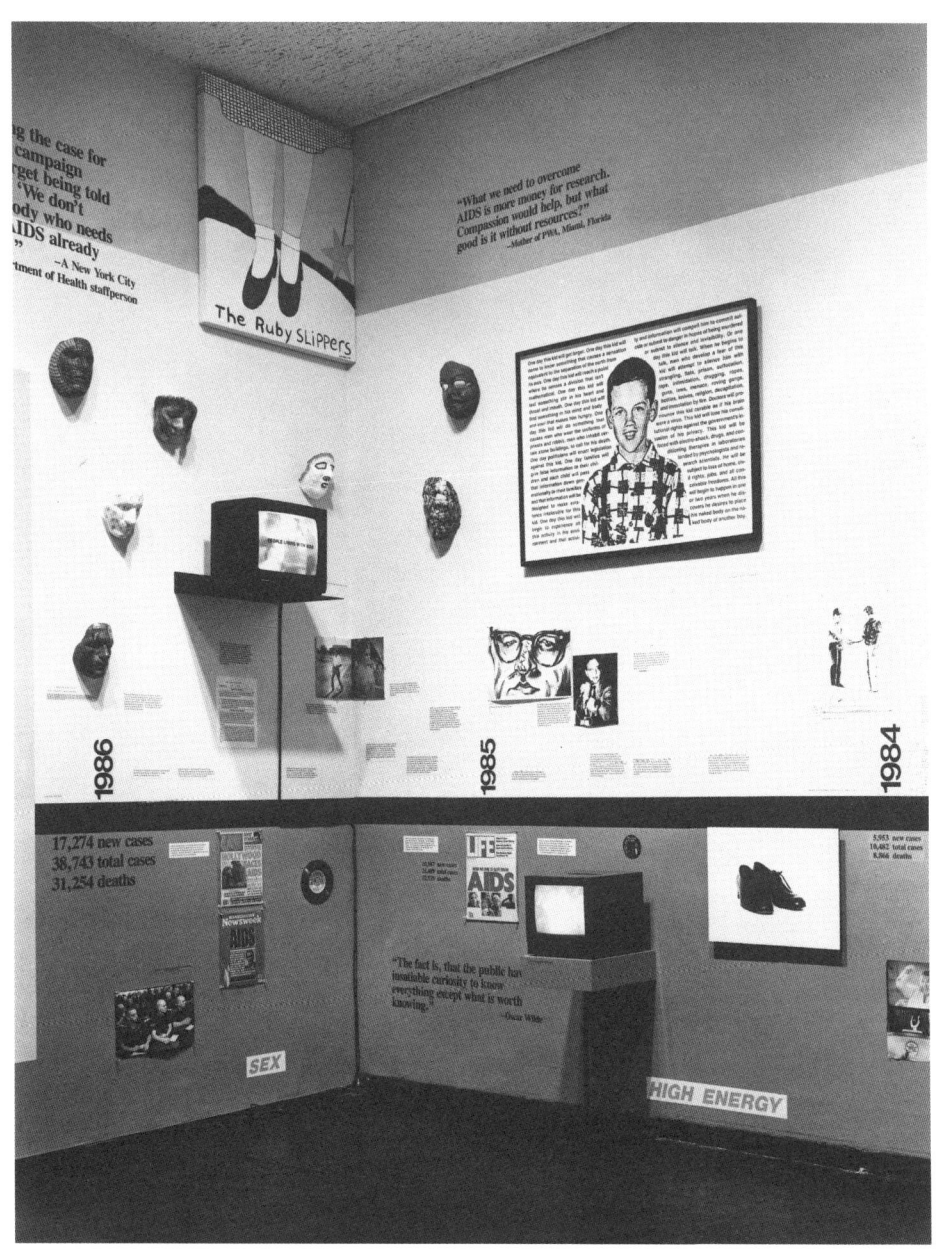

Karen Carson, *Sandwich*, 1994.

"THE EVIL),......
OR
THE STORY
OF
MY LIFE
BY
CPLY   1965

I AM SENT OUT INTO LIFE

I GAIN ETERNAL LIFE

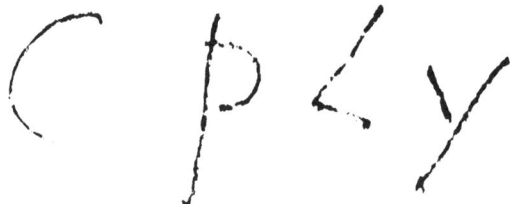

In the late '40s and early '50s, an adventurous new flowering of art bloomed, quite apart from the advent of abstract expressionism, when classical European surrealism pervaded the avant-garde in America. Peggy Guggenheim, whose New York gallery, Art of This Century, opened in 1942, was its most infamous advocate on the East Coast. Out West lived Walter Arensberg—the wealthy poet, collector, and early patron of Marcel Duchamp—and his wife, Louise, who had moved their renowned surrealist salon from New York to Los Angeles in 1924. Man Ray, who had fled the war in 1940, had also landed in Hollywood, and Max Ernst and his wife Dorothea Tanning were living in Arizona.

In 1947, artist and entrepreneur William N. Copley appeared on the scene and became the new movement's most loyal promoter. When he couldn't sell the Joseph Cornells, René Magrittes, Man Rays, and Max Ernsts he exhibited at the Copley Galleries in Beverly Hills, Copley became a collector by default, purchasing the most extraordinary examples of the artists' work himself.

Later, in New York, as the publisher of *The Letter Edged in Black Press*, Copley produced a series of limited-edition multiples by artists ranging from Marcel Duchamp to the younger imagist and pop artists—including a few whose work would not otherwise have been seen.

In his own paintings, CPLY (the name Copley gave himself as an artist) stands as a unique bridge between the Surrealists (who recognized him as an obstreperous young member) and the pop artists who would emerge in the 1960s. Although he died earlier this year, we are still in the process of discovering CPLY, the artist, one of the truly wonderful visual poets of human folly to exist in our time. Humor in the visual arts is all too rare, and there is no one around who can replace him.

WALTER HOPPS

ADAM LEFEVRE

NUMBER THEORY

Nine in the first place means trouble at the gate.
Three can have no consequence beyond the third condition.
Eight is like the anus of an infinite appetite.
In four's place, five cannot remember its own prediction.

Six, at the eleventh hour, succumbs to deep psychosis.
Eleven escapes inherently on the wings of a mirror.
A cough from the tomb where zero lies
means it's safe to believe anything you hear.

Seven, in its own place, weeps to heal like a wounded tree.
In any other place it cures like salt.
Ten paces back and forth, back and forth, a neurotic sentry,
starved for sleep, ordering shadows to halt.

Two defines herself with the smug confidence of a sum.
Every morning, one wakes up alone in a different room.

HALFTIME

October night nesting on the stadium.
The marching band blasts through a medley of moon songs, 4/4 time.
Moon River. Paper Moon.
Out from the ranks this year's appointed maiden spins,
twirling her silver baton.
Clusters of man-made little moons on poles
define the field she dances on.

She's heavy-thighed, not natural to the splits
and pirouettes she halfway does,
stumbling sometimes on the choppy turf.
In this town grace is not divine. It's work.

Her bosom, squeezed in a sequined leotard, heaves for air.
Her brow gleams with little gems of sweat.
She knows what's going wrong, and cares,
but has to keep up with the music till the end,
deferring shame like an inheritance.
Bass drum calmly counts the debt.
The unregenerate horns stampede.
She holds a shaky arabesque, hurls herself spread-eagle
through a wobbly cartwheel.
A smile, immense and frozen, never leaves her face.
Her will to cheer remains sublime
to the tittering of the glockenspiel.

They don't ask much in this factory town.
Pity rises from the smokestacks, acknowledged waste.
All they want from their majorette is the dogged verity of a moon.
She must show,
spread her arms and smile at each degradation.
Bow deeply to the dropped baton.
Stick to it.
Graduate.
Raise sensible children with sensible names
like Jason Jr. and Dawn.
Teach them earthly virtues: bitterness, gravity.
Daughter into mother, always smiling,
reminding them this
is how it is, this
is how it ought to be.

Looking at

Pictures

JOHN SZARKOWSKI / HILTON ALS

INTRODUCTION BY WALTER HOPPS

John Szarkowski became director of the Museum of Modern Art's Photography Department in 1962, and the first of the exhibitions I saw that he had curated was The Photographer and the American Landscape (1963). As a Westerner who loved photography, I was immediately touched by the exhibit. It occurred to me some years later that it had affirmed some of the Photography Department's deepest roots—an American pictoral tradition that was entwined with the documentation of the American Civil War on one hand, and the exploration of the American West on the other.

In the late 1960s, as director of the Corcoran Gallery of Art, I had the good fortune to meet Walker Evans through the young photographer William Christenberry. Evans was the first person to tell me that John Szarkowski was a first-rate curator and a fine photographer in his own right whom I should know and support. (Evans had included Szarkowski's work in a large anthology of the arts called Quality.)

Following in a line of curator-photographers associated with the development of the Photography Department—Edward Steichen, Beaumont and Nancy Newhall—Szarkowski first showed his intelligence and grasp of culture, history, and the relevance of form in his own work, when he presented with insight the birth of modern architecture through the work of its pioneering master in his beautiful book, The Idea of

LEFT Henri Cartier-Bresson, Seville, 1933.

Louis Sullivan (1956).

The extraordinary range of Szarkowski's vision as a curator and his insistence on the dignity of the medium are evident when one considers, on one hand, the four-part Atget exhibition he mounted with Maria Morris Hambourg in the early 1980s, and his acute and sensitive understanding of the works of Diane Arbus, on the other. In his 1972 exhibition of Arbus's work, he never lost sight of the deeply human concerns in what seemed at first, to the public at large, a shocking and sensationalistic series of photographs. By presenting Arbus, as he had Atget, as straightforwardly and clearly as possible, he allowed the photographers to speak for themselves, without apologies and without elaborate notes or arrangements.

Szarkowski has always been uniquely open to looking at the work of young photographers, and his program through which artists could leave their portfolios for review was a model of its kind. One artist to take advantage of this was the then little-known young American photographer, William Eggleston, whose career Szarkowski launched at the Museum of Modern Art in 1976, with a one-person show of color photographs that enraged many within the photographic establishment. As an acquaintance of Eggleston's, I was able to experience firsthand how well Szarkowski understood the editing and presentation of work.

John's concern for the public's understanding of photography led him to maintain the Department's library, which allowed people in the field—working photographers or visiting curators—to make appointments to view the Museum's archives of books, manuscripts, and prints from the collection. On one occasion, when I was there reviewing a box of rather fetishistic photographs, I heard the wry voice of John Szarkowski floating over my shoulder: "Some people will look at anything." He knew I'd consider that a compliment. ■

HILTON ALS: As I look through the exhibition catalogues, it seems to me that what you were trying to do at the Museum of Modern Art was to chip away at the sentimentalization of photography.

JOHN SZARKOWSKI: I wouldn't want to put it negatively like that. My attitude was very simple: it was that if what the best photographers really do is worthy of attention, it is worthy of attention on those terms—as their work. We don't have to use it to illustrate some other notion—or use it as one of the threads with which we weave a tapestry on some extraneous idea. What we need to show is who is Walker Evans? What did he make? Who is Harry Callahan? What did he make? What is their work about? What does it say? What is the nature of its beauty and meaning?

I never thought of my job as cheerleading or of myself as playing an apostolic role. I thought: you edit the work of the best photographers as well as you can, and then put it on a wall as clearly as you can. If you've got something to say about it in words, try to say it simply and precisely. If there is something there for people, they'll figure it out. If you put it up badly, you can make it more difficult for them. If you put it up well, you can help a little. But basically, you can't experience it for them.

ALS: In what state were the photography world and the photo department at the Museum when you arrived in 1962?

SZARKOWSKI: Well, the department was very small. It's still small but it was really small then. The Museum closed for expansion not long after I started, and reopened in the spring of 1964. Before that time, we had a tiny collections gallery called the Photography Alcove. You could hang forty little pictures in it, if you double-hung them. But in '64, we got a much larger space in the east wing. It was a great advance.

Photography at that time had virtually no status in the art business. Although liberal-minded people understood that it was an art of some kind, it wasn't considered a collectible art. If serious photographers made their living at photography, they did it by selling reproduction rights, not prints. You'd be lucky if you could give your prints away to friends—and you'd probably end up having to take prints from them in exchange, so the trunk never really got any emptier. The field was very pure. In that way, it was great fun.

ALS: The field itself was open enough for you to not have any received ideas about it.

SZARKOWSKI: Photographers had received ideas but they were limited to a pretty small in-group. They were often wrong-headed. The photographic community had a lot of ideas that were extremely parochial. In 1950 or earlier, most of the photographers who had some kind of serious ambition thought the picture magazine was where the action was. By the early '60s, photographers were beginning to be much less confident about that. But it was still a prevalent idea. Gene Smith was still the big hero of working photographers. Most people had forgotten Walker Evans, although he was still alive and in good health. All the public knew was The Family of Man show that Edward Steichen had curated in 1955; it was certainly the most successful photography exhibition anybody has ever done. In some ways, one might think of it as Steichen's last great work. But it had more to do with Steichen as an artist than with what intelligent photography was trying to do at the time.

ALS: Many photo people felt that The Family of Man exhibition was detrimental to photography being taken seriously.

SZARKOWSKI: Some may have felt that way. I felt that the exhibition was very much a product of that historical time. In a way, I think it was the last time that one could do an exhibition in that spirit. It persuaded many people who were not already committed to photography that the medium in fact had potential. It showed resources that most people had not yet understood or recognized.

My father saw the exhibition at The Minneapolis Institute of Arts while he was in Minneapolis on business, and he came back and told me that he really understood better what I'd been trying to do with my own photography all of those years. Well, the work in that show wasn't exactly what I'd been trying to do, but nevertheless it gave him access to the medium in a way I had never been able to get across with my explanations. And I was grateful for that.

However, when I came to the Museum of Modern Art, it never occurred to me to try to continue that notion. I thought it had been done. It wasn't necessary to try to do it twice. And I thought also that it was time to let photography speak for itself—with a little less interpretation and a little less hortatory preparation.

ALS: When I was a picture editor at The Village Voice, I always wondered how I would make the

JOHN SZARKOWSKI / HILTON ALS

Diane Arbus, THE JUNIOR INTERSTATE BALLROOM
DANCE CHAMPIONS, *Yonkers, N.Y., 1962.*

same things that worked in the paper work on the walls of a gallery or museum. I started thinking about museum walls as one big layout and stopped being intimidated by them.

SZARKOWSKI: Basically that's what *The Family of Man* was. You might say it was the best photo-story anyone ever did. The individual photographs were not as important as the tapestry that Steichen wove with the photographs, which was both the greatness and also, I think, the limitation of the show. The disadvantage of it was that the meanings that individual photographers might have had in their heads got lost for the sake of the larger general statement.

ALS: Because it became the curator's show.

SZARKOWSKI: Maybe at this point it would be possible to return to a version of the designed exhibition without it being the curator's show. The photographers themselves may be getting bored of a line of pictures on a wall. There are a few photographers now who are very, very serious about photography, but at the same time are sympathetic to the philosophies and techniques of installation art, with which one might communicate a bigger, more coherent idea.

ALS: One of the things you've written is that the history of photography is not really a history per se, but a development. It just keeps developing.

SZARKOWSKI: It has a conscious history now, quite a recent and rather simple history. But basically it began with people trying to figure out what the technical possibilities were. A few people would talk to a few other people. You didn't go to school, and there was no licensing system. There was no canon to learn. You had a couple of friends and you learned from whomever it was you went to work for. Finally, after 1937, you read Beaumont Newhall's book. But that was a hundred years after photography started. So it's a strange history. . . .

ALS: What strikes me is that there are relatively few good writers about photography.

SZARKOWSKI: And most of them have been photographers. Well, no, that's not true. Photographers have been the best critics, in terms of whom they have championed, but seldom in terms of their writings. For example, Berenice Abbott, Man Ray, Walker Evans, and Ansel Adams all championed Atget, but I'm not sure that what they wrote was very useful, except in their insistence that it was necessary to look at his work. James Agee wrote one of the best things ever written about photography—the introduction to the Helen Levitt book—and he was not a photographer, but of course he was the great good friend of both Evans and Levitt, and learned from them. Robert Adams is a marvelous photographer, and has written well about it, although he is very stern. Beaumont Newhall sometimes wrote well, but I think he was handicapped by the traditional art historical training of his day; the intellectual technology that was developed to deal with the history of Western painting didn't necessarily serve well the historical issues that were central to other kinds of traditions.

In the history of painting, when Rubens goes to Italy and sees Caravaggio, quite a simple, clear, linear thing has happened; when he goes home he knows something that nobody else knows.

But, in photography, everything happened at once. Especially after the rise of photomechanical reproduction.

Speaking of writing, I thought your piece on Diane Arbus was very good. It's very easy to write badly about her.

ALS: Why is that? Because of the dramatic element of her work?

SZARKOWSKI: Yes, people think it is just about dwarves and midgets and odd people. It's not about that.

ALS: No, that's not it at all, or not completely. One of the great things about her work is that it is this continuous self-portrait emotionally.

SZARKOWSKI: In a way, yes; I suppose everyone's work is a self-portrait. But Diane was in no way a narcissistic person; she was full of a lively, charming intelligence. I remember once sitting in a bar with Diane and her great friend Marvin Israel, the designer, and he said, "I think we should get Diane a grant to take a portrait of every person in New York." She loved the idea. People don't understand that if you met most of the people in her photographs you wouldn't think they were so peculiar. Even the most haunting of her subjects—the pro-war demonstrators, the people at the masked ball, the dancers, the children, the kid with the hand grenade—of course they're mad, but only in the sense that everybody is a little.

ALS: It seems to me that the interpretations that surround her work are political in a way that the pictures aren't. She was really just interested in humanity. I talked to the filmmaker Shirley Clark's daughter at one point and she said that Diane was the most charming person she had ever met, that she walked on air. She was a great seductress of people.

SZARKOWSKI: Oh, absolutely.

ALS: How did you meet her?

SZARKOWSKI: She sent her portfolio to the Museum in 1962. I remember that I had seen her work published somewhere—in *Harper's Bazaar* or in a photography magazine called *Infinity* earlier the same year. And I wasn't completely convinced. She was working with a Leica then. The pictures were rather grainy and casual, and lacked the kind of precise description that they had later. And I didn't like them very much, frankly. Then she came in to pick them up and I just adored her. Not because she was physically beautiful, but she had such a lively and charming mind. We had a very good time talking. You wouldn't be so frank with most people on first meeting them. But she was clearly extraordinary. She asked me what I thought, and I told her that her photographs were obviously very interesting as documents but I didn't feel that they were really resolved—except for the teenage dancers. That was the only one of the later famous pictures that she'd already done.

I remember saying, "This one is like Sander." She said, "Who's Sander?" So I went and got a couple of boxes of August Sander—and it was like Saint Paul on the road to Damascus or wherever it was that he saw the light. . . . She was just bowled over by him. She'd never seen his work before. His first book had come out in 1929, and the Nazis had prohibited its distribution; almost

August Sander, *Mother and Daughter*, 1912.

JOHN SZARKOWSKI / HILTON ALS

Walker Evans, *Sidewalk and Storefront, New Orleans,* 1935.

nobody had seen it. The second book was published the very year I met Diane.

ALS: So a huge bulb went off in her head.

SZARKOWSKI: That's the story of photography, you know. Ansel Adams wrote Stieglitz in the 1930s and said, "I've seen this terrific new photographer Timothy O'Sullivan." O'Sullivan had been dead for fifty years and nobody had seen his work.

And you know about Brassaï getting a letter from some English eccentric, saying, "Dear Mr. Brassaï, We are enchanted by your pictures in *Paris de Nuit* and are awarding you our bronze medal. Signed Peter Henry Emerson." Brassaï asked himself, "Who is Peter Henry Emerson?" and put the letter in his stocking drawer and forgot about it.*

ALS: I'd like to know how you came to photography.

SZARKOWSKI: I was ten or eleven maybe, growing up in Ashland, Wisconsin, on the shore of Lake Superior, in the mid-'30s, in a generation where all kids collected stamps and did photography and built model airplanes. For me, it was either make photographs or play the clarinet.

ALS: When you started off as a photographer what sort of pictures were you taking?

SZARKOWSKI: Well, when I was a kid, the book that impressed me most was called *The Fun of Photography*. It was done by a couple of people, a husband and wife, I believe, Mario and Mable Scacheri, who were photographers and who also wrote for one of the New York newspapers. I found the book a few months ago at a flea market, and I was astonished at how childish it was. But the good thing about it was that they always talked about the picture. They didn't talk about technique for its own sake, they talked about picture-making. The technique was just a series of tools related to that end.

Later I had an art history professor at the University of Wisconsin named Jack Kienitz. I remember him saying at one point after class, "So, you're interested in photography?" And I said, "I am a photographer." He said, "Okay, go down to the Student Union and buy this book." Being an obedient student of my generation, I went down to the bookstore and bought the book. It cost four dollars, which was a lot of money. It was Walker Evans's *American Photographs*. I took it home to my room and looked at it and I couldn't make head or tail of it. It was so inartistic. It was absolutely a puzzle to me. I went through it over and over again, but most of it looked like plain facts, with no art at all. The one picture I could sort of make some sense of was the one of the lady in the striped blouse standing in front of the barber shop in New Orleans with diagonal striping on the front of the barber shop and pole. There was a kind of design quality I could appreciate. But most of the pictures in that book just looked like absolutely plain facts to me. But I'd paid for it,

---

* *Paris de Nuit* was published in 1933, when Brassaï was thirty-four and Dr. Peter Henry Emerson was seventy-seven. Emerson's great book, *Life and Landscape on the Norfolk Broads*, had been published in 1886. It was illustrated with original photographic prints, and produced in an edition of about two hundred copies. Not surprisingly, Brassaï had never heard of it.

so I kept looking at it, and it kept getting better. And it still does get better.

ALS: What triggered the meltdown when you began to see what Walker Evans meant in his photographs?

SZARKOWSKI: In a sense, I never know what a photographer means. Whenever I think I do, I am always wrong. You know those Cartier-Bresson pictures of the children playing in the ruins in Spain? For years I thought they were made in a bombed-out building during the Spanish Civil War. They were actually made in 1933, and the war didn't start until 1936. It was probably some kind of slum-clearance project!

ALS: But one of the great things about photography is never being certain, going on a hunch.

SZARKOWSKI: Yes, it's totally opaque.

ALS: So you were taking photographs and writing and thinking about photography. How did you get the job at the Museum of Modern Art?

SZARKOWSKI: I don't know. I really don't. One of the trustees, Henry Allen Moe, liked what I had done with my first Guggenheim—a book on the architect Louis Sullivan—and Steichen, who was head of the Photography Department then, liked it too. He had purchased some of my pictures. So he knew who I was. But I don't know who had the original idea. I was in Ontario, working on a book on the Quetico wilderness area, and Monroe Wheeler, who was head of exhibitions and publications, wrote me a letter, saying, "I'm sure you know about the Museum's plans, and if you happen to be in New York . . ." A typical museum letter. If you happen to be in New York . . . and in fact I didn't have any notion what their plans were. So I wrote back, "No, I don't know about your plans and I don't have any intention of being in New York in the foreseeable future. And in any case, I couldn't come until the ground freezes in Western Ontario." Monroe must have thought this was some kind of colloquial expression. He wrote again, saying, "Well, if we didn't make it clear, of course we intend to pay for your trip. And November would be fine." But I still didn't know what they wanted with me. I thought they might want to show my work, or want me to work on an exhibition. I had worked on special exhibitions for several museums. But I had no idea that they wanted me to run the Department.

ALS: What was your first show?

SZARKOWSKI: The first show I did was called *Five Unrelated Photographers*—Garry Winogrand, Minor White, George Krauss, Ken Heyman, and Jerry Leibling. It was not a show that had some big encompassing statement to make, except to the degree that the five photographers were making their own statements. That's the way I like to work.

ALS: Tell me about your show *The Photographer's Eye* in 1966.

SZARKOWSKI: When the Museum reopened in 1964 after the expansion, we had gallery space to hang about two hundred pictures from the collection, but I also wanted to do a temporary show. René D'Harnoncourt, who was the director of the

Museum, said, "I think you should do a show that has to do with your idea of what photography's formal nature is." People had tried before to do something similar but they had tried to do it in terms of a vocabulary that had been established for painting or the traditional visual arts. And their attempts all seemed to me to be really feeble.

I thought, I know about photography, I'm a photographer, I should be smart enough to figure out what you have to deal with in order to talk about the decisions that photographers make. I decided that these issues were intrinsic to the nature of the medium: You have to decide where to go, or not to go anywhere. And you have to decide where the edges are, where to stand, when to push the button. And that's it. The rest is subtleties.

I started fishing for trout around the same time I began photographing, maybe a couple of years later. I didn't get my first fly rod until I was about thirteen. I've been pretty faithful as a fisherman, and it's come to me little by little that I have no talent. People wouldn't realize I didn't have any talent if they watched me fishing. I know how to do it. I cast well, and I have a general idea about where the fish lies. But the real talent is being able to empathize with the fish and to know exactly where it is. Some people are talented and some people aren't. Look at Joe DiMaggio, a great center fielder. If you asked him, "How did you know where the ball was going to come down?" he wouldn't know.

ALS: One photographer who still shows us what we don't know about photography is Cartier-Bresson. How did you begin working with him?

SZARKOWSKI: Cartier-Bresson hadn't been shown at the Museum for a long time when I got there. So I did a show of his current work. It had a little historical section in it, for people who had never seen Cartier-Bresson before, but it was basically work of the time. That must have been about 1968, the time of the student revolution in Paris.

ALS: Maria Morris Hambourg, the photography curator at the Met, told me about seeing him in a café in France when she was going to meet you for a picnic. She went over to him and said, "Oh Mr. Bresson, Mr. Szarkowski and I are having a picnic, you must come along." And he said, "Madame, I am not Henri Cartier-Bresson."

SZARKOWSKI: The photographer Joel Meyerowitz tells another version of that story. He saw Bresson photographing a Saint Patrick's Day parade here and said, "Mr. Cartier-Bresson, I just wanted you to know that I think you're a great artist, and that I'm an enormous admirer of your work." And he said, "Who me? No, you've made a mistake." And then apparently Joel looked so crestfallen that Henri said, "All right, it's true, I am Cartier-Bresson, but don't tell anyone."

ALS: What do you think his reluctance stemmed from? A desire to stay invisible?

SZARKOWSKI: Well, you can't work if people are asking you for your autograph. But there's also something very funny and psychological about it. One story has it that while Bresson was working in India, he registered at the hotel as "Hank Carter." The whole journalist corps knew who he was, but they had to make believe that he was an American journalist. A friend of his once called him "as Norman as a beach tree"; he could be mistaken for a provincial banker perhaps, but never for an American journalist.

ALS: When you've worked with Cartier-Bresson or others, have the photographers generally had a very strong idea of how they wanted the show to look before you started working together?

SZARKOWSKI: It varies. It's rather mercurial. One day they'll say, "It's your show, do what you want, and I don't want to have anything to do with it. I don't even want to go to the opening." But then on other days they feel quite strongly. It's very personal. In 1939, Beaumont Newhall hung a photography exhibition at the Museum in which each photographer's work was hung on a different brightly colored wall. He proposed putting Walker Evans on dull red walls, and Walker just couldn't cope with that. But Beaumont held his ground, so finally Walker said, "Okay, a red wall's all right, if I can hang the pictures." So he took his pictures back and mounted them with immense white mats, then he hung the mats edge to edge.

Basically, I was never interested in trying to make photographs into something else. I was very interested in what the photographers had to say. . . . It wasn't that I was trying to be a nice guy, I just wasn't interested in using their pictures as a raw material for something else. The photographers were the art directors.

ALS: One of the things I've learned from looking at photographers like Garry Winogrand is that it's about you, the photographer, meeting the world.

SZARKOWSKI: That's the way it happens. But the best photographers, it seems to me, the best artists, don't spend a lot of time worrying about self-expression. They have formulated a problem and it's the problem that's interesting to them. Self-expression is more or less unavoidable. What you have to worry about is making the self you express more interesting, more intelligent, more knowledgeable, more alert. Adding something to what the medium has amounted to up to now, that's an interesting problem; that's the thing we call art. People who think they're beginning from ground zero just don't know very much.

ALS: What you are saying reminds me of a beautiful quotation from Jean Rhys's memoirs: "If I didn't write, I would not have earned my life." Literature is a vast body of water and everyone's just a little trickle going into it.

SZARKOWSKI: Winogrand came to visit me at the Museum once and when we'd finished what we needed to do, I walked him out past a couple of people looking at a box of Edward Weston photographs. Winogrand looked over one of their shoulders and said, "Oh boy, isn't that a terrific picture?" The kid turned around and said, "Aren't you Garry Winogrand?" "Yes." "But if you're Garry Winogrand, how come you like Edward Weston?" And Garry said, "Why wouldn't I love Edward Weston? We both do the same thing." He didn't mean they used the same kind of camera or dealt with the same subject matter or had the same kind of technical philosophy, but they both used photography to respond to the world.

ALS: How did Winogrand find you?

SZARKOWSKI: He just came in. Everybody came in. There weren't any photography galleries in those days after Helen Gee closed Limelight. André Kertész came in, too. He was an old man and he had two shopping bags full of big, 250-sheet, 8-by-10 boxes. He must have brought in a thousand photographs. I remembered his work from magazines like Coronet that published a lot of Brassaï and Kertész, but I hadn't heard of him in a long time; nobody had. I thought he'd died a hundred years ago. He had just disappeared. In fact, he had got in very much of a rut working for House & Garden. He did interiors—patios with luncheon tables set with peaches and cottage cheese.

ALS: What was striking to you about Winogrand, personally and professionally?

SZARKOWSKI: Personally, he was a lion. He had so much energy, so much intellectual curiosity, drive, and hunger. It took a while to realize how intelligent he was because he had none of the conventional mannerisms of an intellectual. He didn't even look or sound thoughtful. But, in fact, he was extremely thoughtful. He was extraordinarily intelligent about photography and was capable of thinking about it in a profoundly radical way. His own conception of what he was doing was so strong that he could simply brush aside issues that weren't central to his concerns. And he had a very playful mind, so he wasn't necessarily concerned with explaining clearly what he was doing. People were often put off by

Garry Winogrand, La Grange, Texas, circa 1977–80.

the fact that he tilted the camera; they'd complain that his pictures were tilted and he'd say, "No, no, the picture is never tilted." But he wouldn't explain what he meant by that. Finally, one day, somebody said it once too often and he reached over to a framed picture that was hanging on the wall and raised one corner of it, and he said, "There! Now the picture's tilted...." If you are dealing with a wide-angle lens, unless you are an idiot and refuse to tilt the camera, you are going to have very untraditional perspective effects. Winogrand was an incredible photographer, absolutely astonishing. Every body of work was a new challenge, even to look at.

ALS: Did a lot of photographers socialize with each other in those days? Was William Eggleston, say, particularly friendly with Winogrand?

SZARKOWSKI: They were interested in each other, but Eggleston lives in Memphis and he didn't spend much time in New York.

ALS: I just finished reading your book about Eggleston and I loved what you wrote about him deepening the mystery in the photographs, as opposed to explaining what they are supposed to be.

SZARKOWSKI: When I started out, photographers basically didn't have any idea what to do with color. One learned how to deal with it technically, but that was it. The best color was studio work. And color prints at the time were physically ugly—the carbon process was an ugly process. The prints looked as though they'd been rotting in a damp basement for twenty years. Dye transfer was a little better, but it was pretty ugly as well. Modern color prints are the most beautiful color photographs. The quality of the color is far superior to any of the older processes. Of course, the color always looked better in ink, in the magazines. Much better than the photographic prints, because the ink was transparent enough that you could see the white paper through it a little bit. That gave it some life and vitality, whereas the color prints looked like something made in a chemical factory in Rochester. Anyhow, nobody knew what to do with color then. The best color photographer was probably the early Irving Penn. The still lifes were beautiful. *After-dinner Games, Still Life with Watermelon*, and so on.

ALS: And then Eggleston came along...

SZARKOWSKI: Right. In those days, becoming a photographer had been largely a question of learning how to see in black and white. So when color started, you'd basically compose a black-and-white picture, put color film in the camera and hope for the best. Eggleston, I think, was just about the first person to be able to look at the real world and edit it in color—edit the color sensation not simply as a color sensation, but in terms of its meaning as well, so that the pictures really seem to be about something, about the world, about life.

ALS: What sort of role did Alfred Stieglitz play in your thinking about photography?

SZARKOWSKI: Well, you know, I did a Stieglitz show at the Museum a year ago. I enjoyed it a lot. I learned to come to terms with Stieglitz, who has never really been all that easy for me to deal with, because he was a terrible dissembler. And it finally occurred to me that he was the only person I can think of who was a major artist and also a major art dealer. And that's a pretty interesting combination. I mean, which hat was he wearing at any particular time?

I think that for the first fifty years of his life, certainly for thirty years as a photographer, he was handicapped or crippled by his ambition to have photography accepted as a fine art. To achieve that goal, he produced work and encouraged the people around him to produce work that people would recognize as fine art. But for them to recognize the work as fine art, it had to be similar to what they already knew as fine art.

And he persuaded some people, up to a point, that yes, you could have photography in art museums. His show in 1910 at the Albright in Buffalo was a huge exhibition. But I think when he looked at it, he said, "This is wrong. This is not interesting." After that he did very little for five years, and then his own really great, original, radical photographic work begins. Earlier he had been making *fin de siècle* nocturnes and études and fake symbolist pictures in photography and showing Cézanne, Matisse, and Picasso in his gallery, 291. It didn't make any sense. And eventually I think he stopped trying to persuade people and started to do his own work. The great work doesn't start until he's over fifty. But Stieglitz sort of went out of his way to confuse the issue. If you listened to what he said, you'd think he'd been following a kind of internal principle from the time he was born, that he had never changed. But he changed radically. The end of the teens, the '20s, beginning of the '30s, that's the great Stieglitz.

I am annoyed by the notion that Stieglitz is great because he brought modern art to this country, or that he's great because he married Georgia O'Keeffe—because he was a great lover or a great philosopher. I don't think he was a great philosopher. I think his philosophy is beer-garden Nietzsche. Of course it's remarkable that he showed the European modernists at 291 before the Armory show in 1913. But I expect that European modernism would have come to this country in very much the same shape if Stieglitz had been run over by a bus years earlier.

So I'm not really convinced that he was an original formative influence on the development of modern art in this country. Not at least at that time. Later in his work with the American painters—he probably kept Arthur Dove and John Marin alive—the people he showed were, most of them, the best painters we had. Dove was surely the best American painter at the time. And Charles Demuth, Marsden Hartley, Marin, and sometimes O'Keeffe were artists of substance. But what I mean is that Stieglitz is praised for being this great Renaissance man, but undervalued for the best of his art. Steichen said, "Stieglitz's greatest gift is his work, and the greatest of that is the stuff that began at the end of the 291 days." And that's it. One short sentence.

ALS: Stieglitz and Walker Evans seem to have similar interests, but they come at them in different ways—from the surreal nature to the everyday.

SZARKOWSKI: Walker didn't have much use for Stieglitz. He went to visit him once and I guess Stieglitz didn't say anything very positive. When

JOHN SZARKOWSKI / HILTON ALS

John Runk, *Pine Boards and Frank Stenlund, South Stillwater*, MN, 1912.

Walker was young and very poor, he had a night job at the New York Public Library working in the map room. There's not much to do in the map room at night and because he'd become very interested in photography, he looked at the entire run of Stieglitz's magazine *Camera Work*; and he said that there was only one picture that was useful or meaningful to him. That was Paul Strand's *Blind Woman*—at least according to his memory later on.

ALS: You showed Avedon's series on the death of his father. Tell me about looking at those pictures initially. You had known him, of course, with Diane Arbus.

SZARKOWSKI: Yes. He's a terribly impressive guy, extremely talented. But I said that I thought Stieglitz was handicapped by the nature of his ambition, and I have sometimes thought that Richard also has been.

ALS: That world is a very seductive place. There's no way to excavate your real work from it after a while, because the distinction becomes blurred.

SZARKOWSKI: I liked Avedon's show of the pictures of his father. I also saw a wonderful show that Avedon did in his own studio in midtown, perhaps thirty years ago. If I recall it correctly, there were two rooms: one room had a very modest number of elegantly matted and framed pictures, finished work, wonderful portraits. And the other room was a madhouse of proofs, workprints pushpinned on the wall, telegrams, appointments, and so on that had to do with the nature of the world and the process in which he was working. A fantastic show. And one had the sense that Avedon had a very clear idea of who he was and the nature of the circumstances in which he was working, and the two kinds of product that could come out of it: one where the product and the process were intimately tied together, and the other, which was almost a kind of a residue of the first—the pictures that really lasted on their own terms.

ALS: Was there an enormous response to the show on his father? The cruelty of photography and so on?

SZARKOWSKI: Somewhat, but Diane's work was already known. Robert Frank's work was already known. Even Walker Evans had been wrongly thought cruel. Of course, it was Avedon's father, but that was moving. The show was very sharply focused and it was, of course, not immense—it was only a few prints.

I get to be less and less interested in huge shows. I've always tried to keep shows compact. Nevertheless, I think every show I've ever done was twenty percent too big, and a lot of them more than that.

ALS: Do you like Weegee's work?

SZARKOWSKI: Oh, it's terrific. By the time I met him in 1963 or '64, he had done his great work, and had been doing the distortions and montages—deeply vulgar work—being "Weegee" as a profession rather than being a photographer. But for perhaps ten years, he was wonderful.

I do think that photographers have shorter creative life expectancies than most artists. But come to think of it, there aren't very many Haydns. Even with Haydn, you never hear the

Roger Fenton, *The Shadow of the Valley of Death*, 185

first seventy-five symphonies. Maybe it took him seventy-five to get the hang of it.

ALS: Just like Stieglitz.

SZARKOWSKI: Right. You know, one of the great things about Stieglitz, especially when you get to be over thirty, is that it's wonderful to have a role model who didn't do his best work before he was old enough to shave. One can very easily get enough of that kind of child genius. Edward Weston got better and better, of course, until he got sick. If Atget had died when he was sixty-five, he would have been just another great photographer. But what he did in those last years . . . We did an exhibition after the Museum bought the Atget collection from Berenice Abbott and Julien Levy back in '68. In those days, we didn't have any idea how to date the pictures. We just said "Atget, circa 1910," figuring we couldn't be more than about fifteen years off. So we did a show of about 125 pictures, just on the basis of pulling out the best ones, without any kind of scholarly structure. And years later, after Maria Hambourg figured out how to date the pictures, it turned out that half of the pictures in the show were done during Atget's first thirty years of work, and the other half were done in the last six years of his life, beginning in 1921 when he was sixty-four.

ALS: Do you always have to have an emotional response to the work you're showing?

SZARKOWSKI: Not necessarily. Sometimes you show work because you think there is something in it that's got some vitality to it, or because it is historically important and thus essential to understand. You don't have to love it. Then there is the stuff you really like. When I first came to the Museum, Bruce Downes, the editor of *Popular Photography*, was doing a series called "Critics Choice." He wanted me to pick a photograph and write something about it. So I picked *Pine Boards and Frank Stenlund, South Stillwater, MN*, by an unknown photographer named John Runk. Downes said, "Are you serious about this?" He couldn't believe I was writing about an old picture with no standing at all, by a photographer no one had heard of. But I found it beautiful, and still do, partly because I might have known the old stump that the tree came from, up on the headwaters of the Namekagon. In a peculiar way, it had to do with my life even before I was born, my part of the world.

Photographs never end up quite as you expected. You never photograph what you're trying to photograph. But sometimes what you do photograph is better.

ALS: You never can photograph the whole.

SZARKOWSKI: No, and sometimes you can't even photograph the part. People say that Roger Fenton couldn't photograph the Charge of the Light Brigade in 1855 because his plates weren't fast enough. Well, that's not it. A century later, David Douglas Duncan did the best photographs to come out of the Korean War, and they're portraits—as still and mute as Fenton's cannon balls. The best stuff is always some piece of the unnoticed backside of the issue, that relates to the nominal subject in a way that only a photograph could discover.

—*August 27 and September 13, 1996*

Lynn Davis : Stealing Time

Lumbini, Nepal, 1992.

ABOVE *Pagan, Burma, 1993.*
RIGHT *The Appia Antica, Rome, 1993.*

ABOVE *Gate of Angkor Thom, Siem Riep, Cambodia, 1993.*
RIGHT *Iceberg No. 5, Disko Bay, Greenland, 1988.*

ABOVE Delicate Arch, Arches National Park, Utah, 1991.
RIGHT Cappadocia, Turkey, 1995.

Minaret, Port of Mokka, Yemen, 1996.

Lynn Davis

The sticks are burning in the fire that they feed . . . RAINER MARIA RILKE

Images of silence. Images of erosion and decay. Images caught stealing time. Monumental forms poised in "mid-passage," suspended and illuminated into a "freeze" before their long slide to extinction; a journey that passes beyond history, beyond the lists of time, or, in the case of rock or ice, the geological seizures that spewed them forth.

As a celebration of emptiness and impermanence, the beauty of these disintegrations cannot resonate without pointing beyond itself, toward a final collapse of form into the essence of matter: air, earth, fire, and water. Mysteries that cannot be measured or followed, reduced to echoes from the sublime rot of history. Until, of course, the whole dance is resurrected and begins once again.

An iceberg carved from the edge of a glacier, split in half as it floats down the western coast of Greenland, where it will dissolve into the North Atlantic . . . A natural arch of weathered rock in southern Utah stands like a monolithic sentinel, protecting an empty view . . . Another gate, this one man-made, leads into Angkor Thom, an eleventh-century Buddhist city founded on the Mahayana ideals of wisdom, compassion, and enlightenment, now reduced to rubble, bullet holes, and smashed statutes . . . A stone column built by the Buddhist King Ashoka in 249 B.C., in Lumbini, the place of the Buddha's birth . . . Caves in a Cappadocian mountain that once offered refuge to Christians fleeing the ancient Romans . . . those same Romans who marched forth on the Appian Way, past what is now a crumbling wall . . . A Buddhist stupa in Pagan, part of an abandoned city in Burma which included over thirteen thousand temples as well as seventy thousand monks. Now only silence . . . A sixteenth-century minaret at the end of the Arabian peninsula, once part of a great mosque, its base eroded by sand, desolate and forgotten.

RUDOLPH WURLITZER

FROM **CENTURIA**

GIORGIO MANGANELLI

FOUR

Around ten in the morning, a man of serious learning and somewhat melancholy humor had discovered the irrefutable proof of the existence of God. It was a complex proof, but not so complex that it could not be grasped by a moderately philosophical mind. The learned man remained calm, reexamined the proof of the existence of God from end to beginning, sideways, and from beginning to end, and concluded that he had done a good job. He closed the notebook containing the notes relating to the definitive proof of the existence of God, and went out to occupy himself with nothing—in short, to live. Around four in the afternoon, returning home, he realized that he had forgotten the exact formulation of some sections of the demonstration; and every section was, naturally, essential.

    The situation made him anxious. He went into a bar to have a beer, and for a moment seemed to himself calmer. He recovered one section, but immediately afterward realized he had lost two others. He placed his hope in his notes, yet he knew that the notes were incomplete, and he had left them that way, since he did not want anyone, even the maid, to be certain of the existence of God before he had carefully worked out the full argument. Two-thirds of the way home, he realized that, as the proof of the existence of God was losing its solid, miraculous characteristics, he was running into arguments that he was no longer certain belonged to the original argument. Was there a section concerning Limbo? No, there wasn't; and no Sleeping Souls but perhaps the Last Judgment. He was not sure about it. The Inferno? It did not seem to him likely, and yet he had the impression of having debated for a long time about the Inferno, and of having placed the existence of the Inferno at the culmination of his inquiry. Arriving at the door of his house, he was bathed in a cold sweat. Of what, really, had he demonstrated the existence? For he had reached a result that was indisputably true, invincible, and yet impossible to fix in an unforgettable formula. Only then did he realize that he was clutching the house key in his hand, and, in a belated gesture of desperation, he hurled it into the middle of the deserted street.

SEVEN

The man in a dark suit, with an intent and thoughtful gait, knows that he is being followed. No one has told him; he has no proof that it's so, yet he knows with utter certainty that someone is following him. He doesn't know anything about his pursuer, but he knows that the pursuit began some time ago, that there is a reason for it—though no one, except the pursuer, knows it—and that he is being pursued closely and relentlessly. He knows a few things about this pursuit: in the first place, he is followed less carefully when he is in the open, in a crowd, than when he is at home; he doesn't mean that the pursuer slows down, that the pursuer is hindered by the crowd; rather, the pursuit undergoes a sort of diminution, as if the space in which it operated were altered. He knows that the pursuit is very fast, and that since his pace is slow, it is inevitable that he will be caught, and in fact should already have been caught, and that whatever has to happen when someone is caught should have happened—what that is, he doesn't know, but he does know that the pursuer will never catch him, not even if he stops on a bench and pretends to read the newspaper, in total surrender and defenseless expectation. The pursuer knows that if he caught him, he would cease to be the pursuer, and it's possible that in the scheme of creation there is a place for him only as a pursuer. When the man is in his house, the clamor of the pursuit, the urgency, the pounding of innumerable feet, deafens him—he can't even hear the rustling of papers, he speaks out loud in order to hear himself. In reality, in this rigid and perhaps archaic division of roles, the man who is pursued, although he knows he can't be caught, is unable to free himself from the knowledge that he is the target. He knows that the space behind him is distorted, frustrating any hope of catching him, but he also knows that time is not his friend; its distortion is intended only to preserve his function as target. The target wonders if the pursuer is unhappy, since the horror of their condition lies in a task that cannot be completed. He wonders if there is a way to suddenly turn and begin pursuing the pursuer.

FORTY-NINE

A man loved a young woman madly for three days, and was loved in return for a period of time that corresponded almost exactly. He met her by chance on the fourth day, two hours after he had stopped loving her. At first, the meeting was slightly embarrassing; yet the conversation grew animated when it turned out that the woman, too, had stopped loving the man, exactly an hour and forty minutes earlier. In the beginning, the discovery that their mad love was thus a thing of the past, and that presumably they would stop torturing each other with foolish, painful, and inevitable questions, made the man and woman quite euphoric; and they seemed to see each other through the eyes of friends. But the euphoria was ephemeral. The woman remembered those twenty minutes of difference; she had loved the man for twenty minutes after he—he had confessed it—had already stopped loving her. The woman made of this an occasion for bitterness, frustration, and rancor. The man tried to demonstrate to her how those twenty minutes revealed in her a constancy of affection which classified her as morally superior. She replied that her constancy was not in question, but that in this case someone had taken advantage of it, and coldly, calculatingly, insulted her. Those twenty minutes during which she had loved but had not been loved carved an abyss between them that nothing could bridge. She had loved a frivolous and sensual man; in this life and the next he would suffer the shame of it. He tried to make the point that, since they no longer loved each other, the problem could be considered irrelevant and was not something to lead them to overly bitter remarks, but he said this with a kind of vivacity that betrayed both fear and annoyance. The woman answered that the end of their love was no consolation, but only the sign that they had foolishly committed a depraved act, and it had left her scarred. He let out a brief unfriendly laugh. In that instant, a great hatred arose between the two, a meticulous, overwhelming hatred; in some way they both felt that that difference of twenty minutes was truly atrocious, and that something had happened which made life impossible for at least one of them. Now they began to think they were destined to die dramatically, together, as they had feverishly imagined during their mad love.

FIFTY-SIX

That man with an irritable and on the whole worried look, who seems to be continually confronted by a situation of unbearable gravity, is, generally speaking, in love; more precisely, that's how he would describe himself at this moment, since it's ten in the morning and from now until eleven, eleven-fifteen at the latest, he is in love with a distinguished lady, noble in spirit, cultivated, slightly authoritarian, taciturn, and mildly difficult. The situation, however, is not perfect: from ten-fifteen—the lady gets up a bit later than the man—until half-past eleven, the lady loves a cultivated but cruel student of tarot, who at the same time loves an English lady who is on her thirtieth Sanskrit lesson. Around eleven-thirty, everything changes: the student of Sanskrit desires the irritable man, who for an hour loves no one, although he has a harmless affection for a designer of pillows from the countryside, who for forty-five minutes around midday loves a young tenor of little success but some talent, who until one-thirty is in love with the slightly authoritarian lady. The early afternoon sees a general fading of reciprocal affections, except in the case of the tenor, who nourishes a hopeless reverence for the student of Sanskrit. At five, a middle-aged zoologist comes into the situation, having finally realized that life has no meaning without the pillow designer; the zoologist's young wife goes along with him, racked by jealousy and thinking, alternately, of killing her zoologist husband or the pillow designer—who in truth doesn't even know the zoologist exists—or, if it's a Friday or a Tuesday, deciding to love to distraction the cruel tarot player, who, in the meantime, has written a desperate love letter to a very young stamp collector, a letter that he will not send, however, because in the meantime he has once again fallen in love with the slightly authoritarian lady, who has decided to love the irritable man, who alone now has a presentiment of happiness, having looked into the eyes of the wife of the zoologist, while she mentally devoted herself to a baritone ruined by the hiccups, not knowing that he, rejected by the stamp collector, had decided to enter a monastery and give up the search for happiness, which did not seem compatible with the existence of the clock.

SIXTY

One day a meticulous but somewhat abstracted man received a letter that he had in fact been expecting for some time. The letter came from the Office of Existence and informed him, with laconic politeness, that his declaration of existence was imminent, and that he should therefore prepare himself to enter existence within a short time. He rejoiced at the news, and did nothing, since he had long ago made all the necessary preparations for existence, whenever it started, with or without warning. Almost euphoric at the idea of existing, he considered the point he was at then, that interlude between existing and not existing, a sort of vacation period. Since nothing could happen to him until he had truly begun to exist, he indulged himself: he got up late, he took walks for a large part of the day, he made short trips to relaxing and picturesque places. He waited for the definitive letter without impatience, since he knew that the paperwork was tricky, its workings subtle, the distances enormous, the post office inefficient. Three months after the first letter, he received a second, which informed him of a misdelivery: the preceding letter had been delivered to him owing to a diachronic homonymy—that is, a man with the same name and surname would be born six centuries later in that same city. Therefore the preceding letter was voided; his case had been reopened and was in the process of being decided; although the letter did not mention that existence was imminent, its tone was encouraging. He felt some disappointment, but he did not dare to be offended by it, since in the universe he remained, of course, a very small thing; and he tried to consider the delay as an extended vacation; but he could not deny that his innocent pleasures contained a drop of bitterness. The third letter arrived six months later; obviously it did not concern him, someone must have sent him a letter meant for someone else, since it referred to his death as having already happened, and complained of a failure to deliver his left shoulder to the Central Office. He could not help thinking that in the Office of Existence there were serious inadequacies, and it saddened him. A year later, a new letter, written in a strangely ungrammatical way, again referred to the matter of the left shoulder, and bore a date nine centuries later than the day on which it arrived. Looking carefully at the envelope, he realized that his name had been spelled slightly wrong, and at that instant he ceased both to preexist and to not exist.

SIXTY-TWO

Coming out of a store where he had gone to buy some after-shave, a tranquil and serious middle-aged man realized that they had stolen the Universe. In place of the Universe there was only gray dust: the city had disappeared, the sun had disappeared, no sound came from that dust, which seemed completely used to its career as dust. The man had a peaceful nature, and did not find it appropriate to make a scene; there had been a theft, a larger than usual theft, but still a theft. The man was convinced that someone had taken advantage of the moment when he had gone into the shop to steal the Universe. Not that the Universe was his, but insofar as he had been born and was alive he had a certain right to use it. In reality, when he entered the shop he had left the Universe outside, without putting on the anti-theft device, which he never used, because its enormous size made it impractical. Despite his usual severity with himself, he did not feel guilty of inattentiveness or a lack of vigilance; he knew he lived in a city troubled by an arrogant underworld, but the Universe had never been stolen before. The peaceful man turned, and, as he foresaw, the shop, too, had disappeared. So it was likely that the robbers were still not far away. Yet he felt impotent and slightly irritated; a thief who steals everything, including all the officials and all the street cops, is a thief who is in a position of privilege which does not normally belong to a thief; the man, although calm, was in that state of mind which provokes many men to write letters to the editors of newspapers; and if there had been newspapers, perhaps he would have done so. In the same way, if there had been a police station, perhaps he would have given a statement saying that the Universe was not his, but that he had used it daily, from the moment of his birth, carefully and moderately, without ever being called to order by the authorities. But there were no police, and the man felt embarrassed, mocked, beaten. He was wondering what in the world to do when someone tapped him on the shoulder, unmistakably, clearly, to summon him.

EIGHTY

When he was appointed custodian of the public toilets, he felt at first a certain humiliation; and certainly the job was and is humble. He had to wash the tiles, mop up the water, give toilet paper to anyone who asked for it, open the stall with the bidet for exacting clients. On the social scale of the society he lives in, he was and is at a fairly low level, lower than the street sweeper, who works outside; indeed, he spends many hours of the day in the toilets, and never sees the sun, since the toilets are underground, and are open from morning to night. His toilets are for men only, and he is glad about that, for he is a timid sort and would feel a bit embarrassed opening a stall for a woman. The atmosphere where he works is damp and always warm; the temperature doesn't vary much from season to season. The facility isn't perfect, because often there's no water, or one of the two sinks doesn't work and people who have urinated line up to wash, or they leave with their hands dirty, which doesn't seem right to him. He has a salary, and those who come down to the urinals generally give him a small tip; yet for a long time he suffered. Gradually he has begun not to suffer, not because he no longer feels the poverty of his job but because he now sees it simply as a job. He has, in fact, come to feel a certain pride: occupying a place so low on the social scale gives him dignity, since in the whole city there are perhaps only ten public-toilet attendants and they are at the lowest point, therefore an extreme point, and not everyone is capable of reaching the extreme point of anything. Now another, further change is taking place in him: he realizes that in fact the man who urinates, the man who closes himself in to defecate, is radically different from the man who walks along the streets of the city; he is a man who doesn't lie, who acknowledges himself as a creature, a passage for food, transient; and, at the same time, he sees in that man who is standing on the tiles, urinating, a man made desperate by his own feces, by the sinister efficiency of his body, by uncertainty over the significance of the fact that the human being uses his genitals for urinating. The lowest point is also a catacomb; and the custodian of the toilets realizes that the act of urinating contains a plea: it is brutishness and reality, the lowest and the highest; and he now considers his urinal a church, and himself its priest.

EIGHTY-THREE

The two friends are bound by a singular sort of complicity: the first believes he is a sex maniac, the second that he is suffering from homicidal mania. These conditions, in themselves, are anything but boring, and are complicated by the fact that both consider themselves aesthetes and hence observers of their manias. It follows that the sex maniac is singularly chaste, and the homicidal maniac unnaturally but gracefully meek. In fact, each of the two has delegated to the other the task of pursuing his own mania: thus it's up to the sex maniac to satisfy the homicidal mania of his friend, and up to the homicidal maniac to live out the sex mania of his companion. Naturally, the homicidal maniac is completely inept as a sex maniac, which his friend knows perfectly well; similarly the sex maniac would be incapable of carrying out the most modest and straightforward homicide. Therefore they have decided to trust each other: the sex maniac asks the homicidal maniac to perform a bestial act, and he consents: in the course of twenty-four hours he returns to report, telling of rapes, orgies, young women humiliated: he has done nothing at all, of course—the mere idea is horrifying to him, and if he saw a woman threatened by a brute he would rush to her defense, like an old-fashioned knight; but because of the affection that binds him to his friend, he is willing to pretend that he is an abject criminal; in exchange, the sex maniac almost the very next day will describe to him in minute detail a terrible and ingenious crime, carried out in circumstances so subtle and imaginative, as well as improbable, that no newspaper will carry the story until years later. In this way, the homicidal maniac has a few days of perfect happiness, and gives alms to the poor and offerings to the parish church, in thanks for having met such a good friend. In reality, each knows that his friend is entirely innocent, but realizes that a friendship between two innocents would not be satisfying in the depths of his soul; so each has secretly decided to make himself the dark soul of the other, since only in this way can they cultivate a sensitive, sympathetic, thoughtful relationship.

NINETY-FIVE

He was utterly amazed to see, at the bus stop, a snow-white unicorn. The sight was truly amazing because the unicorn had been the subject of an entire chapter in the treatise on Things That Do Not Exist; he had, until then, been very competent in Things That Do Not Exist and had received excellent marks, and in fact the professor had encouraged him to become a specialist in Things That Do Not Exist. Of course, when one studies Things That Do Not Exist, the reasons that they cannot exist become clear, as do the ways in which they do not: for the Things can be impossible, contradictory, incompatible, outside space and time, antihistorical, recessive, implosive, and can not exist in many other ways. The unicorn was completely antihistorical, yet there it was, at the bus stop, and people did not seem to be paying attention to it; but the wonder was not over: in fact the unicorn was whispering—there was no other word for it—to something that he couldn't see; then a bus came, the unicorn said good-bye to this unseen someone, and got on, "flashing," as they say, a bus pass; and then a basilisk appeared, of medium height, with very thick spectacles. The basilisk was a complicated animal, and its nonexistence was due to "excess"; furthermore it was an animal described as dangerous—its eyes had "impossible" powers—and it occurred to him that this was the reason the basilisk was wearing the spectacles. The basilisk had a purse under his arm, and when the bus drew near he opened it and took something out—was it a Medusa head?—something that looked at the number of the bus and told him what it was, because of course with those glasses he couldn't see anything. The specialist in Things That Do Not Exist was troubled; had he gone mad? He didn't think so. He began to wander without a definite goal, and met a hircocervus, a phoenix, and an amphisbaena on a bicycle; a satyr asked where Via Macedonio Melloni was, and a man with his head in the middle of his chest asked him the time and thanked him politely. When he began to see fairies and elves and guardian angels, he felt that he had always lived in a city uninhabited by human beings, or peopled by extras; now he is beginning to wonder if the World, the very World, is a Thing That Does Not Exist.

NINETY-SIX

A man who was greedy for dreams dreamed so much that in the building where he lived no one else was able to dream, except during the holidays, when the dreamer went to the sea or the mountains. It was an irritating and impossible situation, and the inhabitants of that building, all people of good family, professors, dukes, building contractors, and an international hit man, remonstrated politely; the man did not respond politely, and the matter was exacerbated. No one dreamed at all anymore in that building, and in the neighboring houses as well the dreams were few and feeble and in black and white, because the man dreamed only in color and did experiments in three dimensions. The quarrel ended up in court, where it was demonstrated that the man was illegally using the dreams of others, and he was to stop doing so, because he was violating the rules of good neighborliness. But, naturally, it's not easy to persuade someone to give back dreams and not to steal dreams that do not belong to him. The man continued to dream all the building's dreams, and only the international hit man managed, every once in a while, to have a stupid little dream.

But the greedy dreamer soon realized that something had changed; since he was dreaming all his neighbors' dreams, and the annoyed neighbors, if they could, would have had dreams in which he was a negative figure, he began having dreams in which, besides himself, there was also another self, hateful and cruel. He tried to chase him out of his dreams, but couldn't. And gradually he began to suffer from dream disturbances; he grew restless and started to despise himself. His dreams were full of quarrels, and he often woke from them feeling upset, persecuted, psychologically exhausted. He became ill. He was run-down. He became depressed. In the end, he decided to dream less, and above all not to dream the dreams of his neighbors. In fact, he had often felt uneasy in the duke's dreams, or awoken in a cold sweat from one of the hit man's. Now in the building everyone has started dreaming again. Friendly gestures have been made toward the greedy dreamer, but he is too depressed to welcome them. He doesn't have enough dreams. And now one sees him, sometimes, walking through run-down and disreputable neighborhoods, where he tries to steal dreams from uncultivated, poor people; they are not pleasant dreams, but by now he is addicted to dreams, and will become a thief, a kidnapper, in order to have those dreams every night, even if they are not his own, even if they are ugly and senseless—the very dreams that, in a monstrous heap, are exhausting him and leading him straight to catastrophe.

ONE HUNDRED

A writer writes a book about a writer who writes two books, about two writers, one of whom writes because he loves the truth and the other because he is indifferent to it. These two writers write twenty-two books altogether, in which twenty-two writers are spoken of, some of whom lie but don't know they are lying, others lie knowingly, others search for the truth knowing they cannot find it, others believe they have found it, and still others believed they had found it but are beginning to have doubts. The twenty-two writers produce altogether three hundred and forty-four books, in which five hundred and nine writers are mentioned, since in more than one book a writer marries another writer, and they have between three and six children, all writers, except for one who works in a bank and is killed in a robbery, and then it is discovered that at home he was writing a wonderful novel about a writer who goes to the bank and is killed in a robbery; the robber, in reality, is the son of the writer protagonist of another novel, and changed novels simply because he found it intolerable to live with his father, the author of novels about the decadence of the bourgeoisie, and in particular a family saga that portrays the young descendant of a novelist who is the author of a saga on the decadence of the bourgeoisie, and this descendant runs away from home and becomes a robber, and holds up a bank and kills a banker who was really a writer, and not only that, he was also a brother of his who was in the wrong novel and, through letters of introduction, was trying to change novels. The five hundred and nine writers write eight thousand and two volumes in which twelve thousand writers, to round it off, appear, who write eighty-six thousand volumes, which feature a single writer, a maniacal, depressed stammerer, who writes a single book about a writer who writes a book about a writer, but decides not to finish it, and arranges a meeting with that writer and kills him, causing a reaction which leads to the deaths of the twelve thousand, the five hundred and nine, the twenty-two, the two, and the single initial author, who has thus achieved his primary goal: discovering, thanks to his intermediaries, the only necessary writer, whose end is the end of all writers, including himself, the writer who is the author of all writers.

Translated from the Italian by Ann Goldstein

CLAYTON ESHLEMAN

DE KOONING'S WOMAN I

is the first in a series, probably not
in de Kooning's sense of it primal woman or even
first—earliest—woman, but these facets may have been
on his mind, for we have here a series of "ones,"
a sacrificed and dismembered "goddess,"
a kind of North American Coyolxauhqui
whose circular Stone was discovered at the foot of the Great
    Temple stairway,
as well as Madonna and Child,
the Child at once just born and maybe four,
he is bald and white, is the Madonna's left shoulder and arm,
staring at Her, perched on what appears to be
Her ruddy left thigh, which
on closer inspection might also be
the rump of a flat-snouted or headless animal
lunging to the right, whose back and legs are Her lap and legs,
lunging into the shredding legs of the figure who uses the
Madonna's right shoulder and arm as his breast and stomach
(which is also a red-gartered, chubby, severed thigh)—
he has long, loosely-tied hair, or is "he" a midwife
with face hair—a pirate? sniffing
or whispering to the Madonna's right temple?
His breast-stomach is also his right arm
swinging under the Madonna's haltered and huge right breast,
and out of his splitting hand
another hand emerges
from which shears protrude cutting the Child's umbilicus?
Or is a castration under way?

All this action is simultaneously
splintered and frozen,
once we see the Child, the animal, and pirate-midwife,
there's not much left of *Woman I*, or
let's say she's in sacrificial drag,
all but her head and breasts are others
masquerading as her body parts,
she is a crowned tripod of wedge-head and dome-
   shielded breasts,
dismembered *and whole?* or have her body parts been stuffed
   into new roles?
Oversized Mesopotamian eyes, hypnotic,
teeth like a portcullis beaver-set into her face,
the gaze of one who has been blasted,
the left eye straight ahead, as wide-open animal jaws
   howl at her earless head,
the right eye more inward, averted, maybe reflecting on
   what pirate-midwife is hissing—

to her left, beyond the Child,
a sketchy, wraith-like creature, at attention,
facing her, seems to be tooting or snout-firing into her face,
or is he vying for her attention with pirate-midwife?
She whose body is her retinue,
She who is slaughtered
at the beginning of time, sets time in motion,
whose crate-shaped upper body
contains, like huge pods, food for those
putting on her body,
                        it is hideous,
and magnificent,
                  "Huitzilopochtli
cut off her head,

which was left abandoned
on the slopes of Coatepetl.
The body of Coyolxauhqui
went rolling down as it fell, dismembered,
in different places fell her hands,
her legs, her body . . . "

"Like a black hole in space,
 which destroys all light around it
 but somehow gives rise to galaxies,
 sacrifice is a vacuum at the center of culture
 which somehow spins the web of life."

Sources: Sahagún, *History of the Things of New Spain*, and Patrick Tierney, *The Highest Altar*.

ILYA KABAKOV

THE BOAT OF MY LIFE

A large, wooden, virtually "real" boat, 57 feet in length, 18 feet in width, and 8 1/2 feet in height, is erected in the exhibit hall. Its deck is horizontal, and two sets of stairs lead from the floor to the deck, one for getting on the boat, the other for disembarking. There are special holes cut through the sides of the boat for this.

Twenty-four cardboard crates, the "cargo," are arranged in a disorderly fashion on the deck. All the crates are open, and the viewer can look inside them at their contents. All kinds of residential junk are heaped inside, the things you might gather for any move: children's clothing, toys, dishes, books, more clothing, boots. . . . There are pieces of cardboard inside the crates, like lists of contents, with various things glued to them: pins, buttons, pencil stubs, newspaper clippings, photographs. . . . Under each object is an inscription in Russian and a translation.

As you read these inscriptions, it becomes clear that before you is the story of a life represented day by day, year by year, by this collection of objects and inscriptions. Each crate represents a particular period of that life, and all of the crates, standing one after another in disarray from the stern to the bow, form a material history of that life. The viewer, ascending from the stern begins to read and examine this history from childhood. Moving from crate to crate, he reaches the period when this installation itself was constructed, before descending the stairs at the bow of the boat.

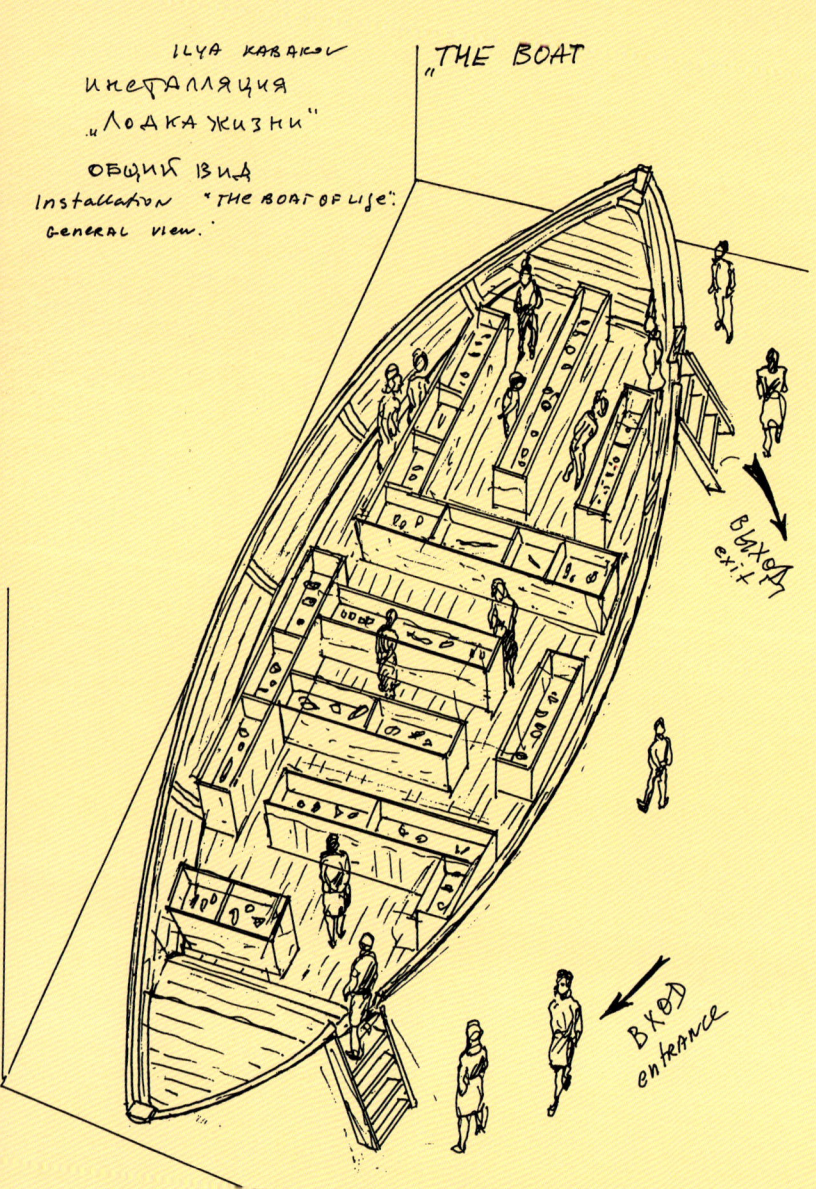

SEPTEMBER 30, 1933
I was born in the city of Dnepropetrovsk, U.S.S.R., and lived there until the age of seven.

SUMMER 1935
Mother said that I would run away all the time, and that it was difficult to catch me.

1935
I don't remember either Mother or Father. I don't remember their faces.

SUMMER 1937
I was given a live white rooster. I never left him, I would always carry him in my arms.

SUMMER 1941
We are crossing the Dnieper in a dense crowd of people. Bomber pilots are attacking from above.

SUMMER 1942
I am running around barefoot somewhere in the white dust. There is terrible heat.

FALL 1943
I find myself in a dark corridor. From afar, coming toward me, is a dark figure that looks like a bird.

SUMMER 1946
We were given a small plot of land to plant potatoes. We planted them but nothing grew; weeds choked everything. We should have weeded, but we didn't know.

WINTER 1948
I ask the best student at art school to tell me in secret whether I have any "talent." The answer: "You are not a colorist."

MARCH 1953
The death of Stalin. I am walking, almost crushed to death in the lines of thousands of people flattened against the wall. They are hurried quickly past the coffin. The feeling in the air is one of a cosmic catastrophe. "What will happen?"

WINTER 1969

The first drawings which will later go into albums. Silence of the studio. I draw because I have nothing to do. No one needs this stuff, it is all "for myself."

WINTER 1969

Metaphysical, higher states come over me. The "white" appears. The mysterious world on the other side of this reality.

FALL 1974

Oscar Rabin calls me to his place and proposes that I participate in an "open-air" exhibit. I am frightened; I refuse. Burning with curiosity and excitement, I go as a spectator to see what will happen. The exhibit is broken up by bulldozers and street sweepers.

FALL 1978

Another person inside of me began to speak. A person from the ZhEK: a small, downtrodden, lying-about-everything Soviet person . . .

THE EXPERIENCE OF TIME IN THE "TOTAL" INSTALLATION

1. You have paused, you cannot exit from it.
2. You stand still in it, but you are waiting tensely and feel that something is about to happen:
3. someone should arrive,
4. but at the same time something has already happened,
5. and something here has already occurred.
6. You end up in the center of all three times, past, present, and future.
7. You are standing at a point where the strongest feeling exists of floods of time passing through and past you, where something is continually happening.
8. This space "spins" you from the past to the future and back again, and this state—of revolution—is dizzying. It doesn't permit you to move from the place where you are standing.
9. But the space surrounding you is not homogenous. It has some sort of clot, a series of objects that concentrate this experience of time.
10. In some objects, the experience of the future is concentrated, in others the experience of the past.
11. And the space around you is itself divided into zones of past and future. When you stand with your face to the future, for some reason the past ends up behind you, behind your back, and vice versa.
12. You see clearly these points of concentration of time and you can identify them: "the object over there—something will happen there later." Or this object here, it already "was" and a feeling of the past emanates from it.
13. But the present is only you yourself, your presence here, your motionless state between these two flows running through you—the one departing into the past and the one running into the future.
14. And there is no break in this revolving flood. It is one and the same winding and unwinding spiral.
15. You are standing among other viewers. But this is happening only for you, and for each person individually.

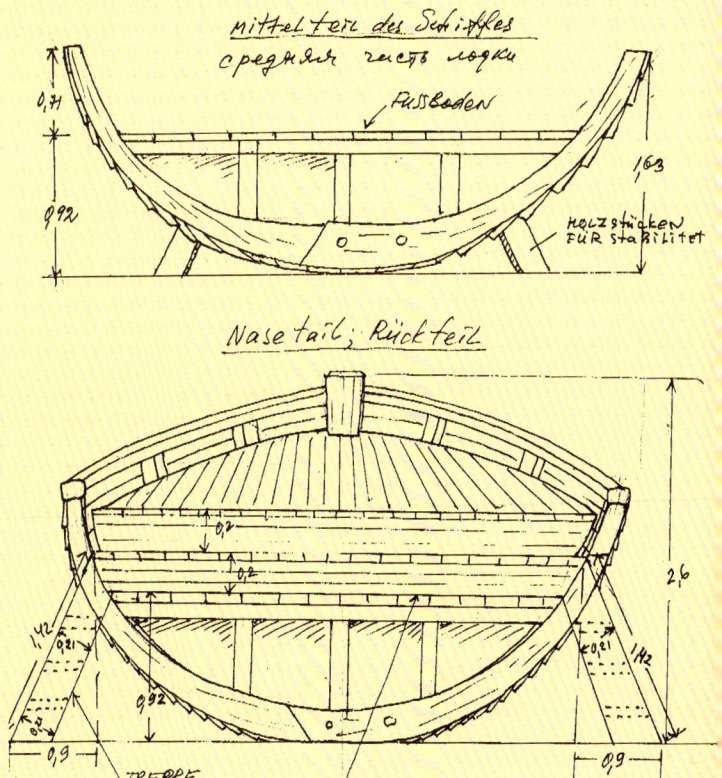

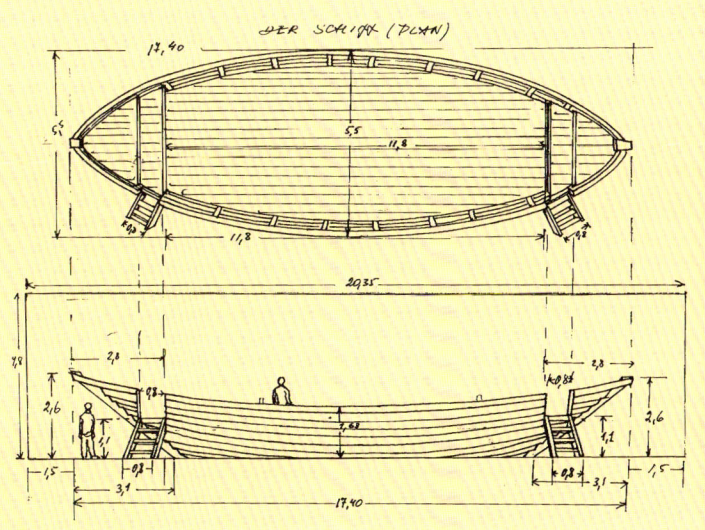

KENNETH ROSEN

DEATH IN MARCH

Just the chevrons whitetail deer
Chew in the thin bark of young trees
Around the vernal equinox,
Snow in a state of surrender,
Melting into rivers and bottomless mud,
Evaporating up through its crust.
Something had to happen. A deer has to eat.
Often the young tree dies on its feet.
And the crystal ashes of moonlight
Melt like love in the languishing
Gaze of the aftermath, whose own
Unprotected nakedness gazes back
Though blind and uncomprehending,
Pale and unable to say for sure:
I know you. You used to love me.

from echoes of an autobiography

NAGUIB MAHFOUZ

A Prayer

I was less than seven years old when I said a prayer for the revolution.

One morning I went to my primary school, escorted by the maid. I walked like someone being led off to prison. In my hand was a copybook, in my eyes a look of dejection, in my heart a longing for anarchy. The cold air stung my half-naked legs below my shorts. We found the school closed, with the janitor saying in a stentorian voice, "Because of the demonstrations there will again be no school today."

A wave of joy flowed over me and swept me to the shores of happiness.

From the depths of my heart I prayed to God that the revolution might last forever.

A Lament

Death paid its first visit to our home when my grandmother died. Death was still something new: I had had no experience of it except in passing on the street. I knew the old adage that it was inevitable, that there was no escaping it, but my real feelings saw it as being as remote as the sky from the earth.

Sobs wrested me from my state of calm as I realized that it had slipped, unbeknownst to us, into that room that had recounted to me such beautiful stories.

I saw myself as small and death as a giant, its breath coming and going in all the rooms, for every person remembers it, every person tells of it.

I tired of the chase and took refuge in my room to savor a minute of quiet and solitude. And then the door opened and the beautiful girl with the long black braid entered and whispered tenderly, "Don't stay on your own."

A sudden feeling of revolt flared up inside me; it was marked by violence and it yearned for madness. I grasped hold of her hand and drew it to my chest with all the sadness and fear that surged within me.

The Good Old Times

We were all boys living in the same street, our ages ranging from eight to ten. He stood out because of a bodily strength that was beyond his years, and he would apply himself ardently to developing his muscles with weight lifting. He was a boorish, coarse, and quarrelsome boy, ready to pick a fight for the most trivial of reasons. No day passed peacefully without a battle and without him beating one of us up. Thus he became in our lives a specter of torment and trouble.

You can therefore well imagine our great joy when we learned that his family had decided to leave the quarter altogether. We truly felt that we were beginning a new life of affection, felicity, and peace. We continued to have news of him, however, for he took up sports professionally and excelled at them, winning several championships, until he was forced to retire because of a heart condition. We then almost forgot him, by reason of the vicissitudes of old age and the passage of time.

As I was sitting in a café in al-Husayn, I was surprised to see him approaching, bearing his long life and visible debility.

He saw me, recognized me, and smiled. Without being invited, he sat down. He appeared to be in an animated state as he began calculating the many years during which we had not seen one another. He went on asking about those relatives and friends he remembered. Then he sighed and asked nostalgically, "Do you remember the good old times we had?"

Forgetfulness

Who is this old man who leaves his home each morning to walk about, getting as much exercise as he can?

He is the sheik, the teacher of Arabic, who retired more than twenty years ago.

Whenever he feels tired he sits down on the pavement, or on the stone wall of the garden of a house, leaning on his stick and drying his sweat with the end of his flowing *gallabiya*. The quarter knows him and the people love him; but seldom does anyone greet him, because of his weak memory and senses. He has forgotten relatives and neighbors, students, and the rules of grammar.

A Message

I came across a dry rose, its petals scattered, behind a row of books as I was tidying up my library.

I smiled. The depths of the remote past gave way to a fleeting light.

And there freed itself from Time's grasp a feeling of nostalgia that lived for five minutes.

A fragrance that was like a whispering escaped from the dry petals.

I recalled the words of the wise friend: "The cruelty of the memory manifests itself in remembering what is dispelled in forgetfulness."

The Specters

After performing the dawn prayers, I went wandering about in the empty streets. How pleasant it is to walk in the quietness and pure air, accompanied by the breezes of autumn. Having reached the heights above the desert, I seated myself on the rock known as "The Lad's Mother" and let my gaze wander in the desolate wilderness garbed in the delicate darkness. Suddenly it seemed that specters were moving toward the city. I told myself they must be policemen, but then the first of them passed right in front of me and I made out a skeleton, with sparks flying from the sockets of its eyes. I was seized by terror as I sat there on the rock and the specters flowed past me, one after the other.

Trembling, I pondered what the day could be harboring for my slumbering city.

The Train of the Unexpected

At the spring festival it is pleasant to amuse oneself.

We stood, a group of pupils, in our shorts in the station hallway, each holding a colored straw basket filled with the food we had been given. We had to choose between two trips and two trains: one that went to the Barrages, and the other that went to an unknown destination and was called the Train of the Unexpected.

"The Barrages are beautiful and we know them," said one of us.

"Venturing into the unknown is more enjoyable," said another.

We could not come to a decision, so most of us went on the train to the Barrages. A few headed for the unknown.

How Impossible!

She never held back from me anything lovely that she possessed, for I imbibed from the spring of beauty until I had quenched my thirst. But ungrateful exultation in that with which one has been blessed may assume the mask of discontent, and one of the signs of my frustration was that I was joyful at parting. In the course of the long path I took, regret did not leave me, and even today her skeleton gazes at me in scorn.

The Man with a Watch

He is always close to me. He never leaves my sight or my imagination, a sparkle in his strong, calm glances. From a neutral face, he shares with me neither joy nor sadness. From time to time he looks at his watch, suggesting to me that I do the same. Sometimes I grow weary of him, but if he is away for a moment I am overcome by a sense of loss. All the fatigue or comfort I have met with in my life has been of his making. And it is he who made me yearn for a life in which no clock strikes the hours.

The Man's Secret

He would pass by where we were sitting, shouting, "It is coming, of that there is no doubt."

Then he would rush off, nothing remaining of him except for the image of his ragged clothes and distracted look.

And the catastrophe did come to pass.

Some people said that he was a saint, others that he was nothing but a secret agent.

A Man Reserves a Seat

The bus started on its journey from Zeytoun at the same moment that a private car set forth from the owner's house in Helwan. Each varied the speed at which it was traveling, speeding along and then slowing down, and perhaps coming to a stop for a minute or more depending on the state of the traffic.

They both, however, reached Station Square at the same time, and even had a slight accident, in which one of the bus's headlights was broken and the front of the car was scratched.

A man was passing and was crushed between the two vehicles and died. He was crossing the square in order to book a seat on the train going to Upper Egypt.

A Whisper at Dawn

At a decisive stage of life, when love brought me to the highest peaks of confusion and longing, a voice whispered in my ear at dawn: "Congratulations to you—the time for making your farewells has been decreed."

Deeply affected, I closed my eyes and saw my funeral moving along, with myself at its head carrying a large glass filled with the nectar of life.

In the Spacious Room

In the dream I saw myself in a spacious, high-ceilinged room, devoid of all furniture except for a round table in the middle, with two chairs around it facing each other. I sat on one chair and a close friend of mine sat on the other. In front of each of us was a cup of coffee. There was a door leading into another room that was extremely dark and I knew nothing of what was inside it.

"We must carry out the task," my friend said.

"We really must carry it out," I agreed.

Suddenly my friend rose, moved toward the dark room, and disappeared. After he left I noticed that the coffee was no longer on the table, so I called out to him. I heard no reply, but a stranger appeared and sat down in his place. His white cloak attracted my attention. Although I did not know him, I told myself that his presence there was better than not. Placing a glass in front of himself and another in front of me, he said, "Let us drink the toast of light and dark."

So I raised the cup to drink. I happened to glance inside it and saw the face of my absent friend staring at me. My hand shook and I said to the man sitting in front of me, "We must carry out the task."

A Trick of the Memory

I saw an enormous person with a stomach as large as the ocean, and a mouth that could swallow an elephant.

I asked him in amazement, "Who are you, sir?"

He answered with surprise, "I am forgetfulness. How could you have forgotten me?"

Dazzlement

It was widely reported that he was knowledgeable about everything. Groups of people went to him at the corner of the street where he sat on a couch. A well-meaning mediator said, "There is no time for simple questions. Let's have some really tough ones."

He was assailed with some truly tough questions. A deep silence reigned so that all might hear the answer that would succor them. I saw no movement of his lips and heard no sound issuing from his mouth.

I came away from his presence amid groups of people dazzled to the point of frenzy by what they had heard.

The Journey

Through a destiny over which I had no power, I had to submit to being away from my homeland. I realized that the event would come about without any doubt, either tomorrow or the day after.

Wait a little and do not anticipate the unknown.

The good-hearted said: Don't be afraid for we have been along the same path before you.

There spread out before me a garden filled with beauty, with enchanting women going to and fro.

I was invited to the singing, but it was as though I had become preoccupied with thoughts and misgivings.

I rid myself of all sensation to cross the gory jungle.

All that remains to me of the crossing are the memories of specters, the echoes of choking nightmares, and the lasting trace of a bloody battle.

They said the time had come for me to roam about in the gardens of the North, but my heart took me to the playground between the public fountain and the hospice.

I arrived, panting.

The face, the skin, the look. Everything had changed.

The loved ones met me, while around them there extended far into the distance the sublime with its special atmosphere and clamor.

My heart said to me: Settle in its shade, and may the Eternal preserve it.

The Detective

I was preparing for bed when there was a knock at the door. I opened the peephole and saw the form of a man shutting off the space in front of my gaze.

"A detective from the police station," he said.

He stretched out his hand to me with a notice ordering me to come with him for some important matter.

It was usual in our quarter for this detective to go to a resident's home to give him a summons. He would go at any time and without observing any consideration, and there was nothing one could do but comply. I found it was futile to argue, so I went back to my bedroom to dress.

I walked at his heels without exchanging a single word.

In the windows I caught sight of the blurred shapes of people following us with their eyes and whispering together.

I knew what they were whispering, for I had often done just that when following those who had gone before.

Give Yourself Up

He came to mind and my heart exploded with longing. I went to his home at the end of the suburban dwellings surrounded by fields. He gave me a friendly welcome and said, "A lifetime has passed since your last visit, but you have come at an appropriate time."

He said this as he pointed to a low table on which had been placed a tray of supper consisting of grilled fish, olives, and hot bread.

He invited me to share the meal, and I sat down.

We had scarcely said "In the name of God" when a voice from a loudspeaker came to us, calling out, "Give yourself up."

He jumped up to the light switch and turned it off, so that darkness reigned. Soon shots poured down on us like rain from all directions.

Trembling with fear, I told myself, "Happy is he who can give himself up."

The Fact of the Matter

The woman on the balcony gazes down from behind the latticework with eyes full of alertness and compassion. The small boy plays below the house and sings. From time to time he goes off to one of the lanes that empty out into the sides of the square coming from the vast areas of the city. At sunset the little boy tears himself away from the world of playing and roaming about and enters the house.

Things do not stay like that for long.

The balcony is emptied of compassion.

And the little boy has penetrated deep into the lane and has not come back.

The Heart's Complaint

My heart grew heavy after time had turned away from me. The doctor went on searching for the secret cause of its malady in the X ray. I contemplated it with curiosity until it seemed to me that it was seeing me as I saw it, and that we were exchanging looks. There also passed through its eyes a look of rebuke, so I said to it apologetically, "For so long I made you bear unendurable torments of love."

To which it replied, "By God, nothing ever made me so sick as being cured!"

The Essence of History

The first time I loved was when I was a child.

I amused myself with my time until death appeared on the horizon.

At the outset of youth I came to know the undying love that is created by the transient lover. I was immersed in the ocean of life; the lover departed, and the memories burned under the noonday sun. A guide deep within me directed me to the golden path that is paved with effort and that leads to unspecified goals.

Sometimes the perfect gentleman makes his appearance; at others the departing lover comes into view.

It became apparent to me that between me and death there was censure, but that I was condemned to hope.

Translated from the Arabic by Denys Johnson-Davies

ADONIS

THE TIME

* Hulagu was the Mongol invader who sacked Baghdad and invaded Syria at the end of the Abbasid period.

    embracing the grain of time and my head is a tower of fire:

        what is this blood coursing through sand
        and what is this waning?
        tell us, flame of the present, what shall we say?

    shards of history are in my throat
    and on my face, the signs of a victim
    how bitter language is now
    and how narrow the door of the alphabet

    embracing the grain of time and my head is a tower of fire:

        . . . / a friend becomes an executioner?
        a neighbor says: how slow is hulagu?!*
        who knocks? a tax collector?
        give him the tribute . . . forms of women
        and men . . . images walking / we pointed
        and whispered—our steps
        are a line of killing /
        does your killing come from your god
        or does your god come from your killing?
    —this mystery bewildered him
            so he bowed, an arch of terror on his bent days

    my brother failed
    my father went mad
    and my children are dead
    on whom shall I lean?
    shall I hug the door?
    shall I complain to a carpet?
    he has become dizzy / bring the hookah
    and revive him
    with the sneezing of theologians

the killer treats corpses as a joke / graineries of bones,
       is this lump a child's head or a piece of coal?
       is this a body I behold or a mass of clay?
       I bow, I sew two eyes and a waist
       perhaps this notion will support me
       and the light of memory guide me
       but in vain I explore the vague pattern
       in vain I piece together a head, two arms, two legs,
            to identify the dead

—for whom does the ant give her lesson?
      and why the surprise?   poetry—
          this mixture of frightful flashing to the eye,
      stunning to see your house raised to god in splinters—
the soothsayer's owl screamed from the minaret
wove from its sound a rainbow
and wept, choking, till joy

embracing the grain of time and my head is a tower of fire:

. . . / the *bahloul** revealed his secrets:
      that this revolutionary time
      is a shop of trinkets,
      a swamp of prophets

the *bahloul* revealed his secrets:
      truth will be death
      and death will be the bread of poets
      and what was called or became the homeland
      is but one moment floating on the face of time

the *bahloul* revealed his secrets:

---

* *Bahloul*, from the Persian, means fool or jester.

        where is your key, oh splendor of the flood?
        have mercy on me, drown me, take the last of my shores, take me
        I am bewitched by a blazing flame
        I am bewitched by a burning straw
        I am bewitched by roads, driving other roads away

embracing the grain of time and my head is a tower of fire:

        my soul has forgotten the object of its passion,
        forgotten its heritage hidden in the house of images
        it no longer remembers what the rain says,
                        what the ink of the tree writes
        it no longer draws
            save a seagull tossed by the waves to a ship's rope
        it no longer hears
            save a metallic screech: "oh the breast of the city
                        is a splitting moon tied
                            to a navel of a spark-spitting ghoul"
        it no longer knows that god and the poet are two infants
                        sleeping on the cheek of a stone

my soul has forgotten the objects of its love
and that is why I am terrified by the shadow—tomorrow's destiny
and that is why doubt consumes me and the dream evades me
bound, I run from fire to fire
        I dive into the sweat flowing from my body and cling to the wall
        insomnia / (the steps of the night are beasts . . .)
        and many times I have told the poetry that settles in my memory:
        what saw against my neck dictates this verse of silence?
        for whom shall I water my ashes?
        I don't know how to rip out my pulse and throw it on a table
        and I refuse to make my sadness a drum for the sky
        let me say: my life
                was a house of ghosts and a windmill

embracing the grain of time and my head is a tower of fire:

> * Kassabin, Adonis's hometown, is located in the coastal region of Syria.

        the trees of love in kassabin* become brothers
        of the trees of death in beirut
        and this forest of myrtle consoles the forest of exile
        as kassabin enters the map of grass
        and distills the vessels of plains
        beirut enters the map of death / graves
        like orchards and shrapnel—fields
what pours kassabin into sidon and into tyre,
                and beirut into itself?
what is this thing—distant and approaching?
what mixes this blood in my map?

        summer has dried up, fall hasn't come
        and spring is blackened in the memory of earth /
        winter as death draws it: the agony of death or bleeding
        a time that comes from the bottle of algebra
        and from the palm of fate
        a time of confusion which improvises time and devours air

        how and from where can you know him:
        an assassin with no face, yet with all faces . . .

embracing the grain of time and my head is a tower of fire:

        exhausted, I turn around and wonder—what are these scraps?
        histories? countries? flags on the cliff of dusk?

right here I read generations in the moment
and in the corpse, thousands of corpses
right here the flood of absurdity consumes me
my body slips from my control
my face is no longer in its mirror

and my blood bursts its veins . . .
am I not seeing the light that carries my dream to him?
am I a distant edge of the universe, blasphemed by myself,
                                      praised by others?
what uproots my depths and goes
between jungles of desires, countries—oceans of tears
        and genealogies of symbols?
between races and species—ages and peoples?
what separates my self from my self?
        what refutes me?
am I a crossroad
and my way, in the moment of revelation, no longer my way?
am I more than one person, and my history my abyss
        and my destination my burning?
what rises in my guffaw, from my strangled organs?
am I more than one person, whom everyone asks:
        "who are you and where are you from?"
        are my limbs deadly jungles
        . . . blood, wind and a body of paper?

is it madness? who am I in this darkness?
        teach me and guide me, oh madness
who am I, my friends,
        oh you downtrodden visionaries
I wish I could molt, to know not who I was
                nor who I was going to be
I am searching for a name, for something to be named,
                yet nothing can be named
        a blind time and a blinded history
        a silted time and a history of ruins
and enslaver is enslaved / praise be to you, oh darkness

embracing the grain of time and my head is a tower of fire:

my semitic grandfather is unraveled by this blind age—
a parrot? or a prophet hollow as a mummy?
oh grandfather, whose way I now leave,
you who live in the microbes of water and strata of sky—
it is wise for you to walk as you walk, arrogantly backward
for you are the secret and the kingdom full
of prophecies—I am one unable to understand you
    and I am the heretic
    and you are the miracle
oh grandfather whom I now reject, I liked the creation
in the name of the creator / you will no longer know me
    and nothing will link me to you
    save those silted ruins in my soul
    which make me weep and weep for you

embracing the grain of time and my head is a tower of fire:

    the end of the epoch that rained stones*
    meets the beginning of the epoch that rains oil
    and the god of palm trees
    bows to the iron god
    and I am between the two, the spilt blood and the arrested caravan
    I explore my extinguished fire
    and see how I confront
    my death waiting in its desert
    and I say, the universe is what my dream weaves . . . /
    the threads of silk are unraveled and I see myself falling
    and I go on in the night of falling,
    and I see things: a wheel of smoke,
    I see the world—a prey
        the table is spread—bodies are vegetables,
            pots are heads
        god sits at the banquet of prey /
    a deer was a baker

---

*A reference to the time during which the Prophet Mohammad established Islam. Legend has it that when the Ethiopian armies were ready to attack the holy places of the Saudi peninsula, flocks of birds dropped stones on the troops and crushed them.

                      and a lizard was a soldier
               is god eating the prey or is the prey god?

deceitful roads, betraying beaches—
how can you not be shocked by madness now?
thus I renounce the eater and the food
               and I seek rest in every labyrinth
my consolation is that I submerge myself in my dream—I break boundaries,
I undulate and sing the desire to rebel and I rave
               the orbit of venus is an anklet for my days
               and capricorn is a bracelet
               and I say: the flowers in their crowns
               are balconies . . .
my consolation is that I leave—I rally the verbs of leaving

saddle these unbridled winds
history is slaughtered and slaughtering is the *fatiha*.[*]
let the slaughterer and the slaughtered and the sacrifice be witnesses,
bury me with its remains and draw me
a ruin among ruins

thus I extract wisdom from its essence
crying welcome to my debris, welcome to the waning
tomorrow death will come yet will not extinguish me
tomorrow I shall pass from one light to another
it is true that I am weaker than a thread
yet I am more sublime than a god

thus I begin
embracing my land and the secrets of its passion—
        the body of its sea is love and its sun is two hands for this love
        a body: the harbor of thunder and the anchor of longing
        a body: a promise I am absent from
        and I am coming out of this bet

---

[*] The *fatiha* is the oft-repeated opening verse of the Koran, and could be variously translated as "opening" or "prelude."

        a body: cover the face of daisies with the light of the loving rain

let it be. . . .
        I embrace the coming age and I walk unbridled
        like a sea captain and I write my country—
        rise in it to its highest summits and
        descend with it to its lowest depths
        you will see neither fear nor chains—as if the bird is a branch
        and the earth is a child and myths are women of a dream

        I leave to those who come after me to open this space

I am not a cottage of ideas
and my longing is not a woodcutter of remembrance—
        my lineage is dissent
        my weddings cross-pollinate the antipodes
        this era is mine
        the dead god, the blind machine and my era mean
        that I live in the pool of desires,
        that my splinters are my flowers
        and that I am the alpha of water and the omega of fire—
        life's madman

        revealing to the time the secret of its passion:
        thus he confesses,
        he is the renegade, the outsider, and the misfit

                        Beirut, June 4 and October 25, 1982

Translated from the Arabic by
Allen Hibbard and Osama Isber

ÉTIENNE-JULES MAREY : CHRONOPHOTOGRAPHS
ÉTIENNE-JULES MAREY : CHRONOPHOTOGRAPHS
ÉTIENNE-JULES MAREY : CHRONOPHOTOGRAPHS
ÉTIENNE-JULES MAREY : CHRONOPHOTOGRAPHS
ÉTIENNE-JULES MAREY : CHRONOPHOTOGRAPHS
ÉTIENNE-JULES MAREY : CHRONOPHOTOGRAPHS
ÉTIENNE-JULES MAREY : CHRONOPHOTOGRAPHS

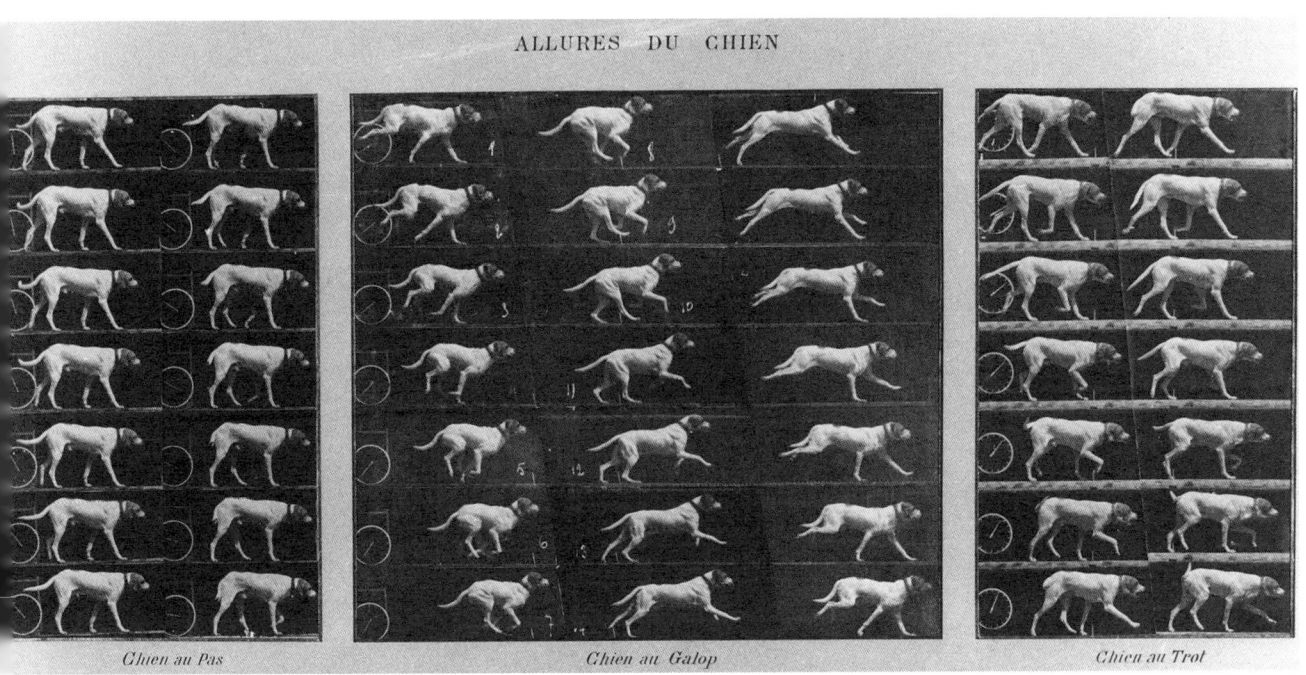

ALLURES DU CHIEN (THE DOG'S GAITS), 1894.

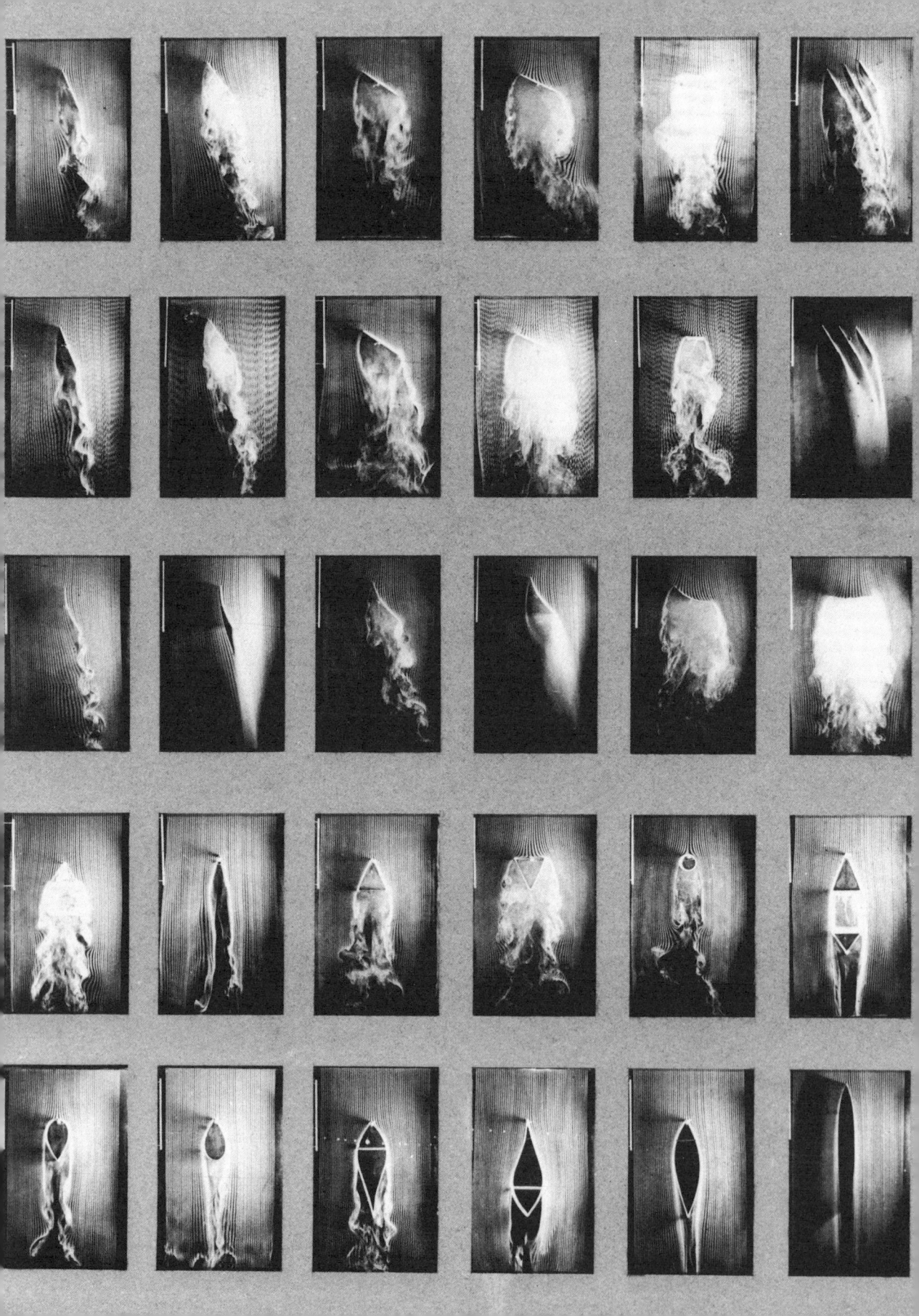

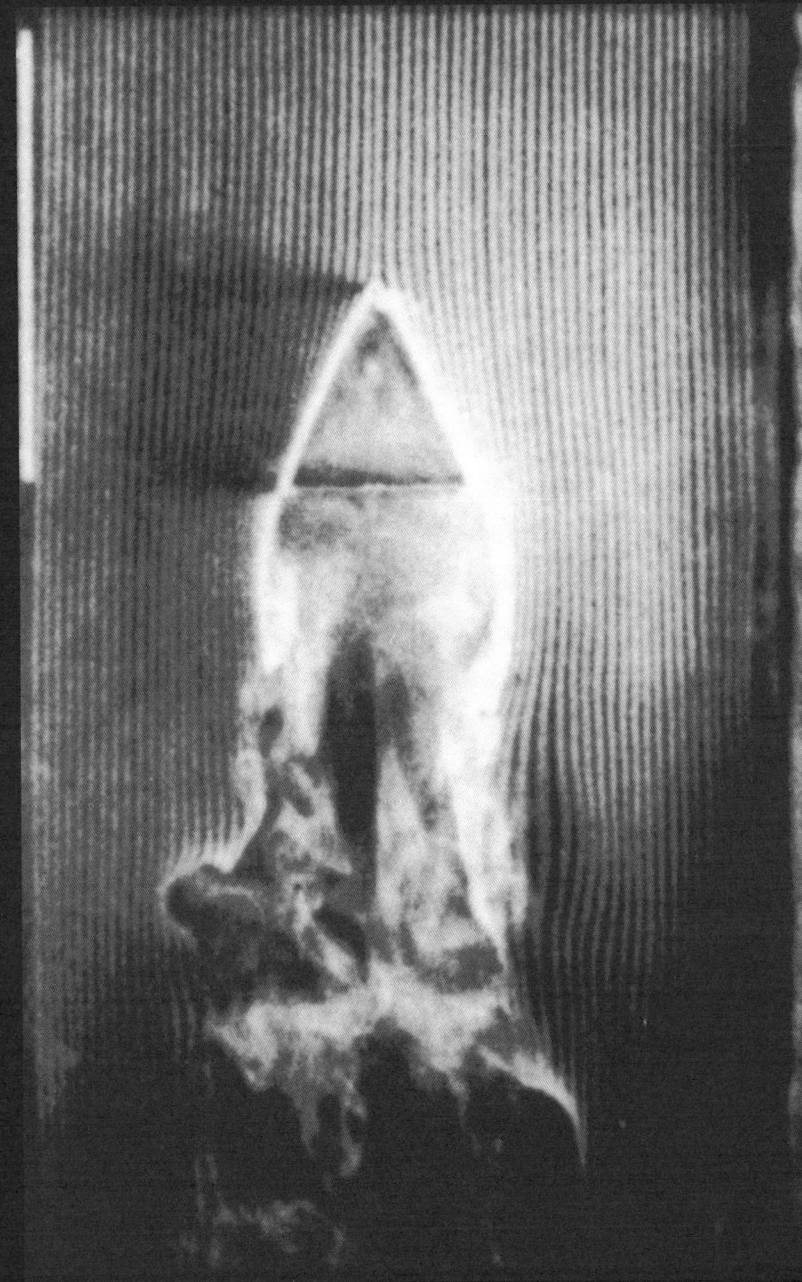

ÉTUDE DES MOUVEMENTS DE L'AIR À LA RENCONTRE DE CORPS DE DIVERSES FORMES

(STUDY OF THE MOVEMENTS OF AIR AROUND VARIOUS SHAPES), 1900.

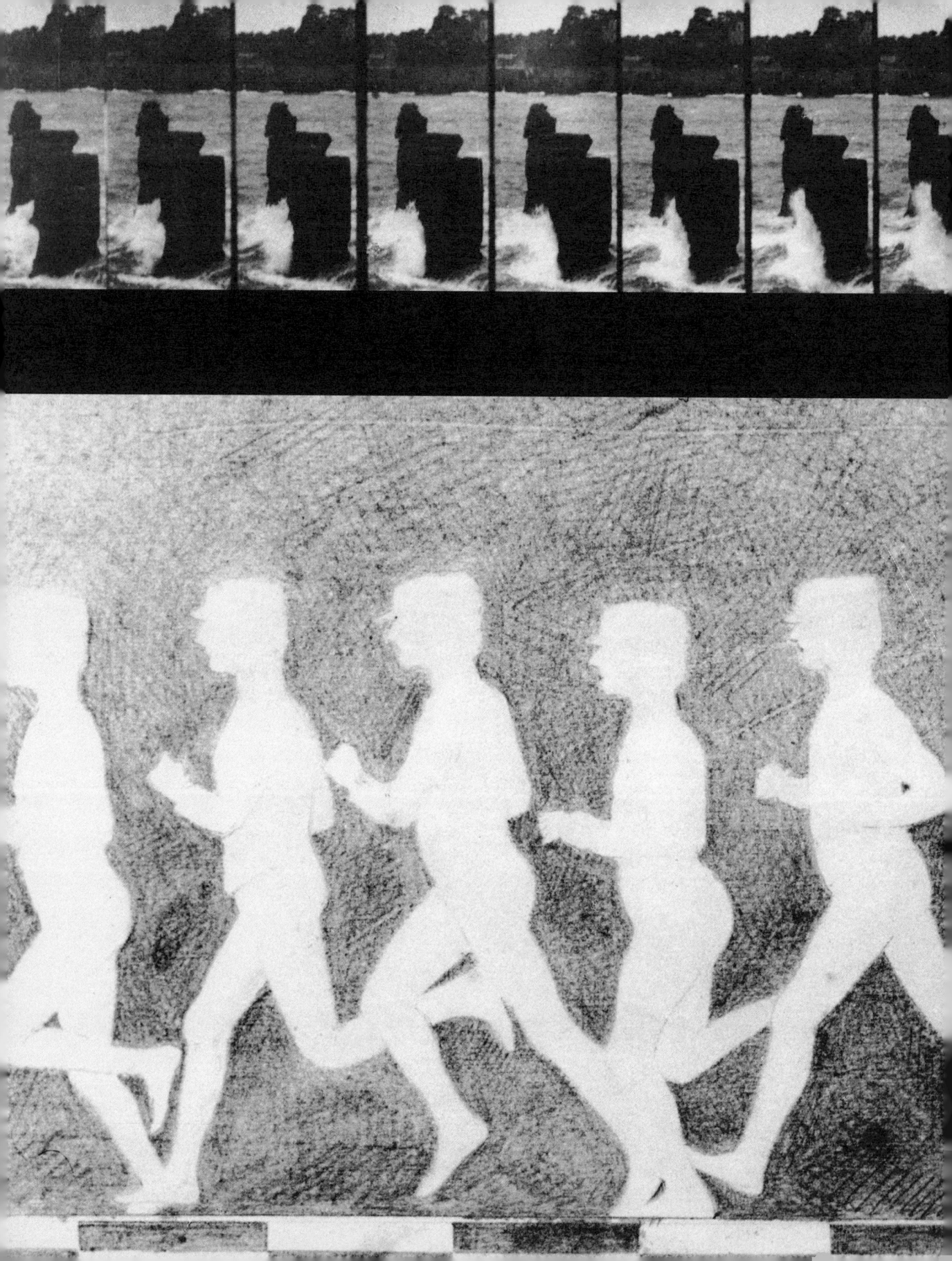

ABOVE LA VAGUE À NAPLES (THE WAVE AT NAPLES), 1890.
BELOW HOMME EN BLANC COURANT DEVANT UN FOND NOIR (MAN IN WHITE RUNNING AGAINST A DARK BACKGROUND), CIRCA 1886.

ÉTIENNE-JULES MAREY

A contemporary of the English-born American photographer Eadweard J. Muybridge, who was his fellow pioneer in the photographic investigation of animal locomotion, Étienne-Jules Marey (1830–1904) was a French physiologist, aviation researcher, pioneer in time-motion studies, and inventor. He studied and transcribed the motions of the bodily organs (heart rhythms, muscle tremors, lung ventilation) before turning to movement in birds, insects, horses, and humans.

At the same time, through his fabrication of new recording devices, he replaced crude mechanical recorders with more sensitive electrical and then chemical ones: the chronophotographic gun, with its barrel housing a lens, and behind it, an ordering clock mechanism, a multiple-aperture shutter, and a replaceable film magazine with twenty-five sensitive plates, could take twelve photographs per second. Aimed at a man with his limbs painted, it produced a linear graph of motion which left its aesthetic trace on the art of the avant-garde: Marcel Duchamp—who most likely came across Marey's work when his brother, Raymond Duchamp-Villon, interned at a Paris hospital with Marey's assistant, Albert Londe—caused a sensation at the 1913 Armory Show in New York when he first exhibited *Nude Descending a Staircase*, which depicts the different phases of motion dissolving into each other; the work's broken lines pressing against each other and the arcs of circles or dots at calf level and at the joints are directly descended from Marey's chronophotographs.

Marey ultimately sought to trace the kinetics of isolated flows, ripples in air, eddies in water, and wave patterns, discovering a world that could not be entirely grasped through human sight—the ultra-inaccessible, the very slow and especially the very fast. At an important junction of scientific, philosophical, and cultural development, Marey's sophisticated techniques for the recording of motion dismantled gesture and stimulated a conscious reconfiguration of corporeal movement.

The technological revolution, and the new realm of relations between the body and the machine it stimulated, echoed Marey's efforts on a much grander scale, as once unruly psycho-motor activites began to be reconstituted through the techniques of cybernetics, ergonomics, standardization, and surveillance.

If the dichotomous relation between mind and body is located between two poles, one dedicated to escape and flight, the other, toward which Marey's work gravitates, is characterized by an ongoing struggle to master the body.

JACKIE MCALLISTER

currents

ANGELA KRAUSS

For a few seconds this morning I experienced a sensation of complete freedom of movement. At the very moment of awakening I was thrown out, cast forth; I spun disoriented in space, in a kind of box, in which there was initially nothing, until, half-blind with dizziness, I made out the outline of the shell of the life I had lived until now. A three-dimensional pattern of strange formations, small celestial bodies, with a noticeable current of air between them where the wind of time blew and eternal twilight prevailed. By dint of the utmost exertion I managed to keep going. And a moment later I was suffused with such an obvious, deep, and total feeling of disappointment that I was unable to move. I had located myself: I lay quite still in bed, and heard music from one of the Sunday morning programs coming from the apartment below. The sun was shining; it was October, and for weeks there had been a stable high-pressure area over Europe, stretching as far as the Urals. There was a great brightness all around me.

    I did not, of course, want to believe it. But over the next quarter of an hour there was no change, other than an almost brutal increase in the brightness of the room. The few objects in my less than mysterious daily life belonged to me, and I to them. For some time, I observed this world establishing its own order in which everything had its place, including me—as if this order were the only possibility, as if it had always been the only possibility. The menace of facts arises from their seeming irrefutability.

I lay utterly still.

There are no longer any mysteries in the neighborhood either. Recently I saw the bloated woman leaving with a flat, plate-like, red hat on her head, and not long ago I met her seven jet-black-haired sons in the cellar passage, where they were attempting to reroute the electric cable, until I took it out of their hands. Electricity is my concern: charges, fields, and currents. Currents consisting of low voltages and wattages. Upstairs cups clatter on saucers, while downstairs doors bang, and a seven-year-old silently holds a match under the wicker bed of the fourth sibling. All surprises deteriorate into routine. There are no surprises here. We know each other too well for that.

Besides, this persistent high pressure is unlikely to produce change; there is no chance of even a small, transient disturbance to provide material for conversations about the weather in stairwells, on streetcars, in staff rooms, or to prompt conversation on the primitive entrails of small basic instruments for measuring voltage and currents. For the past few weeks there has been no talk of the weather, as only those who are absolutely happy can give praise endlessly; everyone else can do so only sporadically. Unallayed suspicion and latent surliness hold them back. Weariness, too, perhaps.

Yesterday evening I acted upon an invitation. Blindly.

The house I was invited to does not lie on my daily route, I had to check the city map and found it in a distant district. Because of the beautiful weather, I walked for over an hour through the old, reddish industrial district in which I live, where some streets have rows of narrow hundred-year-old factories in whose courtyards women come and go in flowery aprons, looking as if they have briefly interrupted a major housecleaning to buy a raspberry soda at the state store opposite, while here and there an older man in those black shoes with acid-proof soles bustles about, carting something off or dumping it on a pile. On such days, the musty family odor of preindustrial manufacturing hangs over the entire district. There are doormen with enlarged irises behind firmly framed glasses, carefully inscribed nameplates in thick, lacquered wood, courtyards, odd collections of by-products, unfinished items, refuse, and warm, porous, inexorably decaying surfaces.

Yesterday, Saturday evening, these streets were quite still, and one could hear leaves brushing against the ancient corner of a dark violet wall, on which there still lingered the stubborn glow of earlier brick-manufacturing practices. Walking through my neighborhood, I had the impression that it was asleep, exhausted, like an old man sleeping with his thermos bottle in the railway station waiting room, long wiry hairs growing like iron filings from his ears. A man without any knowledge of self.

As though automatically adjusting to that deep, labored breathing, I slowed my pace and reached the other district somewhat later than intended. I was admitted into a narrow, high-ceilinged hall, which eventually led into darkness. A man of average size with brown, childlike eyes came up to me. His expectation on meeting me seemed to surpass even mine, and a clamor of anticipation came through the closed door.

Heinrich was the host's first name, though he quickly confided in me that he was known to his friends not by his first name but by his surname. Then he opened the door, where I believed the loud sounds of merriment were coming from, and I had to discard the picture I had tried to form of the evening and replace it with the one now emerging. I would have preferred to linger in the shadow of Heinrich, for I know all too well that I cannot possibly live up to expectations. My responses to my surroundings are evidently quite slow.

The small gathering looked in my direction. Heinrich had laid his arm protectively around my shoulders. I am not the sort of man who ever gets noticed and they must have observed this. And it must have irritated them, as their greeting was reserved and they turned around again quickly to face the large, colorfully laid round table. The advantage of this circular arrangement was that I could not be offered a place that stood out from the others. The room was sparsely furnished; as I entered, it had appeared to be shot through with light, and though the daylight had gone, it still filled the room with an intense radiance. I observed this closely and determined that the effect was due to the almost perfectly reflecting white walls and the tall, bare windows; I was in very beautiful surroundings. Once the sun had set, the room took on a galvanic glow, which was quite weak, yet nonetheless sufficiently strong to make one suspect the presence of voltage. Electrical phenomena are my specialty; I have developed a heightened sensitivity to them. This is obviously something one can live with.

The black-haired woman opposite bared very small, pointed, white teeth each time she laughed.

They simply carried on the conversation, seemingly ignoring me, for which I was most grateful. I gathered that they met regularly, not with scrupulous regularity on a set day of the month, but at such brief intervals that one had a sense not so much of time passing as of a continuous, intensive present. The black-haired woman gazed at me for a long time, as if wishing to discover how I came to be there. I felt relieved, for I did not know the answer and thus her gaze need not concern me. I could remain quite neutral.

I had no longer really been counting on any such invitation. Too many years had gone by. When I thought of those earlier years, I heard subdued rock music, nothing specific, just mid-Seventies rock, sounds coming through the wall. But yesterday evening there were no sounds from neighboring apartments to disturb the excited gaiety of this small group. Before long, Heinrich's wife came in to lay the final dishes on the table, rounding off the exotic repast. Heinrich immediately raised his glass to welcome us. He was enjoying himself, yes indeed, he was enjoying himself. I had fun watching him: few people exude as much joy as did this robust little man through every pore of his body. We drank to each other. Meanwhile, I was discreetly trying to ascertain the rules of the game; there may have been some, but even if this entire event was the product of spontaneous individual reactions, I was aware that I was a novice. I acted with caution.

I am so little accustomed to being noticed that it bothers me when I am. Yes, it bothers me.

It was clear that everyone else was prepared for the evening. The gaunt gentleman on my left drew a couple of wooden chopsticks from the inner pocket of his jacket, held them up in the air, then erupted in soundless laughter, which made his shoulders rise and fall. It was only then that I noticed a penny-sized powdered mole on the black-haired woman's forehead. It lay between her curved brows, only higher up; her small face, which her quick rapacious eyes constantly sought to flee, appeared even smaller on account of the mole. Her husband seemed to be lost in some ancient melancholy, but it was not at all pretentious, since it clung quite naturally to him, enclosing him in a space of its own, a transparent bubble in which he doubtlessly pursued his own thoughts. His gray hair stood out from his head in great waves. He had greeted me like one of those old friends with whom one always sees eye to eye.

What struck me about the couple next to him was the feverish eagerness with which they wheeled about to face each speaker. Yet even before the first hour was over, I knew that I was not the person they wanted. Even if I assumed they were merely being tactfully aloof, I was still quite certain that this was so. I had obviously been invited by mistake. Someone had thought of me by chance and thereby fallen into error. I find it astonishing that in all these years this has never happened before.

Someone had begun to supply names for the contents of the dishes and bottles covering the table, someone who was well versed in the subject: Kela ka raita, Nariyal chatni, Kofta kari, suvar mas ka Vindalu. Of course it was she, but she made two mistakes, which Heinrich corrected. The attentive couple immediately thought of a case in which someone had made a fateful error and based his life on that error; this incident had led relentlessly and consequentially to utter despondency, one of the many minor incidents of human existence that cannot be helped. I have forgotten them as I have forgotten everything that claims the power to affect my existence. My neighbor on the left inquired about the linguistic sources of the two errors, and then, after closely examining the content of the dishes, determined that they should never have occurred. When the mole between her eyes began pointing at him defiantly, he added that, if people are in full possession of their faculties, they cannot come to harm in the world.

Surprised, I turned to him. I was wondering how best to reply to his statement, so as to make myself understood, but he was already smiling at me, raising his eyebrows. "Do you really believe," I began, while Heinrich filled my plate and taught me how to use chopsticks and Heinrich's wife warned us that, given the inevitably protracted nature of a meal eaten with chopsticks, the many tiny portions would have time to expand thrice or fourfold in our stomachs, and consequently we had to reckon with a belated but persistent sense of repleteness.

"Do you really believe," I began, once everyone had begun to eat with great fervor; the unusual cutlery enforced patience and thus enjoyment. (With a start, I fathomed what it is to have nothing escape one.) "Do you really believe," I asked, "that people cannot come to harm?"

"Assuming the optimum," replied the man, who was no longer young and whose reactions, gestures, looks, even the way he sat, were determined by a frugal vitality and a fundamentally stable tension of the mind; our physical proximity ensured that this was transmitted to me with playful ease.

"What optimum?" I asked him.

"The optimum in mutual adjustment," he explained.

I had to chew each bite exactly thirty-two times, she instructed, staring at my mouth. She chewed and smiled, presumably counting for me and for herself. She had great fun performing this little task. She was so appealing. Once she had assured herself that I could chew on my own and savor the juices that one could—she maintained—extract by means of intense devotion from each morsel of dry bread, once she had assured herself of her effect on me, she turned to someone else.

"I no longer feel there is any movement in history," said her husband, emerging briefly from his self-absorption only to sink right back into it again.

"In the lands in which this meal is indigenous," said Heinrich, by way of encouragement, "it is considered good manners to slurp and smack one's lips or eat with one's hands—either one for sure. One of these customs probably stems from the Near East, the other more from Southeast Asia. We shouldn't close our minds to any foreign way of being."

She laughed defiantly, as she had done all evening, with that loud, sharp laugh of hers and those extraordinarily quick reactions. She was being rather inconsiderate. Unlike the rest of us, she—she of all people, with her gaudy blouse—did not pause before responding to Heinrich's suggestion. He called for silence and we listened to the sounds she made while eating.

The women I work with are inconsiderate too. At first this seemed repulsive to me. Their laughter always sounded sharp and shrill, painfully loud, and, if one listened carefully, malicious—as if a long contemplated plan of theirs were soon coming to fruition. They were not afraid of certain words. They were not afraid of anything.

Late in the evening, another guest arrived, an old gentleman who, as became evident, was also expected. The host greeted him as one of the two guests of honor. There could be no question about it: I was the other.

Outwardly, the man made a shabby impression. He had a scrawny white beard, which rested on the collar of a heavy, formless rayon jacket. Yet his gait and his uncertain movements revealed a dignity seldom encountered in this region. He contemplated us for a long time, pensively, each of us, as though we bore hidden messages that he alone could decipher. When he pulled up the tails of his jacket before taking a seat, we could see in the dark, ragged inner lining next to his body a complicated pattern of small objects: pencil stubs of various sizes, pages of a complete timetable folded into tiny packets, a written invitation from a Peking university with a Tibetan charm suspended from it, pieces of maps, a lemon, small and hard as a nut, dictionaries, a ticket for the Trans-Siberian Railway. All of these small objects were arranged according to a transparent yet mysterious, magical system of classification. They referred ambiguously to each other, sometimes through little notes, a word or two in angular cursive written with one of the pencil stumps and surrounded by signs and notations.

The man swayed as he went along, as though staggering under the burden of mental baggage suspended from his clothes.

Oddly enough, from the very outset, I had regarded this evening and this small gathering as a natural phenomenon. Just as one accepts incidents that happen far away and have no bearing on what one has come to accept as one's own life. I am a physicist and I acknowledge the facts; the diversity of phenomena does not confuse me. Each form of diversity is reducible to a formula. The essence is clear and simple—just as the life I lead is absolutely clear and simple, without mystery.

I have essentially reached a point where I can make do with the basics of electrical science: electricity, tension, sparks. Utterly plausible equilibriums. Small sounds, flat in tone, acoustically incapable of expansion. As though space did not exist.

At the time when I still hadn't expanded my not unambitious thesis—a study of spatial specification in selected field theories—into a dissertation that would be readily available through the catalogue of the German Library, it was quite clear to me that one must have a single theme running through one's life if one wants to achieve anything in a field. Wasn't that what I wanted? I was employed in an Institute for Applied Mathematics. In the evenings I went to the library and read about the preconditions for stability in the organization and the autostructuring of complex systems. There, I came across studies on the emergence of tribal hierarchies in Brazilian native peoples and on experiments with workers in a large American automobile factory, who had been observed at work in a relatively autonomous division for over a year.

One day I resigned from my institute so as to devote myself exclusively to my books. I devised a flexible year-long plan. I went to the library at eight every morning and stayed there until four. The food in the small canteen was very reasonable, wurst with bread and sometimes even salad.

The nature, logic, and movement of the organism that comprises reality. The abiding contexts of thought. The relationships. The relationships between all phenomena of animate and inanimate matter. The living and the dead. Life is an infinitely extensible space, about the size of an average heart muscle.

I had saved some money and kept myself supplied with the essentials. A year later I began living off small manual jobs.

In front of the pompous library building, there were several sturdy old chestnut trees, whose top branches I could see through the rectangular window by my usual place in the main reading room. The window was at the end of the gallery, which was usually empty and where I once browsed through reference works on transcultural psychiatry. The window I am thinking of was quite different from the others in that it framed not only its own section of sky but the top branch of one of the old chestnut trees that stretched up into the window area as if it were standing on its toes. I saw it in all seasons. It always seemed quite undisturbed.

Electrically charged fields, positive and negative. Spaces. Powerful, atmospherically charged space. Electricity flows from cloud to cloud. In sheet lightning, most of the surface of the cloud lights up. These discharges occur noiselessly.

After three years without regular employment, I resolved to find work as a physicist again. I did not hesitate for a moment, just as I had not hesitated three years before. I had reached a climax in my stable equilibrium. There is no such thing for there is, of course, no climax in a stable condition. Yet I experienced it.

Prodded by my eager curiosity and believing myself in possession of Promethean qualities, I promptly found six employers seeking someone like me. I visited all six. Each time I watched the secretary in the anteroom of the personnel department typing on a machine connected to an outlet by means of a short, sturdy cable, I was overcome by the sense that I was being admitted into a web of connections, with junctions that could be inspected at all times and reproduced in graphic form as diagrams or as simulation models. I could have defined my own position with great precision. I—that is to say, a high efficiency point inside a model mounted on cardboard, equipped with a small light bulb blinking signals at rapid intervals. Over the past three years I had developed an odd trait: There was no way that I could be intimidated.

But I did not understand them.

To me they simply seemed helpless. I did not recognize their mistrust.

"You are missing those three years," they explained, unless they chose to lapse immediately into expectant silence. But that lengthy, merciless silence was always interrupted by this sentence: "You are missing those three years."

I simply couldn't understand, no, I couldn't understand how I was missing them.

Finally, an older and no doubt sentimental woman offered me work in the assembly section. It was the most she could do for someone like me, she explained. I accepted at once. I was obsessed with the idea of this tiny pulsar, fueled by three amperes, in the universe of social activity. That was how things stood.

Electricity, charges, bangs. As if bubbles of light tin were bursting. Outside the sealed rooms, no one can hear it.

The assembly section: It consisted of nineteen workers, sixteen of them women. We assembled voltage meters and ammeters—those small measuring devices everyone remembers from physics class. Each day lasted until the sound of the final bell, which was still in use and which I had inspected during my first few days there. Ten minutes before that bell rang, everyone laid aside the measuring instruments they were about to solder. There was nothing that couldn't be interrupted at ten to four to allow for a quick reflexive brushing-off of one's body and straightening of one's clothes.

After six days I was indeed tired, though not truly tired. It was as if I were suffering the aftereffects of too much shallow breathing. I carefully analyzed these phenomena. My consciousness, which had been shaped by the idea of holistic unity, registered the incident without the slightest trepidation. It was imbued with an unprejudicial approach to reality. It was inquisitive. It watched over me on the seventh day as I slept.

Today is Sunday.

Yesterday evening a man appeared, an ancient man with a thin beard and with a swaying, sleepwalker's gait, which is just what one imagines it to be: a dance over an abyss, invisible, of course. He observed us all with bright, rather owl-like eyes, each of us at great length, as though each person carried a secret message. When he opened his jacket, small, solid, palpable objects emerged: a tiny set of plastic airplane cutlery, an offset print of the Soviet party secretary, a heavy bundle of keys which had torn the jacket lining in several places and from which hung an especially delicate key with a red ribbon, made for a trunk whose whereabouts could not be ascertained. The old man stood there for a long time with his jacket tails parted. People kept asking to see.

I watched as the black-haired woman's sharp teeth, which reminded me of a young shark's, dug into the chicken's thigh. Encouraged by the expression on her face, I had chewed a portion of rice noodles very thoroughly, without managing to filter out the aroma, to which the conversation kept returning all evening. The rice noodles tasted of their components, water and flour.

At five to four the workers stood there, holding the same bags, waiting for the bell, and each time it sounded exactly like the recess bell at school, automatically yielding wild yells. I could not separate this tone from the wild and strident little screams of that period. Like the shrieks of fleeing seagulls. Being absent for half a day earned one a reprimand.

After about three months I started repeating myself. I moved into another apartment closer to the factory, and as a result did not have to leave the house so early in the morning. Like the other tenants, I now had my work. At some point, from one day to the next, I ceased to remember. This happened when I gave up struggling.

By midnight last night we were all drunk. It was a tenuous drunkenness. A blurring, a slowing down. We had already moved from the great round table to a small oblong one. The light of a wall lamp fell on the neck of the black-haired woman. I could not see her face clearly. She peered at me.

Heinrich served strong coffee. There were large-scale lithographs hanging above the armchairs. One depicted a mountain landscape, the ridge of a rocky mountain chain that emerged from a steep bank of mist, as if it were growing. High above the ridge, in a harsh glare surrounded by darkness, hung three flat, pillow-like clouds, immobile while the bank of mist, which shimmered with all the colors of the spectrum, was driven about by the great wind currents that circle the earth in regular trajectories.

She looked at me, as though she wanted something quite definite from me. With that mixture of penetrating trust, hope, and relentlessness, with which children turn to the person they have been told can help them. And with which they make it quite clear that they will not be shaken off again.

They did want something from me.

They had remembered me.

They must have spent a long time looking for me.

The old gentleman had begun ravenously eating what was left on our plates. Mine was next.

She looked at me.

But at this very moment, I became ill. The choice ingredients in the meal we had enjoyed, the fine, heavy oils, the walnuts, the almonds, the pistachio kernels, and the unfamiliar wine had made me feel heavy and intoxicated. In states such as the one I had been reduced to, one lags so far behind time and the events occurring in it that they are only perceptible as small dots on the horizon. And therefore in the end there is not a trace of anybody who pretends to take an interest in a wretched, marginal existence.

Being noticed is bothersome: it is false.

The current flows sluggishly through the resistors.

You can measure it by taking one of these simple devices for measuring small currents and voltages, and by measuring in turn its built-in resistor. None of this is visible to the naked eye. But it is measurable.

Today, Sunday, I have been lying in bed all morning, immobile. A dazzlingly sunny morning in October. I did not try to move, for everything inside me had separated itself from me. Except for my loudly beating heart. And as time passed, a noiseless, intensifying sensation made itself felt under my cap. As though someone had opened a dovecote and a flock of ringed doves were falling out, skyward.

The resulting din lasted until noon.

Translated from the German by Mark Harman

BRAVO 20
BOMBING
RANGE
NEVADA*
RICHARD MISRACH

PAGE 195
CRYSTALLIZATION OF
MINERALS IN RAIN-FILLED
BOMB CRATER, 1986.
RIGHT MINERAL DEPOSITS
AFTER WATER EVAPORATION
IN BOMB CRATER, 1986.

LEFT UNEXPLODED
ORDNANCE #1, 1986.
RIGHT UNEXPLODED
ORDNANCE #2, 1986.

ABOVE UNEXPLODED ORDNANCE #3, 1986.
RIGHT UNEXPLODED ORDNANCE #4, 1986.

ABOVE UNEXPLODED ORDNANCE #5, 1986.

RICHARD * MISRACH

First the volatile witches' brews when rain mixes the chemicals of war and aridity; then the silt left behind when those brews evaporate in the heat of the day; the dirt itself bombed into craters and clods and dust; the rusting bombs and the unexploded bombs like alarm clocks without hands waiting to go off; and then the horizon that promises respite, difference, and the soft blue of distance; finally, the broad beautiful desert sky, mocking all these mutabilities, pouring its daily light and darkness, its annual brief rain and relentless sun, on the land no matter what.

This landscape is hidden, but everything in it is on view. Bare stone testifies to the uplift of geological forces billions of years ago, and even the traces of death and destruction last far longer out here, where the absence of water slows down the organic processes of both growth and decay. Well into this century, jettisoned furniture and dead oxen from the wagon trains that plodded through at the rate of twelve miles a day could be found in the Great Basin Desert, and the tracks of General Patton's tanks training for the last World War have yet to wear away in the Mojave. In this desert expanse, from New Mexico to Idaho, from southeastern California to Utah, the United States military has concentrated its activity, and though officially it is only practicing the art of war, it often seems that it is fighting a war here, against the desert's sense of time and space that so appalled the early invaders from the East and still overwhelms us. The weapons themselves are strange exercises in scale. There are the sonic booms caused by jets breaking the sound barrier, which were tried out as a weapon that at least made livestock abort and windows break in Dixie Valley, not far from the Bravo 20 Bombing Range (and the other nineteen that preceded it) in northcentral Nevada. Not far from Las Vegas, nuclear weapons have been exploded over and over again, more than a thousand of them altogther, bombs that deal on the scale of the subatomic particle and the apocalypse, and leave behind plutonium with a radioactive half-life of a quarter of a million years to work its strange tricks on any life that comes in contact with it. And there are the conventional bombs—a few years ago, in a desultory cleanup exercise, the Navy picked up 123,375 tons of scrap ordnance on public lands.

This is the landscape Richard Misrach has chosen to work with, and in his vision the conventional landscape as a refuge from or a place before history and politics gives way to something utterly different: the landscape as a battlefield, where the cyclical time of organic nature is eclipsed by the linear march of history. Over and over again, he shows us where our history has been written in huge, incandescent letters, in places where hardly anyone comes to read it.

REBECCA SOLNIT

ERIN BELIEU

NOCTURNE: MY SISTER LIFE

I

Honeysuckles tap soil
    almost anywhere, junkyard
shrubs, able-rooted, attaching
    through rock or sand. From
Evanston to Omaha, their red fish
    roe berries border plots
of zoysia, buffalo, the family portion.
    Lilacs go slowly, their old lady wigs
curling to beige crust; roses might
    develop, but die in extreme weather.
Depend on the honeysuckle
    to maintain where others falter...

II

You were never afraid of the dark, never afraid of each object resolving itself, vanishing into night's good sleeve, benign magic the world performed for you at sundown. You admired the young shepherdess tending sheep at the base of your lamp, coaxing her flock into evening's invisible pen. You wanted the world quiet. Even then, you looked forward to all things shutting their many mouths, interim in the revolving puzzle of light.

III

Scent of an eighth-grader's
    cologne, they strong-arm other shrubs,
are used primarily for husbandry.
    Honeysuckles provide cheap
borders, hide chain-link fences.
    Won't tuck behind your ear, attract
bees bad as marigolds and stand
    awkwardly in floral arrangements.
While not poisonous, the jellied
    berries can be semi-toxic. Some
might not resist the urge to eat them,
    even after being warned against it...

IV

Lying in your twin bed, where cartoon figures stare out from the comforter with their medicated expressions, you realize that you're dying, death includes you. Distant relatives, rodents, and now, suddenly, you. This is the same day you're surprised by a nest of wasps hidden in the neighbors' swing set, their jet bodies burrowing inside your clothes, stinging you between the shoulder blades, one welt bubbling inside your lower lip. Imagine everything dead: your older brother, somewhere in the house, closer to it. Your parents in the den, crunch of the ice bucket as your father fixes his Manhattan (gold anesthesia, issued to the heart), closer still.

V

When stands of honeysuckle
      fade, they reach for the ground,
their nippled flowers pulling close
      to the center of each bush.
Birds abandon old nests
      laid open inside the dying
grove. Eventually the shrubs
      must be stumped, hacked off
below the waist and extracted.
      Do not be shocked by their roots,
how far the honeysuckles' reach is . . .

VI

Now you lie down queen-sized, new husband beside you, paying rent in his dreams. Yesterday, he tells you, you awoke with two questions: Needle? Needle? Who knows, the way you sleep, you might as well be drowning. The dragonfly stuck in a knick-knack's liquid glass. Sometimes you drive a yellow Karmann Ghia through your dreamscapes, clown-mobile with transparent, cardboard windows. Through shopping malls, bordellos, your cousins' basement, you always ferry a passenger. Wake and something else is waking: your familiars at the window, stalking what moves on the ledge.

—for Joseph Lease

György Ligeti

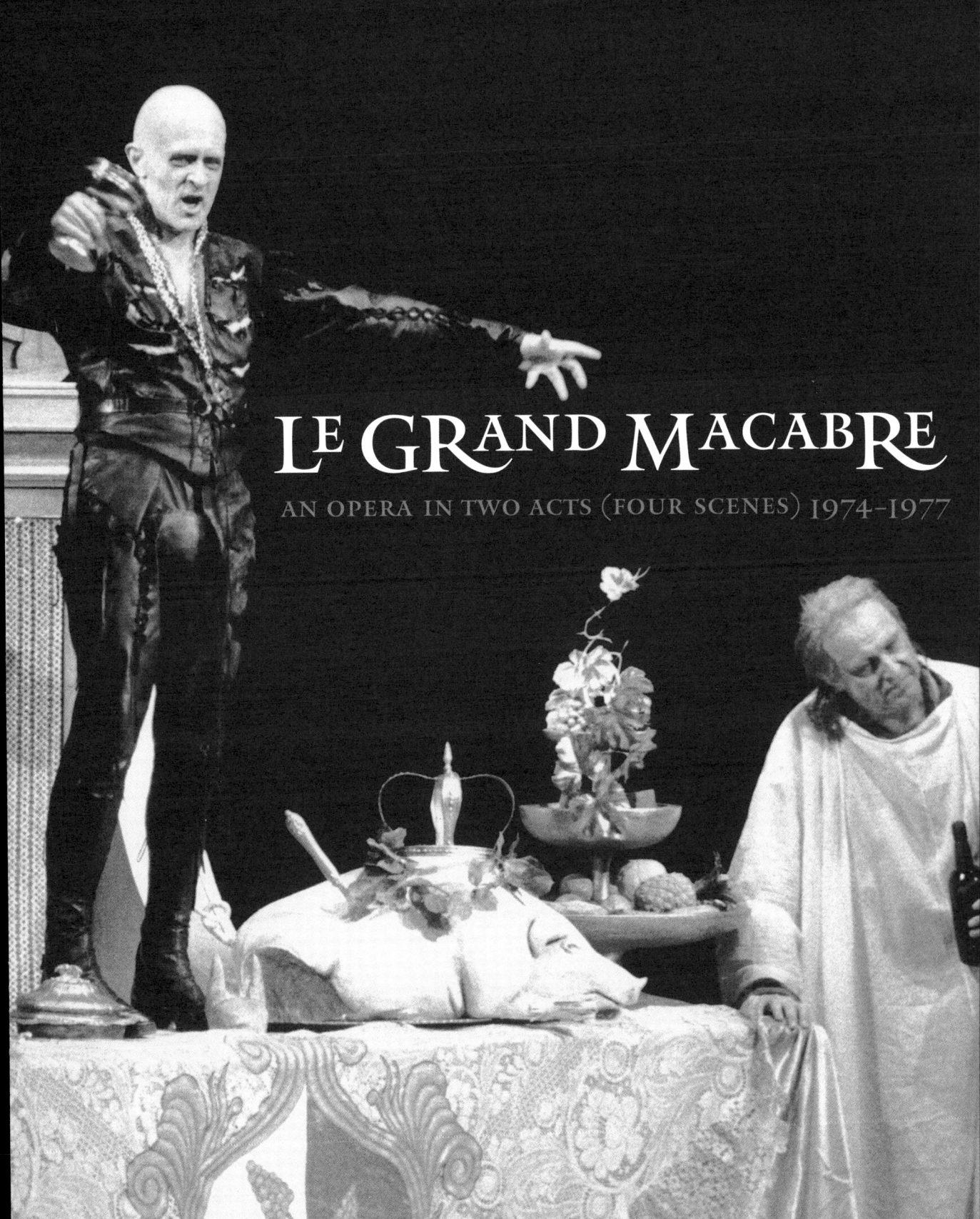

Le Grand Macabre

AN OPERA IN TWO ACTS (FOUR SCENES) 1974–1977

Le Grand Macabre will be staged, in a new production, at the Salzburg Festival in the summer of 1997, under the direction of Peter Sellars with Esa-Pekka Saloner conducting. It was originally commissioned by Stockholm Opera director Göran Gentele in 1965. The opera developed gradually in Ligeti's mind: initially, the action was to take place in "Kylwiria," an imaginary world of daydreams, where emotional states and vocal sounds were to take the place of a coherent plot and comprehensible text. In 1972, Ligeti dismissed this idea as outdated and reworked the opera with a plot structure and libretto (cowritten with Michael Meschke and loosely based on La Balade du Grand Macabre by Belgian playwright Michel de Ghelderode) that revolve around the imminent end of the world. The end of the opera is left ambiguously open: the end has not arrived, or has arrived without changing anything. Le Grand Macabre premiered, in its original version, on April 12, 1978, at Stockholm's Royal Opera.

PAGES 206–207 Performance of *Le Grand Macabre* at the Royal Opera, Stockholm, 1978.

ACT I

SCENE ONE

*In the principality of Breughelland,
an imaginary country, no particular century*
Piet the Pot sings the praises of his native land, while a pair of lovers, Amanda and Amando, look for a place where they can make love. Nekrotzar enters, claiming to be the figure of Death, charged with the task of putting an end to the world. He forces Piet to help him in his mission.

SCENE TWO

In the house of the court astronomer Astradamors
Astradamors is engaged in sadomasochistic love play with his alcoholic, nymphomaniac wife Mescalina. He then goes to his telescope, where he is alarmed by the approach of a comet and other portents. Mescalina falls into a drunken sleep, in which she implores Venus to give her a lover more potent than her husband. Nekrotzar, entering with Piet, responds to Mescalina's appeal and kills her with his violent lovemaking. Astradamors, delighted to be rid of her, joins them as they set off for the palace.

ACT II

SCENE THREE

In the palace of Prince Go-Go
Two politicians are arguing. The Chief of the Secret Police (or "Gepopo") rushes in to announce public disturbances and the approach of a mysterious procession. The gluttonous Boy Prince finds the courage to dismiss his corrupt ministers, the leaders of the opposing Black and White parties, and pacify the people himself. The arrival of Nekrotzar, however, with Piet and Astradmors and an infernal cortège, produces a general panic. As Nekrotzar utters his threats of impending doom, Piet and Astradamors try to divert him by making him drunk; Prince Go-Go helps them. At the last moment, Nekrotzar speaks the words that will bring the world to an end.

SCENE FOUR

Breughelland
It appears that only Go-Go has survived the general destruction. Nekrotzar arrives and, seeing him, realizes that his mission has failed. When he tries to return to the tomb from which he came, Mescalina springs out and pursues him. Go-Go then attempts to assume command, and the group is joined by the two ministers, and by Piet and Astradamors. During the violent scene that follows, Nekrotzar vanishes. While the others are puzzling over his true identity, Amanda and Amando emerge, knowing nothing of what has been happening while they were busy making love. Their mood affects everyone and they all come to the conclusion that it is wrong to fear death. "When it comes, then let it be. . . ./ Farewell till then, live merrily!"

PETER SELLARS
ON
Le Grand Macabre

György Ligeti is a Hungarian émigré, who has been in Western Europe since the 1960s. You know his music from *2001: A Space Odyssey*, where the wild choral voices of the future are in fact his *Requiem*, written between 1963 and 1965. He is now seventy-two and he wrote *Le Grand Macabre* in the mid-'70s. The opera is a shocking, kind of excretory apocalypse. It's not just irreverent, it knows no shame: it is in very bad taste, it's filled with bad jokes, the music is outrageous. And to put this giant mess on the stage of the Salzburg Festival this summer will be one of the great privileges of my life.

Ligeti speaks eloquently about his reasons for making something that is shameless, pornographic, obnoxious, lewd, and excremental. He grew up, first under Hitler and then under the Soviet rule, in regimes that insisted on official cleanliness, on high moral behavior, on family values, on this unbelievably clean image. So he says, "I've seen where *that* leads, and now I want to celebrate dirt. I want to celebrate that which is human, that which is humane, that which cannot be co-opted by ideology."

The other analogy that he gives for his music is African music. African musicians wear bracelets on their wrists and ankles that make noise; the instruments themselves have strange pieces of paper, odd wires, or bits of thong attached to them, so every sound has about five sounds in it, every sound is part of every other sound—so you can't begin to separate or to categorize. You can't set up levels of purity, or of racial purity. *Mélange*, that which is mixed, double, bifurcated, or conflicted, that which is already complex, is the defining condition.

Ligeti's work is based on those kinds of principles. In *Le Grand Macabre*, he's taken a very extreme, elaborate, post-Schönbergian, second Viennese-school compositional approach, but he mixes it with strange tonalities and an absence of tonality entirely, instruments that have no pitch, for example. The opening of the opera is a toccata for car horns; the opening of the second act is a fugue for doorbells and telephones. So it really is about understanding music as not exalted, and yet, in a certain way, transcendental.

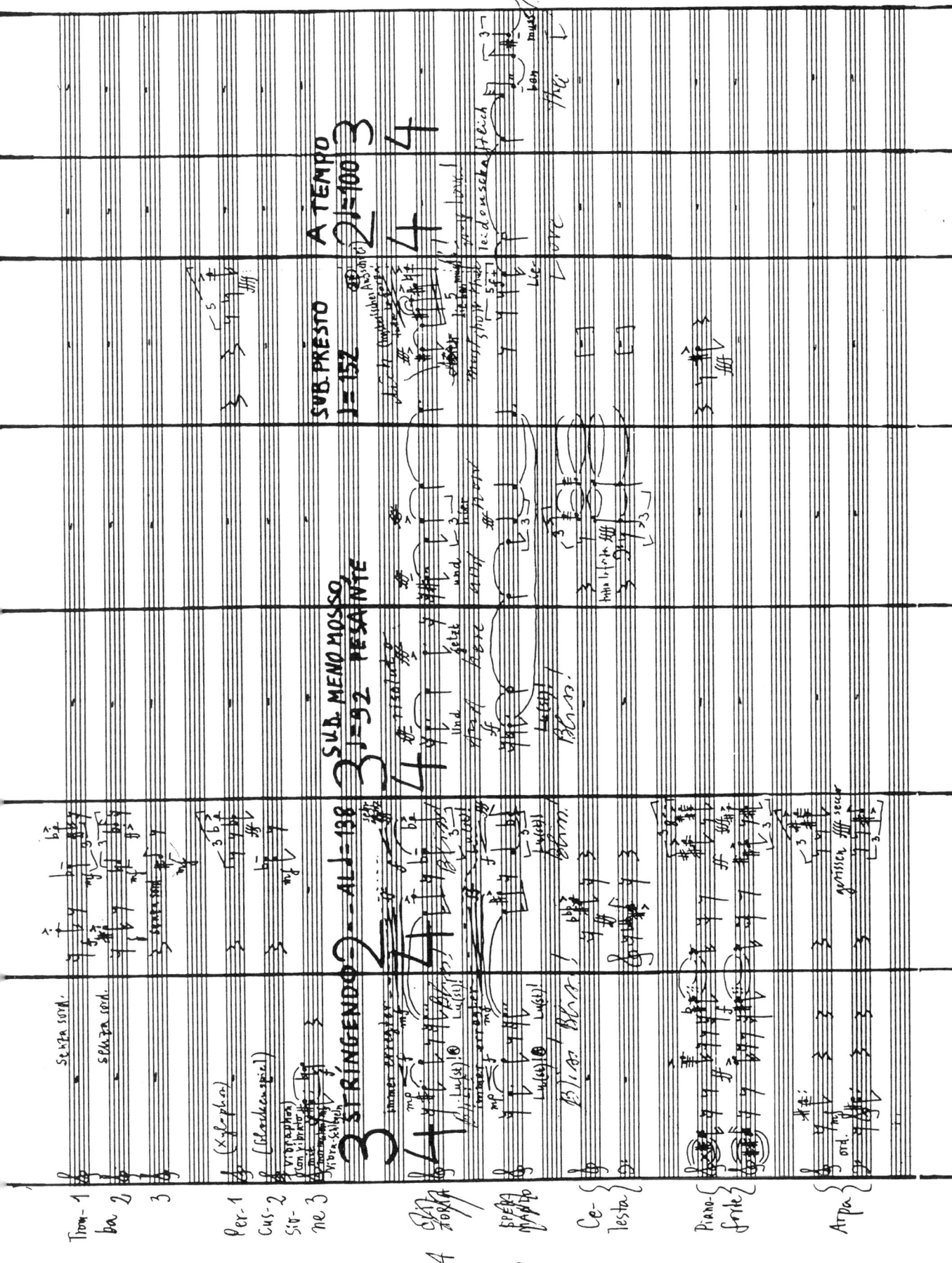

[5]

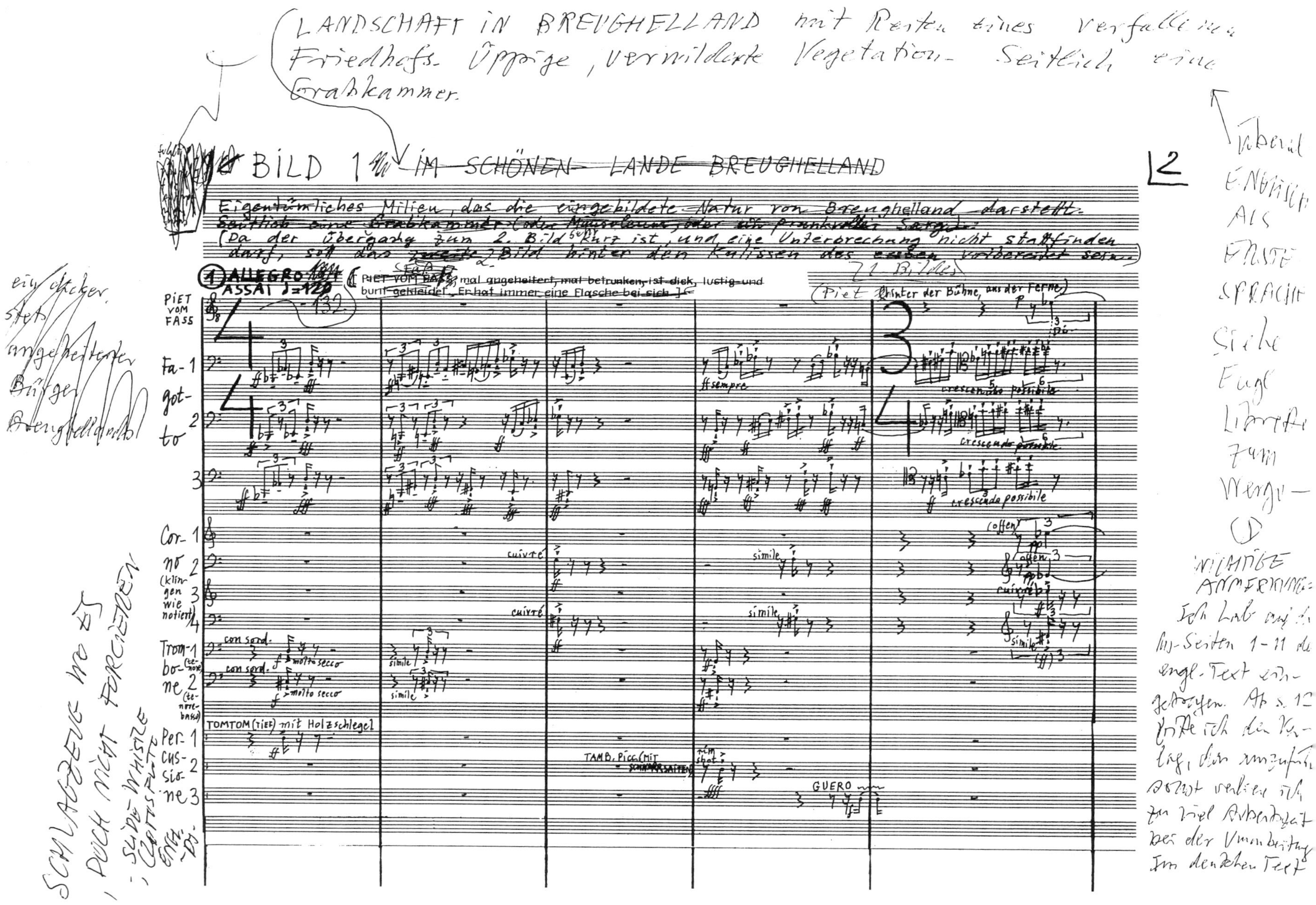
LANDSCHAFT IN BREUGHELLAND mit Resten eines verfallenen Friedhofs. Üppige, verwilderte Vegetation. Seitlich eine Grabkammer.
BILD 1 IM SCHÖNEN LANDE BREUGHELLAND
Eigentümliches Milieu, das die eingebildete Natur von Breughelland darstellt.
Da der Übergang zum 2. Bild sehr kurz ist, und eine Unterbrechung nicht stattfinden darf, soll das 2. Bild hinter den Kulissen des 1. Bildes vorbereitet sein.
2
ALLEGRO ASSAI ♩=120
PIET VOM FASS, mal angeheitert, mal betrunken, ist dick, lustig und bunt gekleidet. Er hat immer eine Flasche bei sich.
Piet hinter der Bühne, aus der Ferne
PIET VOM FASS
Fagotto 1 2 3
Corno 1 2 3 4 (klingen wie notiert)
Trombone 1 (tenore) 2 (tenore-basso)
Percussione 1 2 3
con sord.
molto secco
simile
cuivré
ff sempre
crescendo possibile
offen
TOMTOM (TIEF) mit Holzschlegel
TAMB. PICC. (MIT SCHNARRSAITEN)
GUERO
ein dicker, stets angeheiterter Bürger Breughellands
Überall ENGLISCH ALS ERSTE SPRACHE siehe engl. Libretto zum Vergl.
WICHTIGE ANMERKUNG: Ich hab auf die Seiten 1–11 den engl. Text eingetragen. Ab S. 12 ...
Schlagzeug ... auch nicht forcieren

ROQUENVAL

CHRONICLE OF A CHATEAU

NINA BERBEROVA

1.

Ten years ago, in July of 1926, I first crossed a heavy stone bridge between two rusty chains, the bridge joining Roquenval to the outside world. As I passed over the bridge, a heavy, semicircular door opened in greeting, revealing a glimpse of something greenish-blue resembling a garden. Under the bridge, weeds were growing luxuriantly in the murky damp, pale nettles were blooming, and fat red snails were sitting on the steep walls of the medieval moat. Some creeping bushes, prickly evergreens whose name was unknown to me, were making their way up the old walls, throwing out stiff tendrils from rock to rock, from moss to moss. Three-hundred-year-old trees, their trunks the circumference of three pairs of outspread arms, were rustling their high tops languorously with a silvery sound even in this sultry weather: an avenue of monstrous ancient linden trees planted in four rows lined the way here from the outside world. And as I walked along it to the stone bridge, I had time both to grow nervous and to prepare myself. I prepared myself for that antique and ceremonious thing that awaited me here, and I grew nervous because this avenue of trees planted in the time of my great-grandfathers reminded me of my only image of Russia. It was an image that I had taken with me unwittingly, as people take something not their own, and I discovered it unexpectedly like a hereditary illness—doing so, to my enormous joy, at a time when I had begun to reconcile myself to the fact that I did not know the real Russia, had not seen it, and that I remembered only excruciating and chance moments which had somehow or other moved along with me during our travels.

Our travels had begun many years before the day described here, first taking us around Russia for four years and then, for two years, on sea journeys and across Europe; at the time I had been eight, then twelve, then fourteen years old. My father and Mama sometimes asked me, did I remember Petersburg, Chita, Yalta? But I only had some images of apartments and train cars mixed up in my mind, and I think I finally became aware of my surroundings only somewhere quite nearby: practically in Calais, where we had come down from England shortly before my father's death and my sister's marriage.

But then one day, reading either Tolstoy or Turgenev, or maybe even Chekhov, because Mama had instilled in me a particular appreciation for Russian books—reading a description of the wholly fairy-tale house of some landowner, I suddenly envisioned—at first in very general outlines—the road leading to a house, to its Empire-style balcony and to some low jasmine bushes.

I saw an old avenue of linden trees, eternally dark and eternally alive, with the penetrating bright noonday light shining through them at the end; old, almost frightening trees stood over me. I distinguished with perfect clarity the pattern of sun spots on the overgrown path, the white stone and a large dark-green mushroom by it. And suddenly I noticed that in the book there had been not a single word about anything like this in quite a while, and some strangers were drinking tea on the terrace and a thumping charabanc was audible as a guest rode in from the station. . . . I clapped the book shut and went to ask Mama if I had ever seen such an avenue of trees or a real Russian garden. I think her mind was elsewhere, but she answered me with the tenderness which never left her, that of course I had seen it, it was the house where we had lived for four consecutive summers, the house of my grandfather. She said something else about the swings where the young nanny had seated me, although this was forbidden, and mentioned a gazebo above a pond where my father had proposed to her, but I was no longer listening, I felt like a person who had suddenly got his memory back and remembered his name, and from that day onward when I heard the word "Russia," images of that enchanted corner of densely placed linden trees and the road going at a diagonal from the gates in the field to the white porch of our house invariably surfaced in my mind. I felt especially keenly the black bark of the trees, like black bread, and I touched it with my hands when I walked over to it, and sometimes pressed my face into it until it almost hurt.

As I entered Roquenval that day, I was thus overcome with an unexpected and strong sense of agitation. The tree-lined avenue of my childhood, of my birth, of my preexistence, stood before me wondrous and imposing, hiding the sky, the sunlight and the entire sultry July noon! A dark root snaked unmoving at my feet, a white stone with a marking on it lay on the ground like a faithful hound and looked into my face, and the scratched and peeling bark of the trees awaited my touch. A hushed silence and trepidation simultaneously poured down on me from the tall treetops that leaned in toward each other.... There was no need for me to imagine, no need to summon to mind the sweet and mysterious picture—it was before me. But further on the slow, creaking door opened wider and wider and, seizing my suitcase, I raced toward the château.

Jean-Paul and I had become acquainted during the first year at the lycée, but as often happens, we got to know each other only at the very end, right before graduation—at first we even addressed each other by the formal 'you,' and conversed politely, and I think we both liked this sort of friendship, unusual for the lycée, where everyone around us had either grown sick of each other long ago, or paid no attention to each other at all, and where, as in all schools in the world, curse words and greetings were used interchangeably. We had spoken only a few times, although at such length that conversations begun in class continued outside and then at my house. Finally, Mama would tiptoe in and bring us enormous magenta peaches, which Jean-Paul absentmindedly downed one after the other. The conversations continued at night when I saw him home, and on the embankment, where boards and macadam were tossed in heaps and a grill with a fire going in it rattled in the night as we sat for long hours next to a sleeping watchman. I told Jean-Paul about how I dreamed of becoming a writer and recited my poems to him (the French ones, and then the Russian ones); I was surprised to learn that he had no thoughts of such things at all; the future appeared to him not in the form of something conferred, to which we are all entitled, but rather in the form of a cleverly hidden filigreed knickknack, which some light-fingered person might manage to steal—steal it and then head off to the Arctic Circle with reindeer and dogs, or to forgotten or undiscovered tropical islands, in order "to start life over," as he put it—something that older people so often dream of, and that is so easy to do when one is young. Saying good-bye to me once at the entrance to his home, he smiled at me, wrinkling his nose and crossing his eyes (this grin was uniquely characteristic of him) and said—if he had said it in Russian, it would have been something like this: "I find you very agreeable, Boris," or more loosely, "Let's be friends!" And right after that, he turned and started back—to see *me* off now, and as if making excuses for what he had said, he explained to me that he had made this remark probably because I was Russian and there were Russians in his family, and some of his Russian relatives were still living.

"That's nice," I said, assuming at the time that he must have some cousin once-removed who was married to, say, a Polish woman, and that he was talking this way just to please me. A few days later he visited me again, and I saw from the way he spoke with Mama that it was not only his name which was noble, but that his whole demeanor revealed him as a person of gentle birth and fine old blood.

Yes, his name was at once impressive and pitiful, for now the family title exhaled not only an odor of luxury, but a sense of doom as well, because those who bore it had less money than the average member of the bourgeoisie, and everyone knew that this was the last of the money, not that there was enough to live on for another day or another month, but that there was just enough left for this last generation. I did not compare myself with him; after my father's passing, Mama had received an insurance settlement and on this money my sister was led to the altar and I received my education. That spring when we both became baccalaureates and he invited me to visit him for the summer, he said that the Château Roquenval in the southwestern corner of Île-de-France belonged to his father.

I still did not know at that time who the members of his family were, because that day when I got off the bus in the quiet sunny hamlet and made my way along the linden avenue, I did not yet know the most important thing, which had been the very root, the very basis of this house for the last half-century. I saw a fortress, put in place by a favorite of Francis I, the clock tower, and the château itself, with gray walls and narrow windows set in frames of an unpretentious brick pattern, the dead towers, the broken water pipes, the ivy that had spread across the roofs, and the stillness—it was the stillness of a nocturnal bird on a sunny day. Jean-Paul had told me more than once about his thrice-widowed father, now married for the fourth time (his first marriage had been to Jean-Paul's mother, his second had been to a beauty who was killed in a fall from a horse, the third time he had been married to someone else, and finally, to a woman of loose conduct)—about his father's brother, a monk who had changed his religion twice and had shot at someone and had been to Russia; about his father's sister and her daughters (the younger of whom was named Kyra, to my great surprise). But he talked of all these people somehow in passing, even about his grandmother, who according to him I would like very much (and here he crossed his eyes and wrinkled his nose with a particularly sly look) and it was only later that I learned the story of their lives in detail.

A tall man, heaving open the semicircular door for me—a doorkeeper, footman, butler—apparently knowing who I was, bowed to me and led me through a wide, stone-paved interior courtyard, past empty stables with the glass knocked out of the windows and doors wide open and torn off their hinges. Next to the flagstones at the entrance, worn down by years of being trod upon, a dry marble fountain, a rusty green vase on a slender socle and a headless lion corroded by time stood guard quietly over a low, large sunken hall, where once upon a time the count's sentry had probably warmed himself before a gigantic fireplace. At the end of the room there was a pink stone stairway.

At the top of the stairs stretched a gigantic long gallery with windows looking out on two sides of the house, and I saw a series of terraces which had once descended in a straight and orderly row but which now unfolded, haphazard and unkempt, to a lake overgrown with scum. A woman with disheveled black hair and blazing eyes ran from downstairs, carrying an armload of carrots and turnips wrapped in a soiled pinafore. We went through a corner living room where furniture of all imaginable periods flashed by us, Directory-era silk and cretonne from the Seventies, a clock with a figure of Cupid, and diminutive photographs on the walls. We turned into the corridor, where it smelled of dampness and something sour, and ascended a poorly planed, creaky, wooden staircase to the second floor.

Here the ceilings immediately became lower. I sensed that we were in the living quarters, and there was motley-colored wallpaper from the end of the last century with funny, little, pink human figures covering the walls from floor to ceiling; the door had been coated with varnish and did not give right away, and then I entered Jean-Paul's room, where I would also be staying. The tall man peered into a faience pitcher on the washstand with a serious countenance, used his index finger to remove a spider web artfully woven in the very glass of a kerosene lamp, said that Jean-Paul was with the girls in the garden and that he would look for them (sighing as he said this and assuming an expression of boredom and certainty that his search would be futile) and that as soon as I had rested from my trip I should come downstairs and go see the old countess.

"Why should I go see the old countess?" I asked, growing shy.

"Whoever comes to the house for the first time invariably gets taken to the old countess."

"But she probably doesn't know who I am and when I came, does she?"

"Yes, she does know. She has already inquired about you twice today."

I put down my suitcase by the door and sat on the edge of it.

"Is she very old?"

"Oh yes, *monsieur*!"

"Is she eighty?"

"Oh yes, *monsieur*!"

"Must I call her '*madame la comtesse*'?"

"Oh no, *monsieur*!"

"Then what should I call her?"

"*Vous allez le nommer par son prénom et celui de son père.*"

I looked at him questioningly.

"*Vous allez l'appeler 'Praskovia Dimitrievna.'*"

2.

When in my early youth I thought about the past century, I imagined it as much more distant than it actually was; more precisely, I imagined not the end of the nineteenth century (for such as I, the last thirty years of the nineteenth century were our grandfathers' era), but a dim fantastic period from which no one now remained. Probably the books I read as a child were responsible for this mistake, where the eighteenth century was referred to as "the last century." Then, imagining Nikolai Rostov in *War and Peace* or Germann from *The Queen of Spades*, I still felt too closely in my imagination the twilight of the epoch of Catherine the Great, the epoch of *grossfater*, whose childhood had overlapped with the time of young Rostov, the epoch of the powdered wig which the old countess removed in her bedroom while Germann was standing behind the screens. No, no! The time of our grandfathers was the time of the first automobiles; it was the time of the Paris exhibits; it was the time of the Franco-Prussian War and the mysterious death of Skobelev, Russian military hero and player of the Great Game in Central Asia; it was the time of Tchaikovsky's *Queen of Spades* and of the topical novels of the immoderately productive Boborykin; it was a time quite near, not yesterday, but certainly the day before yesterday. And it was this age, the age of Rostov and *grossfater*, of Germann and the powdered wig, which I saw in the Château Roquenval in the person of Jean-Paul's grandmother Praskovia Dimitrievna.

She was not surrounded by pug dogs or hangers-on; she did not receive calls from grandees with shuffling gait; she lived in the château as anyone might live who is solitary, old, and removed from everything. She had children, she had grandchildren, but she did not participate in their lives, and they remembered her thanks only to their inborn politeness and also because of the obligation to revere all forebears, even those not so very distant. And I do not know whether she loved her children and grandchildren. Probably she did love them but this love was by now only a faint glimmer in her dim soul and gave neither her nor anyone else any joy.

Only the memory of who she herself had been and what sort of life had surrounded her forty, fifty, and sixty years ago was preserved in her, as in Roquenval itself the spirit of old France was preserved, captivating in its liveliness.

The room where she lived had once been one of the parlors, but all that remained from the earlier furnishings were the tapestries on the walls, of which one had been cut away roughly with a knife—in a difficult moment, as I found out later, it had been ripped out and sold by Praskovia Dimitrievna's younger son—and this part of the wall was bare. Two candelabra with candles that had never been lit stood by the mirror; this was a pier glass, the likes of which are no longer made, greenish, with bent legs in the hideous fashion of the Nineties. It exerted a pull on me from the first time I saw it, I do not know why. Whatever the reason, it was not due to the fact that from time to time my own figure was reflected in it. I looked into its greenish streaks and there was something there that I could not see, could not remember, as if it had reflected, once upon a time, somewhere far from here, something that was and was not this furniture, that was and was not these candelabra; in the same way all sorts of little trinkets had stood around it then, pillows, shelves, vases, decorative boxes, and a woman walked in and out and the velvet tassels on the sofa moved back and forth. I looked into the murky glass, and it seemed to me that I had already looked into it when I was a tiny child. I looked into it and waited for Russia to appear before me, that same Russia that rustled in Roquenval's linden avenue and flashed in the name Praskovia Dimitrievna, whose bearer sat behind me in the armchair.

She was of small stature, but once she had been tall and statuesque; her waist had been the envy of the Paris demimonde; as to her beauty, it was now impossible to hazard any guesses about it, looking at her puffy cheeks with their sprinkling of white powder, at her mouth filled with teeth which were too large and too white, and her nose, which came down to her pale mauve lips. She aroused reverence and horror. The high collar of her dress was trimmed with lace, her hands in their lace cuffs were small and plump; her eyes were clouded like those of a newborn baby, they saw, and did not see— she did not wear glasses. On the crown of her head was a small knot of blackish-yellow hair, overwhelmed by a large quantity of tortoiseshell combs.

"Boris," she said, pronouncing my name with a French accent, "thank you and come every day. It has been very nice, Boris"—again that French accent—"to spend half an hour with you."

And that Russian on her lips seemed to me similar to her pier glass, which tried to reflect for me the Russia I had forgotten.

I would begin my visit with a slow circuit of her large, semidark room. Sometimes I would come in when she was still drowsing after breakfast, wrapped in a lap robe, looking like a large, old, powdered bird. I made my way along the walls hung with photographs. "Who is this, Praskovia Dimitrievna?" I would ask. She would open a big, black, dim eye in the direction of my hand and refer to herself in the third person, the remnants of a still-lively, still-warm slyness in her voice, saying:

"That was Pashenka herself, when she had twelve years."

And I tried to find in that dusky-skinned little girl in pantaloons the person I saw before me now.

There was no icon case in the room, and for some reason I wanted there to be an icon case. There was a Catholic crucifix hanging over the bed, and above it, hanging not in a corner or at an angle, but just in the ordinary way one would hang a portrait of someone, there was a large old icon. It was impossible to get a close look at it, but from two round holes in the silver holder, one larger than the other, I guessed that this was the Madonna and Child. Her parents had had this icon blessed for Praskovia Dimitrievna when she married the French count, converting to his faith and leaving her native land forever.

She had wed in secret. . . .

"And who is this, Praskovia Dimitrievna?" I asked once more, pouncing on some more obliterated traces of her life.

"That, *mon ami* . . ." she would begin her answer, barely looking, for she already saw, knowing by heart who hung where. I kept wanting her to say, finally:

"And that is my brother, the one you've heard about," but she did not say it.

She had wed in secret, but not from her father and not from her mother. Praskovia Dimitrievna had had a brother fifteen years older than she, who had since adolescence exerted a strange power over her. When she had told the French count that her brother would never allow her to marry him, he was more than a little surprised. He scrutinized their relations more closely and announced abruptly that he wanted the wedding to be moved up and that there was something abnormal in all of this. They got married and galloped across Europe, and thus began their delirious, impulsive life, full of happiness and brilliance.

Once, as Praskovia Dimitrievna was laying out a game of solitaire, and I was looking at the thick, variegated rings on her fingers, she said, "My husband used to say that there was no point in going broke, spending all one's money on lots of different women, and that only fools didn't understand that. He said, 'I'm going broke spending all my money on one woman and only one, and on my lawful wedded wife at that. . . . ' Was there anything he didn't do for me? Did I yearn for an ermine cloak? An ermine cloak it would be! Did Empress Maria Fedorovna have a necklace made of black pearls? He would have one made. Did I want to learn to shoot, or to gallop on horseback? I would get pistols with silver settings from Gastin-Renetta and he would order racehorses from the horse farms in Tula. We came to our senses with the birth of our first child—that is, when our first child was born, we stopped going to Hamburg several times a year to play roulette. . . . "

"Praskovia Dimitrievna, maybe Dostoyevsky saw you there!" I exclaimed.

But she did not get offended, she merely smiled and intimated that she was not one hundred years old but in fact far, far younger.

And once again I rose and went over to the space between the windows, where I had already learned to distinguish various relatives of her deceased husband (who was related by marriage to Bonaparte), and where in time I also studied daguerreotypes of faded boys holding ridiculous bouquets in their hands, and fine, durable pictures from the last century, pictures of beauties wearing feather boas, and enormous, pale photographs from recent times where Praskovia Dimitrievna's youngest granddaughter Kyra raised her incredible eyelashes over the huge eyes which filled half her face.

Sometimes when the weather was good Praskovia Dimitrievna would go out for a walk in the park; a faceless, ageless female shadow would appear and dress her. In a tall hat with a veil, in a black overcoat trimmed all the way around with thick braid, in felt boots, with a walking stick and an enormous drawstring bag in her hands, leaning on my arm, she would make her way down. Jean-Paul and Kyra, envying us from afar, made faces befitting the occasion: making their eyes bulge out and raising their arms to the heavens, they would silently summon me over to where they were, hinting that a one-of-a-kind event was taking place, and then they would run off somewhere and laugh at me there, and I would threaten them over my shoulder and throw murderous glances at the bushes where they were hiding. We walked down the broad dusty staircase, along the overgrown gravel, past the nearby pond that smelled of decay. Praskovia Dimitrievna's jaw began to work, as if her teeth bothered her; the walk agitated her.

"Right here, one lovely day, my brother came to see us unexpectedly," and she stopped and looked for a long time at the side gate, which had long since fallen down and rotted.

The brother whom she had left behind and from whom she had hidden her nuptials appeared at Roquenval several years after her wedding. The count paid off his debts and housed him in an annex. He lived there only briefly. One day something happened: apparently the count forbade Praskovia Dimitrievna to kiss her brother good night. There was a brief, ugly scene: the count was stronger and more agile, while the brother was older and less nimble, and moreover he did not expect to be tossed out of the château down the steps onto the flagstones of the courtyard....

"It's time to go home, let's get back now," Praskovia Dimitrievna tapped my arm.

"Let's go around this flower bed just one more time," and I drew her over to the high growths of nettles. "And then what happened, what happened next?"

"Let's go home, home, *assez*," and her head began to jerk, she stepped away from me, and I followed her and did not get from her the last lines of this strange story. The sun was above the trees and it was a fragrant, clear summer day, but to her it seemed that evening was already coming on, that it was already damp, and that the felt boots were no longer warming her.

Passing by the dining room, she invariably halted, pointed her stick toward the wireless radio (an enormous box, one of the first models) and panting for breath, said: "Un peu de Schumann?"

And if we couldn't tune in to any Schumann at that particular moment, she would maintain an angry silence, suspecting that someone had taken something away, otherwise how was it possible that today Schumann was not in that box when he had been there yesterday?

Then she would stop before the long, russet-colored grand piano, dulled by damp winters, and I saw that she was burrowing deeply, very deeply, into her thoughts for some particular memories.

"He played here," she said once, "and I made noise on purpose"—here she chuckled—"opening and closing the window, so that he didn't get any fancy ideas."

"Who played here, Praskovia Dimitrievna?"

She looked over the piano, to where, in an ugly frame of Venetian mosaic and ivory, between real portraits from the late seventeenth century, there hung a photograph of a man with a large nose.

"Monsieur Saint-Saëns," she said, and again, already silent, she started burrowing, burrowing, forgetting about me and about everything in the world, as if isolating herself in her own solitary life, distancing herself further and further, alienating herself more and more, becoming in spirit and in body almost a ghost of herself.

The high door closed, and I was alone. Birds were clamoring unbearably in the wild neglected garden, the sun shone oppressively, and I thought about how essentially it was still unclear to whom this all belonged, to her or to us; I thought, here are old stones, here are old trees, and here is an old person, and maybe we are the ones out of place here, not she. And I thought as well: will we really become like her, like her pier glass, like these lindens, will we—or won't we—reflect for someone the Twenties of the present century, I, Jean-Paul, and fifteen-year-old Kyra, whose moist voice makes my heart beat faster?

3.

The thought that I was in love with a fifteen-year-old girl filled me with happiness and fear. I myself was nineteen years old at the time, and my classmates were falling in love with our contemporaries—almost always happily and without stormy scenes—and marrying young. There was also one unmet expectation in my love for Kyra: Jean-Paul and I were not the only young people our age that summer at the château, there were also two girls: Kyra's older sister Madeleine and her friend, a little English girl with the odd name of Una, who for some reason was considered Jean-Paul's fiancée. Clearly I was expected to be Madeleine's, and she was the one with whom I was supposed to fall in love.

That first day, awed by the avenue at Roquenval, awed by my meeting with the Countess Praskovia Dimitrievna, awed by the château and the garden and the silence and the poverty and the magnificence of this old nest, I lay on my bed as evening was coming on. Jean-Paul was sitting on a chair in the dusk, trying to assure me that *la grandmère* had lost her faculties twenty years ago, when his grandfather was still alive, that her origin had been kept secret from the French relatives, and that the only one of her relatives who was known was a certain half-crazy and highly unpresentable brother, whom grandfather had tossed from the staircase like a sofa pillow. And so forth. This story was interrupted by the ringing of a gong: we were being summoned to dinner. And we found ourselves at the table: Jean-Paul, Madeleine, Una, Kyra, and me—all the occupants of the Château Roquenval. The Countess Praskovia Dimitrievna was brought a cup of bouillon on a tray through a little side door by the same manservant who had let me in.

Kyra sat across from me.

No, she had neither the eyes, nor the eyelashes which the photographer had given her in the photograph that hung over the table in Praskovia Dimitrievna's room. She had tender, mobile features the same hue as tea roses sometimes are inside, and her cheeks and forehead were probably always cool, like the petals of a tea rose. Her hair was rosy-colored, and when she smiled, her mouth opened and her tiny teeth appeared, also almost pink. Looking at me longer than was proper, she dropped her fork and while picking it up from the floor, she overturned her glass. When she crawled out from under the table, she was very red and there were tears in her eyes, and then I gasped and dropped a piece of beef in gravy on my lap to ease her embarrassment and put us on an equal footing, and so that Madeleine would not reprove her. Delight spread over her face, she sighed deeply and spread her fingers apart with relief—this was a habit she had, she would spread all ten fingers with ecstasy or joy.

And then she took me around the château, upstairs and downstairs, to the dead towers, to the attic, to the guardhouse, and although it was now impossible to distinguish anything in the dark, I pretended that I was actually examining things. As I was running after her on a staircase, it came into my head that these stairs, these walls, this very air would oblige me to wait with my unexpected feeling for at least three years, to wait until she grew up, as the people who had lived here once upon a time used to wait; and then thinking of that, I caught her in an embrace and forgetting everything in the world began to kiss her, touching the rosy hair over her forehead and over her ear with my lips. She pushed away against my chest with both hands and disappeared into the darkness and I did not know whether she had scampered off to the other end of the house or whether she was standing right behind the black ledge nearby. Walking over to the high window, I saw that the moon was sparkling on the scum of the pond, and an overgrown poplar was moving away from me down the slope there, where the rest of the world began. . . .

"Did you ever have a governess?" she asked me a week later, looking attentively and protractedly into my face, as I tried to catch her long, quivering eyelashes with my lips. We were sitting next to each other in the room that she shared with Madeleine and Una, a low, long room on the top floor, paneled in wood and with a small casement window which kept swinging open and shut that morning.

"No, I did not," I answered.

"You are probably surprised that I don't have a governess, aren't you?"

"A little."

"It's because we don't have any money," she said calmly.

I wanted to object.

"Thank God, we don't have money!" she repeated. "I think that soon, if I don't marry someone rich, I will go to work in an office."

"Why in an office, for heaven's sake?"

"It will be lovely. And when Grandmother dies . . . What do you think, will she die soon?"

"She could live on for another twenty years."

"Come on! Do people really live to be a hundred? . . . So, yes, when Grandmother dies," she stopped, "Roquenval," she stopped again, "will . . . be . . . sold."

"Oh, come on!"

"It will be sold!" she shrieked with ecstasy and spread her fingers. "First they'll sell the trees, that's how it will start. The lindens, the poplars, the pines—the famous ones that the worms never eat, that they use to build all the best buildings in France. Next, the house and part of the garden, as an almshouse or a sanatorium. Then the stone wall will fall apart by itself, and they'll divide up the land into little plots and sell them on the installment plan. And people will start to build awful little houses, all identical, and there will be some bushes left . . . and they'll put up a wire fence around it all. And they'll install gramophones, and hang out laundry to dry, and plant flowers everywhere. . . . "

There was a kind of sad joy in her voice. Suddenly she fell silent and pressed herself to me, putting her arms around my neck. I was sad and content, content as I had not yet ever been with her. Then suddenly we heard a strange rustling, a quiet sound which came now from the ceiling, now from the walls. Amazed, I listened closely.

"Those are the worms," she said. "They're gnawing at the wood. They're gnawing at Roquenval. They gnaw quietly away. Here, you see, they didn't use our pines to build, but just ordinary oak. Grandfather had these rooms built in a hurry, when Grandmother started having children, and they ran out of money."

She said all of this so simply, so calmly, in such adult tones, so thoughtfully, that I wondered, can it be? Is this the same little girl who just yesterday had taken some strong-smelling powder from an ornamental box belonging to Praskovia Dimitrievna and tried to convince us that it was snuff? (It had turned out to be dried lavender.)

"Come here," I said to her, although it was impossible to be any closer than we were. I wanted to dispel the impression of adultness which always so disturbed me in her. "Come here. Why are you saying all this? Why do you want your grandmother to die, and why do you want them to sell Roquenval?"

"It's kind of . . . unfashionable."

"And do you like only things that are fashionable?"

"I don't like anything."

"But it's partly yours, after all. If it's sold, there won't be anything."

"Big deal! So there won't be anything."

"Won't you be sorry?"

"Sorry?" she asked cruelly, in a ringing voice. "I'm never sorry about anything."

I took both of her hands, pressed them in mine, and I don't even know why I suddenly became unbearably sad, to the point of tears. I wanted—I myself did not know what I wanted at that moment—maybe not to live now, but to be a contemporary of Praskovia Dimitrievna, or not to have been born yet, but to be born sometime later, when all of this would be settled.

"Why were you given a Russian name?" I asked, in order to hide the terrible sorrow she had found in me.

"Just because. For Grandmother. She asked them to do it. She was very sick, and Mama agreed."

"Do you want to go to Russia?"

"With you?"

"With me."

"I do."

"And what about without me?"

"Isn't it all the same, where one lives?"

And again, in the hush, in the lull of our conversation, we heard the worms gnawing at the thick beams of the ceiling and rustling among the plinths, as if someone were rustling tissue paper in an old cardboard box, rustling and not finding what they needed, rustling and searching, unable to find, and time was passing, passing. . . .

We kissed in the garden, under the trees, and on the chipped stone staircase. Sometimes she infected me with her cruelty, her cheerfulness, and her shamelessness. She was a little girl, but unexpectedly I saw that the same ruinous traits that she had, impossible to overcome, existed in Jean-Paul and in Madeleine as well. The main one was indifference to the family collapse, a kind of secret hardness toward the rest of the world, and an evil joy coupled with a lack of desire to change or improve anything, even for themselves.

Waist-deep in grass, we went far into the garden where the overgrown hazelnut tree stood and where the nettles, as tall as human beings, gave off a wild sound, where thistles caught at Kyra's dark blue dress, where apple trees trailed along the ground, choked by creeping wild rose bushes. Somewhere in another corner of the garden, Jean-Paul and Una were apparently deciding their fate, and somewhere alone, silent and frowning, with a walking stick in her hand, and wearing an enormous soft straw hat which fell over her face, Madeleine walked, probably in search of us.

Yes, she was in search of us, and I do not know precisely which of our conversations she heard, what she understood of my confessions and Kyra's arch answers, or what she saw of our first long and tender embraces. And I don't know what precisely she wrote in that letter to her mother which determined the outcome of the summer for both of us.

One morning, a telegraph man's bicycle bell rang in the courtyard. Madeleine walked past me with an annoyed look. Kyra ran upstairs and froze on the last step in a ballet arabesque.

"Mama orders you to pack," said Madeleine, returning.

Kyra, without moving, continued to stand on one foot and I left the room.

Madeleine was sending her away from Roquenval. Perhaps she wanted to stay there alone with me. Kyra went away to her father's relatives—the family of a small provincial banker—near Grenoble. "You're not a little child," I cried, "you can say no!" But she shrugged her shoulders and looked past me. And in those minutes I saw that she could not say no, that she did not even know what she should do. I took her by the shoulders, I brought my face close to her sweet pink one, and her eyes filled slowly with tears, but did not look into mine. And she moved away from me, as a cloud moves away, and probably, if she could have at that moment, she would have willed herself to become transparent.

The next day she went to bid Praskovia Dimitrievna farewell, and then Monsieur Maurice—the unchanging Monsieur Maurice—dragged the high, green 1911 Dedion out of the stable, seated her, seated himself, and with an infernal din, in a cloud of gasoline smoke, with the car making shooting sounds and jumping up and down, drove out of the courtyard to the railway station; few live prejudices remained here—they were swept out of all the corners each year like dead flies—but to take the bus was still considered impermissible for the heirs of Roquenval.

"I don't understand why myself," Jean-Paul said to me at night, shrugging his shoulders.

And she was gone. She was already far away. Somewhere her train was chugging away.

4.

One early August morning I woke feeling a peculiar anxiety and was completely unable to fall back asleep. Everything was as always: sunlight came crookedly into the room, past Jean-Paul, who slept with his arms flung apart; the clock said ten to seven and there was a nighttime stillness in the house, but I couldn't sleep. I rose, dressed soundlessly, and went out, trying not to make noise. (Jean-Paul and I slept in one room, as did Madeleine and Una, not because there was any shortage of rooms in the château—in our corridor alone there were at least six—but they had been neglected, there was no one to clean them out, and there probably wouldn't have been enough kerosene lamps and washbasins for all of them.)

I went down and unlocked the oak door, patched with pieces of iron, that led into the park. Birds whistled in the bushes. The day was off to a clear and bright beginning. I walked by the ponds, covered with greasy, unmoving scum, which had been laid out once upon a time in imitation of Versailles; past thick tree stumps—the trees had grown right up to the house, fallen onto it, covered it, and a year ago they had had to be cut down. Further on there were overgrown hazelnut trees, lilacs, and tall weeds, through which we had beaten a path this summer, all covered with convolvulus and hops.

I walked for a fairly long time. All the while the park grew denser, damper, and darker. I was still a long way from the end, which was supposed to be marked off by a high stone wall, a country road which ran alongside it, and a distant field. I walked and walked, at times making my way with difficulty through the brambles, jumping over streams as I came to them; and off to both sides of me at times I heard something running or rustling away or flying out of the dense trees. I encountered some old stones heaped in a pile—as if someone had wanted to construct a little bridge out of them, and had then had second thoughts—then I glimpsed something more substantial to the left, and looking closer I saw something that was either a hut or some kind of booth with a door torn off by time and a window which had been knocked out by a human hand.

The floor was laid with the same tiles as the floors of the château, a sticky spiderweb adhered to the corners, a round, black fungus had grown on the door, and a bat hanging by one wing swung from the ceiling near a wide crack. I glanced at the door which held by a single hinge and ventured to give it a push. On the doorjamb it said in Russian letters, "Robert. Olga. 1897." The words had been carved with something sharp.

"Robert. Olga," I said loudly, and something ran away from me into the grass, and something moaned in the branches of an enormous elm tree. Once again I had come across a Russian clue in this French château, another of the clues—which included even Kyra—left by Grandmother Praskovia Dimitrievna. "Olga. Robert," I repeated again. And suddenly in the quiet of the garden there was a sound—the peaceful sound of an automobile going along the country road. Yes, here, twenty steps from where I was standing, Roquenval ended, and the old stone wall went around the property. And, here, right here, someone was driving by, the grocer perhaps, or the owner of that enormous new white villa of which we had heard wonders recounted: all the bedrooms had hot running water, and lunch was sent up from the kitchen to the dining room by dumbwaiter!

The return seemed shorter to me. The clock in the village bell tower chimed nine times. I went back to the house. The unchanging Monsieur Maurice met me in the pantry with that expression of absentmindedness and haughtiness I knew so well and had seen him wear so many times.

"Is Jean-Paul up?"

"No, *monsieur*."

"Who is in there?" (There was nothing audible from the dining room, but it was clear that there was someone there.)

"*Monsieur l'abbé, monsieur.*" And bowing to me, he passed by.

The village priest had not been in the house before, but I decided that this was of course the same one who had ridden past the château on a bicycle a number of times—young, jolly, with rough hands and a basket under his seat. He had probably come to Praskovia Dimitrievna to get some kind of donation. It would be interesting to get a closer look at him.... I opened the door, and what I saw disconcerted me for a moment.

Sitting at the end of the table was a man of about fifty, black-haired, with gleaming eyes and a red, slightly puffy face, with his elbows placed at a wide distance and a knife gripped in his fist, cutting a steak.

He was wearing a cassock, with the right sleeve tossed back, and he was eating fast and greedily, drinking red wine, wiping himself off with a napkin and once again hunching over the plate where blood oozed out of a thick piece of meat (it seemed to me that it squealed under his knife). Eyes flashing, he chewed loudly—and something crunched in the room—poured more wine into his glass, fastened his lips to the glass and slurped. This was highly unusual at nine in the morning when no one else had come down to the dining room, the sun had not yet risen to that low branch of the apple tree over there, and the hour hand had not yet reached the upper part of the clock face; and I myself, unwashed, hastily dressed, stood there smoothing my uncombed hair.

"*Bonjour, Monsieur,*" said the person in the cassock. "And who are you, may I be so bold as to ask?"

"I am a friend of Jean-Paul's," I answered.

"Visiting?"

"Yes."

"*Un lycéen?*"

"*Un bachelier.*"

He frowned, tossed down the knife and placed his heavy arm on the table.

"Say this: *ronronner.*"

"*Ronronner.*"

"You are not French," and with satisfaction he seized the mustard jar and helped himself to its contents. "You cannot say *ronronner.* Who are you?"

"I am Russian."

His face suddenly expressed alarm, but he suppressed something in his eyes, compressed his mouth, folded his hands, and bent his head down. "Well," he said resignedly, "my wife was Russian, too. And her lover was also not French. My friend, of whose death I was accused by the Paris rumor mill, was your countryman. And my mother, as you know, is also Russian."
He chuckled again and tossed his napkin on the table.

This was the Countess Praskovia Dimitrievna's youngest son, Jean-Paul's uncle, the very same Uncle Robert who had cut down the tapestry in his mother's room and sold it.

As he finished chewing the last piece of runny Camembert without even removing the rind, he rose from the table. He turned out to be smaller than I had expected. "Maurice!" he cried in stentorian tones, and Monsieur Maurice appeared right away. "Well then, let's not lose precious time, shall we? Have you apprised her of my presence?"

"The countess awaits you."

The abbot took a small, round mirror out of his pocket, studied it carefully and then passed a broad hand over his face and squeezed his nose and cheeks hard. "I'm coming," he said and the nails of his heavy shoes banged on the mosaic floor. "Farewell, young man. I wish you a speedy return to Russia."

Exactly one minute later the door opened—as it does only on stage and nowhere else.

"Has he cleared out?" asked Jean-Paul.

"Yes, but he'll probably be back. You know, his appetite is really something. . . ."

"No, he's a creature of habit: he always goes straight to catch the bus after he's seen Grandmother. So now you've seen him!"

And with a squeamish look Jean-Paul pushed away the empty wine bottle and the plate containing the remnants of the cheese. . . .

I had seen him for the first and last time. He had come to bid his mother farewell before setting off on some distant journey; he was leaving to be a missionary. He was the only person in the whole family who spoke Russian and who had been in Russia, but this I learned only in the evening when he was already gone. A full moon shone in the room, Jean-Paul was smoking, having unbuttoned his shirt collar and put his feet up higher than his head—he said that all famous travelers loved to do this. . . . I sat on the windowsill and kept looking down into the garden, as though waiting for a white female shadow to appear there; once upon a time, long ago, people had believed that this happened during the new moon. Madeleine, somehow revolting to me since Kyra's departure, and Una, whom we were both sick and tired of, were playing pinochle next door in their room, and they were arguing—we could hear their voices—and we were both secretly afraid that they would come to us with their stupid chatter and their idiocy and senselessness. Jean-Paul was telling a story, as he alone knew how, and it seemed long, yet at the same time one wanted it to be even longer, and it seemed detailed, yet one wanted it to be even more detailed.

"Yes, Uncle Robert was a degenerate and an adventurer. . . ."

"But you want to be an adventurer yourself!" I inserted.

He paused in thought. "Yes, Uncle Robert was a person without a nationality."

"But you yourself sometimes . . ." I wanted to insert, but restrained myself.

He was Grandmother Praskovia Dimitrievna's youngest son and had come into the world when financial ruin was already coming to a head and nothing could be done to set things right or save the situation. He graduated from L'École Normale with flying colors and went to Russia where he learned the language and converted to Orthodoxy. He traveled through Siberia and then disappeared, and for six years the thread of his existence was lost. It was said that he was breeding martens somewhere, then headed for Alaska where he sojourned with an Indian chieftain who conferred a high rank upon him. When he returned to Paris, people called him "the Russian count," despite his French name and his youth passed in Paris. Here in France, he married a daughter of the Russian nobility, whom he met while taking the waters. In their second year of married life, this woman took a shot at him, missed, and ran away with an officer. Half a year later, she gave birth to a child, whom he did not acknowledge. Half a year after that she came back to him—he did not accept her. After that his trace was lost again. Before the war he surfaced, now as a high church official, and in his cassock had an audience with high-ranking military officials (he had returned to Catholicism again). His incredible valor became a legend, and in 1919 a book was written about him, after which he entered the monkhood. By this time nothing remained of his zeal or his youthful restlessness and he denied any affiliation with Russia; however, it was said that during the years when the Catholic Church was persecuted in the U.S.S.R., he visited the Pope and presented a thorough report.

"When I encounter that person anywhere," said Jean-Paul in a cloud of smoke and moonlight, "you cannot imagine how he violates everything that is in me, absolutely everything; he is somehow revolting to me, and at the same time, I cannot brush him aside. I have to, how can I say it, take him into account."

Silence. I look down again—no, there is no one there, although there should be, although there has been on precisely such evenings as this.

"Please draw the curtain and just sit in the armchair," says Jean-Paul. "It's just a touch too poetic for me. That moon is just unbearably crass!"

"Onegin thought so, too," I mumble, sliding down off the windowsill.

"What are you mumbling about? Listen, let's talk about something sensible. Hey, recite that poem to me, you know the one. It reconciles me . . . to everything."

I look past him and recite in Russian:

"Do you recall, Maria / An old and stately home / And rows of ageless linden trees / Where we used to roam?"

And I immediately translate into French—and it seems to me that I don't do a bad job of it, either.

"A slumbering pond, a grove so still, / Fleecy clouds in azure sky. / Up a gently rising hill / Alone we wandered, you and I."

"Again," says Jean-Paul. And I recite it again.

"'nd roze of ain-shent lin-den treeze . . . " he repeats, paying close attention. "After that, I can't get it, there are too many of those zz, sh sounds. . . . I swear to you, those lines somehow reconcile me to Roquenval!"

5.

I was dissatisfied, I was nearly unhappy, and nothing was the way I thought it should be. Roquenval, with its Russian avenue, with Grandmother Praskovia Dimitrievna's past, with the pier glass which preserved some hazy Russian reflections in its damp depths, was headed off somewhere away from all of us. And it was impossible to follow it down its old, romantic, and ruinous path.

Summer was ending. It was the end of September, that time when raging windy nights are followed by clear, still-hot days; and you go out in the morning and look for clues of the storm heard beyond the shutters upon waking, when something flitted and wailed in the chimney, scraped and banged in the garden and swept against the window in the wind and the rain. But all is calm, all is clear; someone raised a clamor and has now gone into hiding. The sky is blue and high; the tall trees gleam and are silent and the gravel in the courtyard is moist. The rusty greenish vase by the entrance, literally full to the brim, lets fall the last drop, and the headless stone lion has already dried in the sun. Not wishing to be deceived, I descend to the densest part of the garden with a businesslike air, for I need proof of the first inroads of fall, made last night; I am going to look for confirmation. And here I receive it when a torrent of water falls on me from a branch, my foot gets swamped in something rotten, and, as dreadful evidence, a heavy branch from the apple tree is lying on the walk on top of the red worms that have emerged from their holes; and with its fall the branch has changed the dear familiar profile of the tree I know so well.

And so, through Roquenval, which was hiding itself away, past the people —not those, no, not those who it seemed to me were supposed to live here!—past the living, alien to this house, past myself and all of us, I went in search of those clues which in the first weeks of my life here had held out so much promise to me. Yes, the avenue of lindens stood before the entrance, resurrecting, as before—or no, giving birth in my memory to my past which had disappeared; in Praskovia Dimitrievna's bedroom next to the crucifix an icon hung in its old Suzdal chasuble; a woman's name was scratched in Russian letters on the gazebo wall. Now I tried to imagine "Uncle Robert," the Russian count, now that rosy girl with the artificial Russian name, now other unknown people, living and dead, about whom I could only hazard guesses. But those who were around me, those people who had lived here or came here to visit, were already distant from the powerful allure that lived on in names and objects.

Of course guests couldn't come here, as I might have wished, on troikas with sleigh bells, with a fat coachman wearing a feather in his hat. A chauffeur in driving gloves helped Jean-Paul's father out of a long automobile, then his wife, and then Una's father—a gaunt Scotsman in checked stockings, as dry and clean as cardboard. They had come for the young ladies—for Una and Madeleine, but standing at the window, I gathered that prior to the general departure a certain event would be celebrated, about which Jean-Paul kept silent, but of which he was well aware.

I looked at the young countess. I recalled Jean-Paul's words: "My father's fourth marriage was to a woman of loose conduct," and because of my agitation I could see nothing in front of me. She apparently had gone to show the park to the Scotsman while her husband, in a hunting outfit with game bag and dog, shot at rabbits in the field. Then tea was brought in.

"So your engagement is being announced today?" I asked, turning to Jean-Paul.

"Yes, yes, you see how it is . . . but then again . . . "

"But did you propose?"

"Oh, everything was quite clear without a proposal! No, I did not propose."

"And when is the wedding?"

"Oh, God! There isn't going to be any of that."

The last several days he had not been himself at all, and it was impossible to talk to him because he would immediately start shouting. Just then Una walked in and laid her head on Jean-Paul's shoulder without a word.

No, these guests were completely inappropriate to this old, proud, quiet house. And Praskovia Dimitrievna did not come out to greet them, and they—except, I think, for the count—did not go in to see her. Enormous vases from the Imperial Porcelain Factory stood at both ends of the table, and thick red dahlias drooped from them onto the tablecloth. The roast beef was dried out, canned peas rolled around the plate, the village bread left flour on one's hands. The champagne, brought from Paris, shot its cork dolefully and released its light momentary puff of smoke.

I sat next to my friend's stepmother, his father's fourth wife, and each time I looked at her, I had trouble looking away. It wasn't that she was especially attractive or beautiful; women would probably have found in her appearance more flaws than merits.

She was rather fat, but her face, to the contrary, had remained slim and long, as happens with women who put on weight suddenly. Her hands were very small and revealed total idleness; her hair she wore pulled smoothly back. But I find it difficult to describe her. I remember that she was wearing a bright blue dress of that merciless shade which leaves not a shadow of warmth in the face.

The Scotsman was nodding and listening to the count's hunting tales; Madeleine and the countess were leaning across me and discussing people I didn't know; Una, her eyes wandering, leaned toward Jean-Paul, chewed, opening her mouth wide and raising her eyes to Jean-Paul's face from time to time, and laid her hand on his shoulder. He did not look at her hand. Toward the end of lunch, when Monsieur Maurice brought coffee in filigreed cups (under our cups Madeleine and I received crude saucers made of faience), the Scotsman rose, let his monocle drop from his eye, and gave a speech, which started out, "My dear children," but which contained no other hints. He looked at his daughter and at Jean-Paul, and we turned involuntarily toward them. Now, right before me, and very close, I saw this woman's forearm, neck, blue silk, her knot of dark-blue hair, and the corner of her dark eye, narrowed by wine. I felt the smell emanating from her and was close enough to count the diamonds in the buckle on her shoulder, and it seemed to me that I could hear her shoulders and breast living and breathing under her dress. "She will arrange a rendezvous with me," the thought flashed through my mind, shameful in its unaccountable stupidity, "that is how this dreary evening will be resolved." And I had an urge to go downstairs into the garden, into the dark where we would be unable to see each other.

We all went out together; it turned out to be cooler than we thought and the sky was black and on the whole the night had no desire to seem any better than it in fact was. It did not want to pretend to be the continuation of the Scotsman's speech, the count's exclamations, or Madeleine's smiles. Everything on the earth and in the air was quiet, crepuscular. We went toward the ponds—Una, Jean-Paul, Madeleine, and I—and behind us the countess hurried to catch up. Leaving the men behind and not listening to us, she gave us news of Lord knows what: of Paris, of seamstresses, of someone's funeral, about whether one could bequeath what one wants to whom one wants, about how much it cost to travel around the world.... Fog rolled in, and the windows of Praskovia Dimitrievna's bedroom grew redder and redder, where the light burned, where she was not yet sleeping, and the old garden became more and more treacherous and more and more autumnal. We passed under the elms, the countess now walking with us; I was not listening to her, I was thinking what would happen now if we remained alone in the garden together, in the château, in the world, under these trees, where rain had already quietly begun to fall. What would happen if I pulled that dreadful rain slicker off her....

But we returned to the house and the farewells began. Madeleine kept shoving her heavy suitcase somewhere, catching the floors with her thick woolen coat which kept sliding off her transparent dress; Una placed her cheek on Jean-Paul's lapel, and Jean-Paul said nothing. "*Prenez soin à la grand-mère*," the count shouted, and two bright yellow lights sliced through the air and came up against the grass.

"My little, sweet, furry, baby tiger," said Una, "my little chicken, my tender little sparrow won't leave his tiny one for too long, will he?"

"No," answered Jean-Paul.

"I had an umbrella," cried the countess.

"That was a most pleasant picnic indeed," the Scotsman's voice was heard from the darkness, and then the ignition caught.

"It seems to be raining," I announced in a hoarse voice, when the automobile had plunged through the gates and everything had fallen silent, but Jean-Paul did not reply. (The count himself had grabbed the umbrella and handed it to her, and everything was over, and all that remained was a rushing sound inside my head from a vanished, futile joy.)

I cleared my throat and went into the house.

"So when are we off to Paris?" I asked carelessly. Jean-Paul was groping for the lock on the door.

"Well, when do you need to go?"

"If you want to know the truth, I really have no place to go until the fifteenth: Mama is moving to a new apartment."

"Well, then stay here until the fifteenth, if you're not sick of it."

Water was already streaming down the black gallery windows, and the garden was bending noisily back and forth, waving and threatening to overtake the house: this was autumn coming on, impossible to catch red-handed during the day.

I listened to it as I undressed in the darkness in our room. Something cried out loudly in the garden, and although Madeleine had assured me more than once that this was the sound of frogs, I imagined in the trees an enormous, half-blind bird, which somehow resembled Praskovia Dimitrievna. Finally I lay down and, surprised that Jean-Paul did not come, I fell asleep. I was awakened by a rustling sound: he was getting ready for bed in his corner; it was quiet outside the window.

"What time is it?" I asked.

He did not answer.

"Will you think it hopelessly piggish if I go before you do, and leave you here alone with grandmother and Maurice?"

"Not in the least," I answered quickly. (Did he really miss Una already?)

"I'm not going to Paris," he continued. "Please don't say anything to me about the Slavic soul awakening in me or about my complicated heritage and Uncle Robert. Oh, there's a lot you could say, but don't say anything. You remember how we walked around at night on the embankments and sat by the fires?"

Now I was silent.

"Listen, are you sleeping? I want to be good and kind to you at parting. If you like her, call her up on the phone. Papa isn't at home in the mornings. She'll probably agree to have breakfast with you. . . . "

I let out a fake snore, too loud, and he fell silent, and although I wanted very much to change position—my leg ached and my elbow was numb—I continued to lie still until I really did fall asleep. . . .

"Praskovia Dimitrievna!" I cried, running in to Grandmother in the morning. She had not yet emerged from behind her high, painted screens. (Sometime back in the Eighties, some cousin of hers had drawn on them an ostrich with its tail fanned out, some lilies, two rabbits, and a swampy expanse with snowy mountains on the horizon.) "Praskovia Dimitrievna, did he say good-bye to you? When did he disappear?"

"I em eel," said a calm voice and I realized that she was lying on her high bed, under the faded satin canopy. "I em very eel today, Boris," she said, pronouncing my name as always with a French accent. "You mustn't disturb me so. He said good-bye, and he said that he will never marry. He vants to roam. . . ."

This dear familiar room, with all its tattered, antique or simply ancient objects, seemed to know something, to know more, at any rate, than I did. I looked at its resplendent, cumbersome furnishings, the lackluster Poussin landscape in the space between the windows, at the bronze candelabra, and at the tiled fireplace which had been described in a travel guide to the Île-de-France. . . . And suddenly, I realized that here again, for a second time, something unlawful and irrevocable had occurred: the second of four magnificent, three-hundred-year-old tapestries had been taken down and removed from here today, but not cut with a knife as Uncle Robert had done once upon a time, rather it had been taken down, painstakingly and with care; and under it, as under the first one, an unplastered wall was revealed, with dark streaks and a network of fungus near the high, molded ceiling.

"End now I em eel," said Grandmother's voice, "I hev a dreadful cold and I em very jittery. Leave me, Boris. I don't vant anyone to come in here, no one may come here at all. End," she added, agitatedly, almost angrily, "now is forbidden to look in zis room!"

6.

The bell at the gates squeals with a thin, penetrating sound; someone jerks on it a third, a fourth time; someone is ringing, ringing, and the sound peals out into a long, sharp trill. It is nighttime, a black September night in the courtyard, a night fallen almost without twilight in cold and gloom among the trees, and the first leaves have been torn off the trees by the storm. I am alone in the house, and my heart is beating hollowly and fast because I have realized that Monsieur Maurice and his wife in their shallow underground bedroom with windows looking out on the garden do not hear that someone is ringing at the gates and demanding to be let in at this late hour. I leap out of bed, grab my coat off the hanger and, putting my felt shoes on over bare feet and striking matches as I go, holding in my hand the candlestick with its melted candle, I run down the dark corridor, down the stairs, past the first living room, the second (where it is cold and the slipcovers are fading), next into the gallery where I think for a moment that my light is already visible to the person standing at the gates. But the bell trembles again, unclearly, anxiously, and I hurl myself down past the guardhouse and into the courtyard; a cold wind grabs me by the hair, and I cut diagonally across the courtyard; black sky, black trees rustle on the other side of the wall; up close, the black gates I'm heading toward turn out to be lighter than this entire night.

"Who's there?" I cry.

The bell has stopped its harsh knelling.

"Open up," says a female voice in French. "Are you all deaf in there, or what?"

I turn the enormous key with both hands and heave open the door. Out of the darkness a woman I don't know comes toward me—I see that she is a woman, but what she looks like, who she is, I do not have time to see—she walks around me and goes ahead of me to the château, as if she is familiar with every stone of this old courtyard. I follow her, and thus in silence we come to the entrance; on the stone stairs, on the wide banister, I have left the candle. A fearful shadow prepares me for what I am about to see; before me is an unfamiliar face with large, angry eyes; she is a woman of about thirty, exhausted and drained, with a large belly and with those inexpressibly pale cheeks only pregnant women have.

She stood apprehensively at the foot of the stairs knitting her brows, looking at the candle and not glancing in my direction. Her shoes were muddy, her coat wrinkled as if it had recently got wet and dried while still on her shoulders. Under her hat, straight hair was visible; its color reminded me of something; it was red with a rosy glow.

"Take me to Grandmother," she said, continuing to mistake me for the butler and treading heavily on the first step of the staircase.

"I am sorry, but the countess was taken away yesterday."

She caught the wall with her left hand and finally fixed me with a fierce look.

"If you don't take me to Grandmother, I will go myself. You have orders not to let anyone up?"

I explained to her that Praskovia Dimitrievna had been taken to Paris yesterday, that I had summoned the count, and that I had telephoned him today: it turned out that she had pneumonia and that she would most likely not live through it.

Suddenly tears flowed down the woman's pale face.

"Who are you?" she asked quietly.

"I am a guest who has overstayed his welcome. I am leaving tomorrow. I will wake Monsieur Maurice now."

But she flew toward me and seized my sleeve.

"No! Don't go. Don't get Maurice. He'll tell everyone that I was here and what I have become."

She caught her breath.

"I'll sit here until the first light. Give me a chair. When does the first bus depart?"

She said something else, but so quietly that I did not catch it. And that murmuring again reminded me of something, and such pity toward her suddenly awakened in me—pity, mixed with curiosity—that I said:

"Please come up to the second floor where we have been staying. There's no one in the house. You are probably hungry. I'll bring the leftovers from dinner that are in the kitchen; I apologize, things are modest here. Then I'll make up a bed for you."

Of all that I had said, she understood only that there was no one in the château.

She now sat in the light of the kerosene lamp at our table upstairs. At her request I had firmly closed the outer shutters. She was eating cheese and drinking red wine—all I had been able to find in the cold kitchen.

"So Grandmother is on her deathbed?" she suddenly asked me. "Just a week ago she wrote to me and she was healthy."

"Did she summon you here?"

"Yes, she wrote to me that she had been left alone, and that I could come to her whenever I wanted—I haven't seen her in over a year, since I quarreled with all of them."

She looked around anxiously.

"I'm telling you all this, but I do not trust you, although you are so gracious and kind. Did I wake you? That's because I came on foot from Le Roi."

I did not sit down and I tried to keep at a certain distance from her, step softly, and speak little.

"Whose room is this?"

"Your cousin's and mine."

"And next to it?"

"Madeleine stayed in the next room."

Again she began to cry soundlessly, sitting still, covering her face with neither her hands nor a handkerchief.

"And Kyra was here?"

"And Kyra."

And suddenly I understand once and for all, who she was: that rosy hair, that tender face, so early faded, that weak voice gave her away to me finally. This was Kyra's older sister, who was never mentioned in the château.

She sat there and cried. And I stood—still in my coat and shoes—by the door, and was unable not to look at her.

"What will happen now?" she asked.

"Now you will lie down and go to sleep. And I will take this bed right here and quietly, very quietly, please don't get upset, I will take it out into the corridor and I'll lie down, too."

And I made up Jean-Paul's bed for her and moved mine out into the hall.

For a long time she did not turn off the light, and from the darkness I watched the strip of light under the door and the star shining at me through the keyhole. Right in front of me at the end of the corridor on the landing there was a window with matte glass, and gradually a cloudy silverish hoarfrost began to filter through, this was deep into the night, it was practically morning, and at some point the moon rose and around an hour later it fell. And then something strange happened to me; I lost my sense of time. At first it seemed to me that it was daybreak, then I imagined that this was not a corridor at all, but a narrow hospital ward where I was lying, only not now, but rather God knows how many years ago. Something northerly filtered through the window. Ghosts came out of the white walls. Surgical ward, morgue, purgatory—all seemed somehow right nearby. It was most likely a dream, because during waking hours I could never have felt so cut off from the present.

I slept in my coat, and when the door opened slightly in the morning, I leapt up right away. She was already dressed.

"I will see you out, just let me dress," I said to her, and she came out. "Wait for me downstairs."

As soon as I had dressed, I looked for her around the house; she was standing in the middle of one of the rooms and again there was such sorrow in her face that once more I felt something grip my heart.

"Twenty years ago," she said, without addressing herself to me, but nonetheless probably glad that there was a person who was listening to her, "twenty years ago, when I was very small and Grandfather was still alive, there were enormous armchairs standing here that one could curl up and sleep in. And how everyone loved each other then!"

I listened without speaking.

"I'm the oldest granddaughter, you know. All of them came later. And as in any family, everyone wanted me to have nothing but happiness, they wanted everything to turn out well for me, and, most important, they wanted everything to be proper; and as it's turned out, things haven't been happy, they haven't turned out well, and they haven't been proper at all, and only Grandmother, she is the only one . . . She has no money herself, but she sent me some. And she even wanted to see me."

She walked over to the window.

"Oh my God," she looked at the withered garden in the blue-gray morning. "What has become of Roquenval! How wild everything is, how dreary! And outsiders"—now she was not talking for my benefit—"strangers receive me here. . . ."

I waited.

She turned round, remembered something, and then quickly, as quickly as she could, she walked past me, went down the stairs, no longer afraid to be seen, and crossed the courtyard. I opened the gates for her.

"Farewell," she said. "Thank you."

But I accompanied her down the narrow street to the village square, and helped her get into the high, dark-blue, almost-full bus (it was market day in Le Roi, and old women in black aprons and straw hats were chattering among themselves). For a second all went silent, and then a man rose and gave her his seat. She sat down without looking at anyone.

When the bus pulled away, rocking from side to side, I felt that I too must leave here this very day and not a single day later.

In the square just opposite the church, women were wailing and lamenting as they carried their household goods out of a two-story village house. A large yellow poster announced in legalistic language that the property of Monsieur Dupont would be auctioned off this morning due to nonpayment of debt. Plates, pillows, a coffee grinder, an old stove, an armchair without legs, and a sideboard already stood in the yard in a heap, and people were beginning to gather. At first they did so timidly, embarrassed at the proceedings, then more and more boldly, and then people came up fearlessly to look, pawing through property not their own; they sat in the armchair, opened and closed the squeaky doors of the sideboard, and turned the handle on the coffee grinder. Two small boys stood there tearlessly bidding farewell to the things among which they had lived up to now.

I returned to the château.

No, nothing had been carried out of here yet, and Roquenval's proud and famous furnishings had not yet been tossed out to be laughed at by passers-by. Everything was still whole and in place, although Praskovia Dimitrievna was dying in Paris, although the worms were gnawing at the beams of our old ceilings. And this house had not yet fallen like the House of Usher, and there was no fairy tale behind these high walls overgrown with moss. It was just that autumn was coming on, and I was returning to Paris; summer was staggering to a close and the ghostly spirit, dear now to me alone, of the old and alien dust of this place, was flying away. Impressions were evaporating, certain images were assuming a false aspect. That which lay ahead acquired a more distinct outline: the university, Mama, a new apartment, perhaps a rendezvous with Jean-Paul's stepmother, perhaps a postcard from him, from Alexandria, Lima, or . . . Moscow. Maybe—at her grandmother's funeral—a forbidden encounter with Kyra. All of this seemed so pleasant and ordinary: I knew that it would be, that it was possible. I packed up my books, locked my suitcase and went to say good-bye to Monsieur Maurice, and everything that I was leaving behind at that moment fell silent behind me so sorrowfully and so hopelessly: our rooms fell silent, the slipcovered living rooms fell silent, the staircase fell silent; in the drawn-out whi-s-s-per of autumn, the park fell silent; the gates banged and fell silent for the last time, and the key creaked and above me my avenue went still, resembling on that morning a monument to something which had not existed for a long time, not here, not in my country, nowhere on earth.

—1936

Translated from the Russian by Laura E. Wolfson

CONTRIBUTORS

ADONIS was born in the Alawite mountains of northern Syria in 1929. From 1956 to 1986, he lived in Beirut, where he founded, in 1968, the avant-garde literary magazine, *Mawaqif* (*Situations*). One of the greatest poets in modern Arabic literature, known for his formal innovation and his revolutionary poetic language, imagery, and approach, Adonis is the author of ten books of poetry, as well as criticism and translations. A selection of his poetry, *Orbits of Desire* (Jonathan Cape), was published in the United Kingdom in 1992. His *Introduction to Arab Poetics* (Dar al-Saqi) was published there in 1990. Other selections of his poetry, *The Blood of Adonis* and *Transformation of the Lover*, both translated by Samuel Hazo, have also appeared in English.

HILTON ALS is an advisory editor to *Grand Street*. His first book, *The Women*, was recently published by Farrar, Straus & Giroux.

ERIN BELIEU is the author of *Infanta* (Copper Canyon Press), which was selected as one of the best books of poetry in 1995 by the National Book Critics Circle and *Washington Post Book World*. She is an editor at AGNI magazine and will begin teaching in the Creative Writing Program at Washington University in the spring of 1997.

NINA BERBEROVA was born in St. Petersburg, Russia, in 1901. She attended the Institute of Art History in Moscow before leaving the country in 1922. She then lived in Germany, Czechoslovakia, and Italy, settling finally in Paris in 1925, where she attended the Sorbonne. After moving to the United States in 1951, she worked as a language instructor at the Berlitz school, as a radio announcer for the "Voice of America," as an office-machine operator, and finally as an instructor at Yale University and later at Princeton University. She is the author of *The Tattered*

Cloak and Other Novels, The Accompanist, Three Novels, her autobiography The Italics Are Mine, and a biography of Pyotr Tchaikovsky, among others. In 1989, she was named a Chevalier de l'Ordre des Arts et des Lettres by the French government. She died in Philadelphia in 1993.

LUIS BUÑUEL was born in Calanda, Spain in 1900. From 1920 to 1923, he studied entomology at the University of Madrid, where he became close friends with Salvador Dalí. Together, they established Spain's first film club, and, in Paris in 1925, Buñuel collaborated with Dalí to write and direct his first film, the silent, twenty-five-minute An Andalusian Dog, a series of unconnected images intended to achieve a "poetic" effect similar to that achieved on canvas by the Surrealists. After a brief, fruitless stint in Hollywood, Buñuel returned to Spain in 1932. In 1940, he began work at the Museum of Modern Art in New York, reediting footage from Leni Riefenstahl's pro-Nazi films to be used as American propaganda. He resigned from this position, however, after Dalí publicly revealed that Buñuel was both anti-Catholic and a member of the French Communist Party. Buñuel then returned to Hollywood, where he worked for Warner Bros., and, in 1947, he moved to Mexico. Several movies followed, including Los olvidados, The Devil and the Flesh, The Daughter of Deceit, El, Illusion Travels by Streetcar, Nazarín, and The Exterminating Angel. In 1966, Buñuel returned to France, where he directed Belle de Jour, The Discreet Charm of the Bourgeoisie, and That Obscure Object of Desire, among others. He died in Mexico City in 1983. Why I Don't Wear a Watch was originally published in Spanish in Alfar in May 1923, and will appear in Christ With a Switchblade: Selected Writings of Luis Buñuel, to be published by the University of California Press in the fall of 1997.

WILLIAM S. BURROUGHS is the author of Naked Lunch, Queer, Junky, The Western Land, The Cat Inside, My Education: A Book of Dreams, and Ghost of Chance. He is a member of the American Academy and Institute of Art and Letters. He lives in Lawrence, Kansas.

DENNIS COOPER is the author of the novels Try, Frisk, and Closer, as well as The Dream Police: Selected Poems 1969–93 (all Grove Press). His most recent book is Horror Hospital Unplugged (Juno Books), a graphic novel created with artist Keith Mayerson. His fourth novel, Guide, will be published by Grove Press in the spring of 1997. He is a contributing editor to Spin magazine. An Interview with Charles Ray is an excerpt from an imaginary interview with Charles Ray written by Dennis Cooper for Charles Ray, a catalogue accompanying Ray's exhibition at the Newport Harbor Art Museum, Newport Beach, in 1990.

CPLY (WILLIAM N. COPLEY) was born in New York in 1919. Orphaned as an infant, he was adopted by the newspaper tycoon, Ira C. Copley. He attended Yale University and worked briefly as a reporter for The San Diego Tribune. In 1947, he opened the Copley Galleries in Los Angeles, and showed the work of Man Ray, Joseph Cornell, Max Ernst, and René Magritte, among others. The gallery closed the following year, but Copley purchased a number of the works himself: the first acquisitions in what would become a legendary collection of surrealist art. Nineteen forty-seven was also the year that Copley began to make his own artwork, and in 1951 he traveled to Paris with Man Ray, who had been living in Southern California since the war. Copley stayed in Paris for the next thirteen years, meeting and becoming friends with the Surrealists and painting under the name of CPLY. In 1965, he returned to the United States and settled in New York. In 1980, an exhibition of his work was organized by the Kunsthalle Bern, and traveled to the Centre Georges Pompidou, Paris, and the Stedelijk van Abbemuseum, Eindhoven. In 1995, a retrospective of his paintings was presented by the Kestner-Gesellschaft, Hanover. Copley died in 1996 in Florida, where he had been living since 1992. His estate is represented by the Nolan/Eckman Gallery, New York.

DENYS JOHNSON-DAVIES has published translations of over twenty volumes of short stories, novels, and poetry from modern Arabic literature, most recently Naguib Mahfouz's *Arabian Nights and Days*. His translation of Mahfouz's *Echoes of an Autobiography* will be published by Doubleday in January 1997.

LYNN DAVIS studied at the San Francisco Art Institute and worked as a freelance photo-journalist before moving to New York in 1974. In 1979, she had her first major exhibition with Robert Mapplethorpe at the International Center for Photography. A 1989 solo exhibition entitled *Ice*, which featured photographs from Davis's two trips to Greenland in 1986 and 1988, established her as a major contemporary photographer. In 1989, Davis traveled to Egypt where she photographed the great pyramids and statues favored by nineteenth-century travel photographers. She has since photographed landscapes and ruins in Cambodia, Thailand, Syria, Jordan, Turkey, Yemen, Lebanon, and the American West. She is represented in New York by the Houk Friedman Gallery.

MIKE DAVIS is finishing *Ecology is Here*, a new book on Los Angeles's recent trial by riot, flood, and earthquake. He is a contributing editor to *Grand Street*.

CLAYTON ESHLEMAN's most recent collection of poetry is *Nora's Roar* (Rodent Press). His translation of some of Artaud's late works, *Watchfiends & Rack Screams*, was recently published by Exact Change Press. Eshleman is a Professor in the English Department at Eastern Michigan University, where he edits *Sulfur* magazine.

ANN GOLDSTEIN's translation of Aldo Buzzi's *Journey to the Land of the Flies* was published in 1996.

BRION GYSIN was born in England in 1916. His name is listed alongside Dalí, Duchamp, Ernst, Miró, Picasso, and others in the catalogue of a 1935 show of surrealist drawings at Aux Quatre Chemins in Paris, but Paul Éluard took his work down at the orders of André Breton, who apparently suspected Gysin of "deviationism." In 1940, after holding a one-man show at the same gallery, Gysin moved to New York where he worked in the New Jersey shipyards and as a costume designer on Broadway. He studied Japanese in the Army during the Second World War and his subsequent art was influenced by Eastern and Arabic calligraphy. In 1950, Paul Bowles convinced Gysin to visit Tangier, where he stayed for twenty-three years. In a 1962 show at the Musée des Arts Decoratifs, he exhibited the

DREAMACHINE, which he had invented with Cambridge mathematician Ian Sommerville, and which attempted to reproduce with a paint roller the patterns and dream elements of interior visions produced in the alpha band of brain activity. His novel, *The Process*, was published by Doubleday in 1969, and *The Third Mind*, a joint work with his close friend and collaborator since 1958, William S. Burroughs, was published by Viking in 1979. Gysin was named a Chevalier de l'Ordre des Arts et des Lettres by the French Ministry of Culture in 1985. He died in 1986. His paintings are currently in the collections of the Museum of Modern Art, New York, the Institute of Fine Arts, Boston, the Centre Georges Pompidou, Paris, and the Musée d'Art Moderne de la Ville de Paris. The interview with William S. Burroughs that appears in this issue of *Grand Street* was first published in a different form in the catalogue for Gysin's exhibition at the October Gallery, London in 1981.

MARK HARMAN is an Irish-born critic and translator who lives in Lancaster, Pennsylvania. He has taught German and Irish literature at Dartmouth College, Oberlin College, and the University of Pennsylvania, written widely on modern authors, and translated works by Hermann Hesse and Robert Walser. He is a frequent contributor to the book pages of newspapers in the United States and in Ireland. His translation of Franz Kafka's novel, *The Castle*, based on the new critical edition, is forthcoming from Schocken Books.

ALLEN HIBBARD has lived and taught in Cairo and Damascus. He is the author of *Paul Bowles: A Study of the Short Fiction*, and has published many stories, reviews, and translations in journals such as *Cimarron Review*, *Passport*, *Digest of Middle East Studies*, *Edebiyat*, *The Partisan Review*, and *Sulfur*. He currently teaches at Middle Tennessee State University and is collecting material for a biography of Alfred Chester. He would like to thank Mustafa Ouaffi for assisting with the final editing of Adonis's poem, *The Time*.

OSAMA ISBER is a Syrian writer who has been an editor of the innovative literary journal *Alef*. He has published collections of his own stories and poems as well as Arabic translations of Eduard Galeano's *Memory of Fire*, Michael Ondaatje's *The English Patient*, and Allen Hibbard's *Crossing to Abbassiya and Other Stories*.

ILYA KABAKOV was born in Russia in 1933. An artist with an "official" career as an illustrator of children's books, Kabakov was affiliated with Moscow's underground avant-garde, and emerged during the post-Stalinist era as one of the U.S.S.R.'s most sophisticated dissident artists. His complex installations of drawings, paintings, structures, and detritus present scenes from typical Soviet environments, emphasizing the contradictions and absurdities inherent in life in an oppressive society. Kabakov's work was first shown in the West in 1985. Since then, his installations have been exhibited at the Museum of Modern Art, New York, the Jewish Museum, New York, Ronald Feldman Fine Arts, New York, Donald Judd's Chinati Foundation, Marfa, Texas, the Stedelijk Museum, Amsterdam, the Ludwig Museum, Cologne, the Venice Biennale, and Documenta IX, Kassel. Kabakov is represented in New York by Barbara Gladstone Gallery. He lives in New York City.

JOHN KING was born in 1960 and lives in London. His second novel, *Headhunters*, will be published by Jonathan Cape in the United Kingdom in May 1997, and he is currently working on his third novel, *England Away*. *The Football Factory* is excerpted from his novel of the same name (Jonathan Cape, 1996).

ANGELA KRAUSS was born in Chemnitz, Germany, in 1950. She received the Ingeborg-Bachmann Prize in 1988, the Lessing-Förder Prize in 1995, and the Berliner Literature Prize in 1996. *Currents* appeared in German, in a longer form, in *Kleine Landschaft*, a collection of short stories published by Suhrkamp Verlag in 1989.

JOSEPH LEASE's new book of poems, *Human Rights*, is forthcoming from Zoland Books. Poems from *Human Rights* have been published in *Grand Street*, *Colorado Review*, *Talisman*, *Pequod*, *AGNI*, *Boston Review*, and *Denver Quarterly*. A winner of the Academy of American Poets Prize, Lease is Poetry Editor of *The Boston Book Review*. His first book of poems, *The Room* (Alef), was published in 1994. He also coedited *On the Verge* (AGNI Press), an anthology of emerging poets.

ADAM LEFEVRE's book of poetry, *Everything All At Once*, was published by the Wesleyan Press. His play, *Waterbabies*, won the 1995 Heideman Award. He makes his living as an actor on stage, screen, and television.

GYÖRGY LIGETI was born in Transylvania, Romania, in 1923. He studied composition at the Conservatory in Cluj from 1941 to 1943, and, from 1945 to 1949, at the Franz Liszt Music Academy in Budapest, where he also taught until 1956. He settled in Vienna in 1959. In the 1960s, Ligeti was a yearly lecturer in Darmstadt and a guest professor at the Music Academy in Stockholm. With his early orchestral works, *Apparitions* (1958–59) and *Atmosphères* (1961), he developed a new musical style that was marked by a dense polyphony and static formal development. His important works of the 1960s are *Requiem* (1963–65), *Lux aeterna* (1966), *Continuum* (1968), *String Quartet No. 2* (1968), and *Chamber Concerto* (1968–70). In the 1970s, his polyphonic writing became more transparent and melodic, as can be heard in *Melodien* (1971) and in his opera *Le Grand Macabre* (1974–77). His works in the '80s and '90s, such as *Trio for Violin, Horn and Piano* (1982), *Piano Concerto* (1985–88), *Piano Etudes* (1985–95), *Violin Concerto* (1990–92), *Nonsense Madrigals* (1988–93) and *Sonata for Viola Solo* (1991–94), have been based on a more complex polyrhythmic composition technique. He currently lives in Hamburg and Vienna. *Le Grand Macabre*, which premiered at the Royal Opera, Stockholm, in 1978, is currently undergoing revisions and will be staged, with Peter Sellars directing and Esa-Pekka Saloner conducting, at the Salzburg Festival in the summer of 1997.

TIMOTHY LIU's books of poems are *Vox Angelica* (Alice James Books) and *Burnt Offerings* (Copper Canyon Press). A new book, *Say Goodnight*, is forthcoming. He will be the Holloway Lecturer at the University of California at Berkeley in the spring of 1997.

NAGUIB MAHFOUZ was born in Cairo, Egypt, in 1911. From 1930 to 1934, he studied philosophy at Fuad I University (now Cairo University). He then worked in a variety of government departments as a civil servant until his retirement in 1971. His first novel, *The Game of Fates*, was published in 1939, and was followed by thirty-four more novels and fourteen collections of short stories. He received the Egyptian State Prize twice, as well as numerous other awards, including the Nobel Prize for Literature in 1988. In 1992, he was elected an honorary member of the American Academy of Arts and Letters. In 1994, he was stabbed in the neck outside his home. He is making a slow recovery and has not yet regained full use of his right arm. He and his wife have two daughters and live in Agouza, a suburb of Cairo. The meditations published in this issue of *Grand Street* are taken from his new book, *Echoes of an Autobiography*, which will be published by Doubleday in January 1997.

GIORGIO MANGANELLI (1922–90) was a writer, critic, translator, and professor of English at the University of Rome. He was one of the principal exponents of Gruppo 63, a movement of writers determined to break with the existing literature through formal experimentation. In addition to his strictly creative works, *Hilarotragoedia* (1964), *Centuria* (1979, reprinted by Adelphi Edizioni in 1995), and *Amore* (1981), he wrote several volumes of essays in which he reflected on writing and the figure of the writer. In his 1994 introduction to the French translation of *Centuria* (Christian Bourgois), Italo Calvino called Manganelli "a writer unlike any other, unmistakable in every sentence, an inexhaustible and irresistible inventor in the game of language and ideas," adding, "no one represents both tradition and the avant-garde more than he does. Tradition, because he always departs from a constructed and cultivated formal idea, in the syntax of his sentences and in the logic of his arguments and inventions. (One could say that his fundamental model is Swift, a Swift who lets his saturnalian humor and his obsessions go to the most extreme of consequences.) The avant-garde, because, in the use of thought and forms of expression, there is no challenge before which Manganelli will back down. The subversive charge of his writing exploded in the early 1960s, at a time when Italian literature was bubbling, like a huge cauldron, on the fire of a long-restrained desire for radical renewal."

ÉTIENNE-JULES MAREY was born in Beaune, France, in 1830. He wrote extensively on the circulation of the blood, cholera, terrestrial and aerial locomotion, and experimental physiology. His interest in studying the movement of the heart and lungs, the locomotion of animals and humans, and the kinetics of flow and turbulence in smoke and water led Marey to invent increasingly sophisticated recording devices. In 1882, he invented the chronophotographic gun, a camera shaped like a rifle with magazine plates that recorded photographs at the rate of twelve per second. His chronophotographs had an enormous influence on cubist and futurist artists. He died in 1904.

JACKIE McALLISTER, an artist and writer who lives in New York, recently contributed a catalogue note on the respective *weltanschung* of Baron Georges Cuvier and Walt Disney to a retrospective exhibition of artist Mark Dion's work to be held at the Ikon Gallery, Birmingham, England, in 1997.

CARLO MCCORMICK is a senior editor at *Paper* magazine. He was the cocurator, with John Carlin, of the 1993 exhibition *Comic Power* at Exit Art, New York. His writing has appeared in *Spin*, *High Times*, and *Artforum*.

RICHARD MISRACH has been working on his epic photographic project *Desert Cantos* for eighteen years. The Museum of Fine Arts, Houston, has organized a national traveling exhibit and publication of the first eighteen cantos entitled, *Crimes and Splendors: The Desert Cantos of Richard Misrach* (Bulfinch Press). Misrach has exhibited and published widely and is the recipient of four National Endowment for the Arts Fellowships and a Guggenheim Fellowship. He is represented by the Robert Mann Gallery and the Curt Marcus Gallery in New York. In his 1991 publication, *Bravo 20: The Bombing of the American West* (Johns Hopkins University Press), Misrach proposes the conversion of a military bombing range into a national park. The photographs reproduced in *Grand Street* are previously unpublished examples of the proposed site exhibits along the park's walking tour, "Boardwalk of the Bombs."

CHARLES RAY was born in Chicago in 1953. He currently lives in Los Angeles and teaches sculpture at the University of California at Los Angeles. Some of Ray's pieces, incorporating his own body, have blurred the line between sculpture and performance, and he often concerns himself, in both his figurative and nonfigurative work, with questions of vulnerability, perception, and subjective reality. In 1990, Ray had a one-person exhibition at the Newport Harbor Museum, Newport Beach. Another show, organized by the Rooseum Center for Contemporary Art, Malmö, traveled to the Institute of Contemporary Art, London, Kunsthalle Bern, and Kunsthalle Zurich. Ray's sculptures have been included in Documenta IX and the 1989 and 1993 Whitney Biennials. He is currently working with 16 and 35 mm film, and his movie, *FASHIONS Spring 1996*, was shown at the Hirshhorn Museum and Sculpture Garden, Washington, in 1996.

KENNETH ROSEN's latest collection is *No Snake, No Paradise* (Ascensius Press). In the spring of 1997, he will be the Balkan Scholar at the American University in Bulgaria, in Blagoevgrad, in the mountains south of Sofia. His poems will appear in *Chelsea*, *Ploughshares*, and *The Paris Review* in 1996 and 1997.

PETER SELLARS has directed more than a hundred productions in the United States and abroad. A graduate of Harvard University, he studied in Japan, China, and India before becoming the Artistic Director of the Boston Shakespeare Company. At twenty-six, he was appointed Director of the American National Theater at the Kennedy Center in Washington, D.C. A frequent guest at the Salzburg and Glyndebourne Festivals, he has specialized in contemporary operas, most notably Olivier Messiaen's St. François d'Assise and John Adams' and Alice Goodman's *Nixon in China* and *The Death of Klinghoffer*. Sellars was Artistic Director of the 1990 and 1993 Los Angeles Festivals and is a Professor of World Arts and Cultures at the University of California, Los Angeles. He is a recipient of the MacArthur

Prize Fellowship. His production of György Ligeti's *Le Grand Macabre* will premiere at the Salzburg Festival in the summer of 1997.

REBECCA SOLNIT is a critic and a writer whose works include *Savage Dreams: A Journey Into the Landscape Wars of the American West* and the forthcoming *A Book of Migrations* (Verso), as well as essays in many museum catalogues. She is on the board of Citizen Alert, Nevada's statewide environmental organization.

SPAIN (MANUEL RODRIGUEZ) was born in Buffalo, New York, in 1940, and attended the Silvermine Guild School of Art in New Canaan, Connecticut. His professional career started in 1967, when his work was published in the comic-strip tabloid, *Zodiac Mind Warp*. He began to draw comic strips and covers for *The East Village Other* in the same year, and in 1969, he became a regular contributor to *Zap Comix*. Spain is the creator of the *Trashman* and *Mean Bitch Thrills* comic books, and his book, *Trashman Lives!*, was published by Fantographics Books in 1990. He has illustrated a comic-book biography of Stalin, histories of the Spanish Civil War, the French Commune, and the 1887 general strike in the United States. In 1991, Spain designed sets for the movie *Cool World*. He is currently working on graphic novels based on the books *Nightmare Alley* by William Lindsay Gresham and *Boots* by Jim Madow. Spain lives and works in San Francisco.

JOHN SZARKOWSKI was born in Ashland, Wisconsin in 1925 and received his bachelor's degree from the University of Wisconsin in 1948. He taught at the Albright Art School, Buffalo, from 1951 to 1953, and sold several photographs to the Museum of Modern Art, New York, in 1952. After completing two books, *The Idea of Louis Sullivan* and *The Face of Minnesota*, and receiving two Guggenheim Fellowships for his photography, he became the director of the Department of Photography at the Museum of Modern Art, New York, in 1962. The major surveys he organized there include *The Photographer and the American Landscape* (1963), *Mirrors and Windows: American Photography Since 1960* (1978), and *Photography Until Now* (1990). The solo exhibitions he organized include *Cartier-Bresson* (1968), *Brassaï* (1968), *Walker Evans* (1971), *Diane Arbus* (1972), *William Eggleston* (1976), *Harry Callahan* (1976), the four-part *The Work of Atget* (1981–85), *Irving Penn* (1984), and *Garry Winogrand* (1988). Szarkowski has published several books, including *The Photographer's Eye* (1966), the highly acclaimed *Looking at Photographs: 100 Pictures from the Collection of the Museum of Modern Art* (1973), *Irving Penn* (1984), and *Winogrand: Figments from the Real World* (1988). He has taught at New York University, Harvard University, and Yale University, among other institutions, and served as the Andrew D. White Professor at Large at Cornell University from 1983 to 1989. He retired from the Museum of Modern Art in 1991 and was appointed Director Emeritus. His book, *Mr. Bristol's Barn: With Excerpts from Mr. Blinn's Diary*, will be published by Harry N. Abrams in 1997, and he is currently assembling a collection on American photography and land use for PaineWebber, New York.

JAMES TATE's *Selected Poems*, for which he received the Pulitzer Prize and the William Carlos Williams Award, was published in 1991. His latest volume of poems, *Worshipful Company of*

Fletchers (Ecco Press), won the National Book Award. In 1995, the Academy of American Poets presented Tate with the Tanning Prize for mastery in the art of poetry. A new book of poems, *Shroud of the Gnome*, is forthcoming in 1997.

GARRETT WHITE is a translator and film and art journalist who has written for the *Los Angeles Times*, *Premiere*, and *The Hollywood Reporter*. In 1995, the University of California Press published his introduction to and translation of *Hollywood: Mecca of the Movies* by French modernist poet and novelist Blaise Cendrars. *Why I Don't Wear a Watch* was originally published in Spanish in *Alfar* in May 1923, and will appear in White's translation, from Spanish and French, of *Christ With a Switchblade: Selected Writings of Luis Buñuel*, to be published by the University of California Press in the fall of 1997. He lives in Hollywood.

LAURA E. WOLFSON is a conference interpreter and literary translator from Russian. Her translation of *Dermo! The Real Russian Tolstoy Never Used* by Edward Topol will be published by Plume in August 1997. She lives in Philadelphia.

RUDOLPH WURLITZER is the author of four novels, a collection of essays, and many screenplays, including those for *Pat Garrett and Billy the Kid*, *Candy Mountain* (which he codirected), and *Little Buddha*. He has also written three short films and directed two, and has published stories and articles in *Esquire*, *The Atlantic Monthly*, *The New Republic*, *Rolling Stone*, *The Paris Review*, and *Harper's Bazaar*, among other publications.

Grand Street would like to thank Neil Printz for his contribution to *Art Charts: Timelines by Artists*.

Grand Street would like to thank the following for their generous support:
EDWARD LEE CAVE
CATHY AND STEPHEN GRAHAM
BARBARA HOWARD
DOMINIC MAN-KIT LAM
THE NEW YORK STATE COUNCIL ON THE ARTS
SUZANNE AND SANFORD J. SCHLESINGER
BETTY AND STANLEY K. SHEINBAUM

ILLUSTRATIONS

FRONT COVER
Charles Ray, *Clock Man*, 1978. Wood, paint, and artist as clockworks, 30 x 30 x 54 in. Photograph courtesy of the artist.

BACK COVER
Richard Misrach, *Unexploded Ordnance #3* (detail), 1986. Dye-coupler print, 30 x 38 in. Copyright © Richard Misrach. Copy print courtesy of the artist and Curt Marcus Gallery, New York.

TITLE PAGE
Charles Ray, *Clock Man*, 1978. Wood, paint, and artist as clockworks, 30 x 30 x 54 in. Photograph courtesy of the artist.

PP. 2–3 Étienne-Jules Marey, *Vol du Pélican (Flight of the Pelican)*, 1886. Chronophotograph on fixed plate. Courtesy of the Musée Marey, Beaune, France. Copy print copyright © J. C. Couval.

PP. 6–7 Film still from *Earthquake*. Copyright © 1974, Universal Pictures. Courtesy of Photofest. **P. 9, P. 12, P. 13, AND P. 15** Books from the author's collection. **P. 16** Film still from *War of the Worlds*. Copyright © 1953, Paramount Pictures Corporation. Courtesy of Photofest.

PP. 24–32 Charles Ray, 1953 . . . . Titles, dates, materials, and dimensions appear with images. Photographs courtesy of the artist.

PP. 57–66 Spain, *Libidinous Boulevards*. Titles and dates appear with illustrations. **P. 57** Detail from image on **P. 63**. **P. 58 AND P. 59** Ink and Zipatone on board. First page 14 9/16 x 11 3/4 in., second page 12 9/16 x 8 1/16 in. Published in Blab! #6, Summer 1991. **P. 60** Pencil and ink on board, 17 x 11 1/2 in. Unfinished cover for *The East Village Other*. **P. 61** Ink on board, original dimensions unknown. Published in *The East Village Other*, Vol. 2, No. 18, 1967. **P. 62** Ink and Zipatone on board, 9 7/8 x 12 in. Published in *Screw*. **P. 63** Ink and Zipatone on board, original dimensions unknown. Published in *Zap #11*, February 1985. **P. 64 AND P. 65** Ink on paper, each 10 x 7 3/4 in. **P. 66** Ink on board, 13 7/8 x 8 7/8 in. All images copyright © Spain Rodriguez. Courtesy of the artist and Psychedelic Solution Gallery, New York.

P. 70 Black-and-white photograph by François Lagarde. Copyright © François Lagarde. **P. 73** Colored ink on paper, 13 5/8 x 10 7/8 in. Courtesy of the Musée d'Art Moderne de la Ville de Paris. Photograph copyright © Photothèque des Musées de la Ville de Paris, by Spadem. **P. 74** Oil on canvas, four panels, each 19 11/16 x 24 in. Courtesy of the Musée d'Art Moderne de la Ville de Paris. Photograph copyright © Photothèque des Musées de la Ville de Paris, by Spadem. **P. 76** Photograph copyright © Paul Bowles. Copy print courtesy of The Paul Bowles Photographic Archive, The Swiss Foundation for Photography, Zurich. **P. 77** Watercolor on paper (paper circa 1810), 8 1/16 x 10 7/16 in. Courtesy of Jason Weiss. **P. 78** Photograph by Loomis Dean/Life Magazine. Copyright © Time, Inc.

P. 81 Lithograph, 17 x 11 in. Courtesy of the artist.
P. 82 Copyright © Estate of Ad Reinhardt/Artists' Rights Society (ARS), New York. First published in P.M., June 2, 1946. Reproduced from *The Art Comics and Satires of Ad Reinhardt* by Thomas Hess, Kunsthalle Düsseldorf/Marlborough Rome, 1975. Courtesy of

The Tony Smith Estate, New York. **P. 83** Silkscreen on canvas, 57 x 75 in. Edition of 12. Courtesy of Tony Shafrazi Gallery, New York. **P. 84–85** Black-and-white photocopy, dimensions variable. Copyright © Peter Nagy. Courtesy of the artist. **P. 86** Ink on five cloth napkins, dimensions variable. Courtesy of American Fine Arts, Inc., New York. **P. 87** Installation, 1991 Biennial, Whitney Museum of American Art, New York. Photograph courtesy of Doug Ashford. **P. 88** Enamel on vinyl, 72 x 56 1/2 in. Courtesy of Rosamund Felsen Gallery, Santa Monica.

PP. 89–97 CPLY, *The Evil I or The Story of My Life*. Excerpted from a book of the same title. One thousand copies printed. Privately published, New York, 1965. Copyright © The Estate of William N. Copley. Courtesy of the Nolan/Eckman Gallery, New York.

P. 102 Gelatin-silver print, 9 3/16 x 13 9/16 in. Collection of the Museum of Modern Art, New York. Gift of the photographer. Copyright © Magnum Photos, New York. Copy print courtesy of Magnum Photos, New York. **P. 106** Gelatin-silver print, 20 x 16 in. Copyright © 1972, The Estate of Diane Arbus. Copy print courtesy of the Robert Miller Gallery, New York. **P. 109** Gelatin-silver print from the series *Men of the 20th Century*, 11 1/2 x 9 3/16 in. Collection of the Museum of Modern Art, New York. Gift of the photographer. Copyright © August Sander Archive/SK Stiftung Kultur, Cologne; VG Bild-Kunst, Bonn. Copy print copyright © 1996, Museum of Modern Art, New York. **P. 110** Gelatin-silver print, 9 1/4 x 7 in. Collection of the Museum of Modern Art, New York. Purchase. Copyright © The Walker Evans Archive, The Metropolitan Museum of Art, New York. Copy print copyright © 1996, Museum of Modern Art, New York. **P. 115** Negative number 13610. Developed and proofed, but not printed in artist's lifetime. Copyright © The Estate of Garry Winogrand. Courtesy of Fraenkel Gallery, San Francisco. Copy print provided by the Center for Creative Photography, Tucson, Arizona. **P. 118** Gelatin-silver print, 9 1/2 x 7 1/4 in. Collection of the Museum of Modern Art, New York. Gift of John Runk Historical Collection, Stillwater, Minnesota. Copy print copyright © 1996, Museum of Modern Art, New York. **P. 120** Salt print from a glass negative, 10 3/8 x 14 in. Collection of the Museum of Modern Art, New York. Anonymous gift. Copy print copyright © 1996, Museum of Modern Art, New York.

PP. 123–130 Lynn Davis, *Stealing Time*. Eight gelatin silver prints. Titles and dates appear with images. **P. 123** Gold-toned, 19 x 19 in. **P. 124** Split-toned, 28 x 28 in. **P. 125** Selenium-toned, 19 x 19 in. **P. 126** 80%-toned, 28 x 28 in. **P. 127** Untoned, 28 x 28 in. **P. 128** Selenium-toned, 45 x 45 in. **P. 129** Selenium- and gold-toned, 28 x 28 in. **P. 130** Selenium-toned, 40 x 40 in. All images copyright © Lynn Davis. Copy prints courtesy of the artist and Houk Friedman Gallery, New York.

PP. 147–154 Ilya Kabakov, *The Boat of My Life*. Installed at the Salzburger Kunstverein, Austria, 1993. Le Magazin, Centre National d'Art Contemporain, Grenoble, France, 1994. Hillerau Foundation, Dresden, 1995. **P. 147** Drawing of the boat. **PP. 148–149 AND P. 154** Installation views, Salzburger Kunstverein, Austria. Photographs by Margherita Spiluttini. **P. 150** Perspective drawing, first concept. **P. 151 AND P. 152** Installation views, Hillerau Foundation, Dresden, Germany. Photographs by Emilia Kabakov. **P. 153** Construction plans for the boat. All images courtesy of the artist and Barbara Gladstone Gallery, New York. Collection of Ilya and Emilia Kabakov.

PP. 175–179 Étienne-Jules Marey, *Chronophotographs*. Titles and dates appear with images. Copy prints copyright © J. C. Couval. **P. 175** Chronophotograph on moving film. Detail from a poster made for the 1900 Exposition Universelle. **P. 176 AND P. 177** Black-and-white photographs. **PP. 178–179 (TOP)** Chronophotograph on moving film. **(BOTTOM)** Chronophotograph on fixed plate. Courtesy of the Musée Marey, Beaune, France.

PP. 195–202 Richard Misrach, *Bravo 20 Bombing Range, Nevada*. Seven dye-coupler prints. Titles and dates appear with images. Each print 30 x 38 in. All images copyright © Richard Misrach. Copy prints courtesy of the artist and Curt Marcus Gallery, New York.

PP. 206–207 Photograph by Enar Merkel Rydberg, for the Royal Swedish Opera, Stockholm. Copyright © 1978, Sverihes Radio Informationstjänsten, Stockholm. **PP. 211–214** Manuscript score of György Ligeti's *Le Grand Macabre*. Opera in two acts (four scenes), 1974–77, 1996. Libretto by Michael Meschke and György Ligeti, freely adapted from Michel de Ghelderade's play *La Balade du Grand Macabre*. Courtesy of the composer and Schott Musik International, Mainz/Germany.

Green Mountains Review

New Series   Spring/Summer 1996

Now in its tenth year of publication, the *Green Mountains Review* is an international journal, featuring the poems, stories, interviews and essays of both well-known writers and promising newcomers.

▼▼▼▼▼▼▼▼▼▼▼▼▼▼▼▼▼▼▼

Neil Shepard, Poetry Editor
Tony Whedon, Fiction Editor

$5/back issue
$7/current issue
$12/one-year subscription
$18/two-year subscription

"*GMR* is solid, handsome, comprehensive."   – *Literary Magazine Review*

"*GMR* ... has a strong record of quality work ... many exciting new voices."
     – *Library Journal*

"*GMR* possesses character, vision and energy...The production is beautiful and the space crisp and clear."   – *Magazine Rack*

CONTRIBUTORS

Julia Alvarez	Maxine Kumin	Lynne Sharon Schwartz
Hayden Carruth	Denise Levertov	Ntozake Shange
Stephen Dobyns	Larry Levis	Alix Kates Shulman
Mark Doty	Phillip Lopate	Gary Soto
Stephen Dunn	William Matthews	David St. John
Donald Hall	David Mura	Diane Wakoski
Lynda Hull	Naomi Shihab Nye	Derek Walcott
Galway Kinnell	Grace Paley	David Wojahn

Send check or money order to:
Green Mountains Review, Johnson State College, Johnson, Vermont 05656

Terra Nova: Nature & Culture

Edited by David Rothenberg
New Jersey Institute of Technology

"One of the Top Ten New Magazines of 1995"
— *Library Journal*

Terra Nova: Nature & Culture covers the ethical, metaphysical, and aesthetic aspects of the human relationship with nature. Dissolving the borders between the academic and the readable, **Terra Nova** seeks to revolutionize academic culture and show how environmental issues are part of the mainstream of cultural critique and commentary.

Terra Nova features incisive writing coupled with provocative reflection. Essays, fiction, poetry, art, philosophy, literature, history, anthropology, geography, environmental studies, psychology, politics, and activism all appear on its pages.

Terra Nova crosses the boundaries between disciplines to show how serious discussion of nature appears in many fields of creative inquiry.

Published quarterly in winter, spring, summer, and fall.
ISSN 1081-0749.

Television Planter: Andrew Wermuth

1997 Rates:
$34 individual, $98 institution, $24 Student & Retired. Outside U.S.A. add $16 postage and handling. Prepayment is required. Send check drawn against a U.S. bank in U.S. funds, American Express, MasterCard, or VISA number to:

MIT Press Journals
55 Hayward Street
Cambridge, MA 02142 USA
Tel: 617-253-2889
Fax: 617-577-1545
journals-orders@mit.edu
http://www-mitpress.mit.edu

THE

"Elegant, Fearless, Stunning!"
— A Reader

publishing daring new writers
and the more radical established writers

Kay Boyle, Mark Doty, Olga Broumas,
Marge Piercy, Ursula LeGuin, Li-Young Lee,
Kate Braverman, Isabel Allende, Chaim Potok,
Lily Tuck, Suzanne Gardinier, Eduardo Galeano,
Cristina Peri Rossi, and others.

Frederick Smock, Editor

Available At Bookstores
Or By Subscription ($15)

The American Voice
332 West Broadway
Louisville, Kentucky 40202
USA

BOOKFORUM

ARTFORUM'S SEMIANNUAL BOOK REVIEW

ELVIS **ART** BELLHOOKSDOUGLASCOUPLAND
WILLIAMBURROUGHSPETERSCHJELDAHL
VIVIENNEWESTWOODHAROLDBLOOMLINDA
NOCHLINLISALIEBMANNBARBIEPAULBOWLES
GARYINDIANA **AND** PETERPLAGENSDAVID
WOJNAROWICZANDYWARHOLARTHURDANTO
DIDEROTJOHNASHANDREWSOLOMONBRUCE
HAINLEYMANRAY **CULTURE** QUENTINTARANTINO
ANDRÉBRETONRICHARDPRINCENANGOLDIN
GUYTREBAYBIGHAIRE.H.GOMBRICHDIANE
ARBUSLOUISEBOURGEOIS **COVER** WAYNE
KOESTENBAUMCHUCKCLOSEBARBARA
KRUGERANDREWHULTKRANSDAVID
RIMANELLIDENNISCOOPERMAYA **TO** ANGELOU
YVE-ALAINBOISGEORGBASELITZARTHURELGORT
PHILIPTAAFFERICHARDAVEDONDAVEHICKEY
JASPERJOHNSDAVIDSALLEBRIAN **COVER** ENO

ARTFORUM

ON YOUR NEWSSTAND IN NOVEMBER '96
TO SUBSCRIBE CALL 1 800 966 2783
ADVERTISE DANIELLE McCONNELL 212 475 4000

New York University

Master of Arts Program in Creative Writing

PERMANENT FACULTY

E. L. Doctorow • Galway Kinnell • Paule Marshall • Sharon Olds

FACULTY FOR 1996–1997

POETRY

Deborah Digges
Marie Howe
Galway Kinnell
Philip Levine
William Matthews

FICTION

Nicholas Christopher
Edwidge Danticat
E. L. Doctorow
A. M. Homes

Raymond Kennedy
Paule Marshall
Dani Shapiro
Ted Solataroff

A number of fellowships and work-study grants are available.

Application deadline is January 4, 1997.*

For more information about our program,

call **(212) 998-8816** or write

New York University

Graduate School of Arts and Science

M.A. Program in Creative Writing

19 University Place, Room 200L

New York, NY 10003-4556

*Applications for the fall 1997 semester will be accepted if they are received by Graduate Enrollment Services, Graduate School of Arts and Science, New York University, P.O. Box 907, New York, NY 10276-0907, on or before Febuary 4, 1997.

New York University is an affirmative action/equal opportunity institution.

A MAJOR LITERARY EVENT

Introductions by an American literary who's who, including Toni Morrison, Kurt Vonnegut, E.L. Doctorow, Arthur Miller, Willie Morris, and many other eminent writers and scholars

Facsimiles of the first American editions, including many rare or long out-of-print volumes

All the original illustrations, some by Twain himself, many not seen for over a century

A spectacular price, for a limited time only only $295 for 29 volumes, through January 31st, 1997

The twenty-nine volume OXFORD *Mark Twain*

At better bookstores. Or charge 1-800-451-7556 (M-F, 9-5 EST)
OXFORD UNIVERSITY PRESS www.oup-usa.org

Explore the Prehistoric Cave Art of the Dordogne

with **Clayton Eshleman**

American Poet and winner of the National Book Award

 "No one knows the caves and the archaic regions of the soul in our times as does Clayton Eshleman. He is a guide among the animal images of the primordial psyche." — *James Hillman*

&

Special Guest Lecturers

Anne Waldman & Andrew Schelling

Award winning Poets and Directors at the Naropa Institute

A rare travel-study opportunity for writers, artists, or anyone who wants to explore this magical region of France, its caves and regional specialties.

May 27–June 10, 1997

(4 days in Paris, 10 days in Les Eyzies)
Tentative Cost: $3,500 plus airfare

For information, call Academic Programs Abroad at
800/777-3541 or 313/487-2424.
E-mail: programs.abroad@emich.edu
Early registration is encouraged - space is limited.

EASTERN MICHIGAN UNIVERSITY.

STATEMENT OF OWNERSHIP

Statement of Ownership, Management, and Circulation (Act of August 12, 1970: Section 3685, Title 39. United States Code). No. 1. Publication Title: Grand Street. No. 2. Publication Number: 692-070. No. 3. Filing Date: October 1, 1996. No. 4. Issue Frequency: Quarterly. No. 5. Number of Issues Published Annually: 4. No. 6. Annual Subscription Price: $40. No. 7. Complete Mailing Address of Known Office of Publication: 131 Varick Street, Room 906, New York, NY 10013. No. 8. Complete Mailing Address of Headquarters or General Business Office of Publisher: 131 Varick Street, Room 906, New York, NY 10013. No. 9. Name and Address of Publishers: Jean Stein and Torsten Wiesel, Grand Street, 131 Varick Street, Room 906, New York, NY 10013. Name and Address of Editor: Jean Stein, Grand Street, 131 Varick Street, New York, NY 10013. Name and Address of Managing Editor: Deborah Treisman, Grand Street, 131 Varick Street, Room 906, New York, NY 10013. No. 10. Name and Address of Owner: New York Foundation for the Arts, 155 Avenue of the Americas, New York, NY 10013. No. 11. Known Bondholders, Mortgagees, and Other Security Holders: None. No. 12. Tax Status: Has Not Changed During Preceding 12 Months. No. 13. Publication Title: Grand Street. No. 14. Issue Date for Circulation Data Below: September 1996. No. 15. Extent and Nature of Circulation. Average No. of Copies of Each Issue During Preceding 12 Months.

No. A. Total Number of Copies: 8,000. No. B. Paid and/or Requested Circulation (1) Sales Through Dealers and Carriers, Street Vendors, and Counter Sales: 4,500. (2) Paid or Requested Mail Subscriptions: 1,600. No. C. Total Paid and/or Requested Circulation: 6,100. No. D. Free Distribution by Mail: 350. No. E. Free Distribution Outside the Mail: 50. No. F. Total Free Distribution: 400. No. G. Total Distribution: 6,500. No. H. Copies Not Distributed (1) Office Use, Leftovers, Spoiled: 1,000. (2) Returns from News Agents: 500. No. I. Total: 8,000. Percent Paid and/or Requested Circulation: 94. Actual No. of Copies of Single Issue Published Nearest to Filing Date. No. A. Total Number of Copies: 8,000. No. B. Paid and/or Requested Circulation (1) Sales Through Dealers and Carriers, Street Vendors, and Counter Sales: 4,505. (2) Paid or Requested Mail Subscriptions: 1,613. No. C. Total Paid and/or Requested Circulation: 6,118. No. D. Free Distribution by Mail: 375. No. E. Free Distribution Outside the Mail: 30. No. F. Total Free Distribution: 405. No. G. Total Distribution: 6,523. No. H. Copies Not Distributed (1) Office Use, Leftovers, Spoiled: 1,000. (2) Returns from News Agents: 477. No. I. Total: 8,000. Percent Paid and/or Requested Circulation: 94. No. 17. I certify that all information furnished above is true and complete. Deborah Treisman, Managing Editor.

GRAND STREET
BACK ISSUES
AN ESSENTIAL COLLECTION

36 Edward Said on Jean Genet; Terry Southern & Dennis Hopper on Larry Flynt
STORIES: Elizabeth Bishop, William T. Vollmann; PORTFOLIOS: William Eggleston, Saul Steinberg; POEMS: John Ashbery, Bei Dao.

37 William S. Burroughs on guns; John Kenneth Galbraith on JFK's election
STORIES: Pierrette Fleutiaux, Eduardo Galeano; PORTFOLIOS: *Blackboard Equations*, John McIntosh; POEMS: Clark Coolidge, Suzanne Gardinier.

38 Kazuo Ishiguro & Kenzaburo Oe on Japanese literature; Julio Cortázar's HOPSCOTCH: A Lost Chapter
STORIES: Fernando Pessoa, Ben Sonnenberg; PORTFOLIOS: Linda Connor, Robert Rauschenberg; POEMS: Jimmy Santiago Baca, Charles Wright.

39 Nadine Gordimer: SAFE HOUSES; James Miller on Michel Foucault
STORIES: Hervé Guibert, Dubravka Ugrešić; PORTFOLIOS: *Homicide: Bugsy Siegel*, Mark di Suvero; POEMS: Amiri Baraka, Michael Palmer.

40 Gary Giddins on Dizzy Gillespie; Toni Morrison on race and literature
STORIES: Yehudit Katzir, Marcel Proust; PORTFOLIOS: Gretchen Bender, Brice Marden; POEMS: Arkadii Dragomoshchenko, Tom Paulin.

AVAILABLE NOW

41 Nina Berberova on the Turgenev Library; Mary-Claire King on tracing "the disappeared"
STORIES: Ben Okri, Kurt Schwitters; PORTFOLIOS: Louise Bourgeois, Jean Tinguely; POEMS: Rae Armantrout, Eugenio Montale.

42 David Foster Wallace: THREE PROTRUSIONS; Henry Green: An unfinished novel
STORIES: Félix de Azúa, Eduardo Galeano; PORTFOLIOS: Sherrie Levine, Ariane Mnouchkine & Ingmar Bergman—two productions of Euripides; POEMS: Jorie Graham, Gary Snyder.

43 Jamaica Kincaid on the biography of a dress; Stephen Trombley on designing death machines
STORIES: Victor Erofeyev, Christa Wolf; PORTFOLIOS: Joseph Cornell, Sue Williams; POEMS: Robert Creeley, Kabir.

44 Martin Duberman on Stonewall; Andrew Kopkind: Slacking Toward Bethlehem
STORIES: Georges Perec, Edmund White; PORTFOLIOS: William Christenberry, Fred Wilson; POEMS: Lyn Hejinian, Sharon Olds.

45 John Cage: Correspondence; Roberto Lovato: Down and Out in Central L.A.
STORIES: David Gates, Duong Thu Huong; PORTFOLIOS: Ecke Bonk, Gerhard Richter; POEMS: A. R. Ammons, C. H. Sisson.

46 William T. Vollmann on the Navajo-Hopi Land Dispute; Ice-T, Easy-E: L.A. rappers get open with Brian Cross
STORIES: David Foster Wallace, Italo Calvino; PORTFOLIOS: Nancy Rubins, Dennis Balk; POEMS: Michael Palmer, Martial.

ORDER WHILE THEY LAST.
CALL 1-800-807-6548

Please send name, address, issue number(s), and quantity. American Express, Mastercard, and Visa accepted; please send credit card number and expiration date. Back issues are $15 each ($18.00 overseas and Canada), including postage and handling, payable in U.S. dollars. Address orders to GRAND STREET, Back Issues, 131 Varick Street, Suite 906, New York, NY 10

47
Louis Althusser's ZONES OF DARKNESS; Edward W. Said on intellectual exile
STORIES: Jean Genet, Junichiro Tanizaki; PORTFOLIOS: Barbara Bloom, Julio Galán; POEMS: John Ashbery, Ovid.

OBLIVION **48**
William T. Vollmann: UNDER THE GRASS; Kip S. Thorne on black holes
STORIES: Heinrich Böll, Charles Palliser; PORTFOLIOS: Saul Steinberg, Lawrence Weiner; POEMS: Mahmoud Darwish, Antonin Artaud.

HOLLYWOOD **49**
Dennis Hopper interviews Quentin Tarantino; Terry Southern on the making of DR. STRANGELOVE
STORIES: Paul Auster, Peter Handke; PORTFOLIOS: Edward Ruscha, William Eggleston; POEMS: John Ashbery, James Laughlin.

MODELS **50**
Alexander Cockburn & Noam Chomsky on models in nature; Graham Greene's dream diary
STORIES: Cees Nooteboom, Rosario Castellanos; PORTFOLIOS: Paul McCarthy, Katharina Sieverding; POEMS: Nicholas Christopher, Robert Kelly.

NEW YORK **51**
Terry Williams on life in the tunnels under NYC; William S. Burroughs: MY EDUCATION
STORIES: William T. Vollmann, Orhan Pamuk; PORTFOLIOS: Richard Prince, David Hammons; POEMS: Hilda Morley, Charles Simic.

GAMES **52**
David Mamet: THE ROOM; Paul Virilio on cybersex and virtual reality
STORIES: Brooks Hansen, Walter Benjamin; PORTFOLIOS: Robert Williams, Chris Burden; POEMS: Miroslav Holub, Fanny Howe.

FETISHES **53**
John Waters exposes his film fetishes; Samuel Beckett's ELEUTHÉRIA
STORIES: Georges Bataille, Colum McCann; PORTFOLIOS: Helmut Newton, Yayoi Kusama; POEMS: Taslima Nasrin, Simon Armitage.

SPACE **54**
Born in Prison: an inmate survives the box; Jasper Johns's GALAXY WORKS
STORIES: Vladimir Nabokov, Irvine Welsh; PORTFOLIOS: Vito Acconci, James Turrell; POEMS: W. S. Merwin, John Ashbery.

EGOS **55**
Julian Schnabel: THE CONVERSION OF ST. PAOLO MALFI; Suzan-Lori Parks on Josephine Baker
STORIES: Kenzaburo Oe, David Foster Wallace; PORTFOLIOS: Dennis Hopper, Brigid Berlin's Cock Book; POEMS: Amiri Baraka, Susie Mee.

DREAMS **56**
Edward Ruscha: HOLLYWOOD BOULEVARD; Terry Southern and Other Tastes
STORIES: William T. Vollmann, Lydia Davis; PORTFOLIOS: Jim Shaw, ADOBE LA; POEMS: Bernadette Mayer, Saúl Yurkievich.

DIRT **57**
John Waters & Mike Kelley: THE DIRTY BOYS; Rem Koolhaas on 42nd Street
STORIES: Mohammed Dib, Sandra Cisneros; PORTFOLIOS: Langdon Clay, Alexis Rockman; POEMS: Robert Creeley, Thomas Sayers Ellis.

DISGUISES **58**
Anjelica Huston on life behind the camera; D. Carleton Gajdusek: THE NEW GUINEA FIELD JOURNALS
STORIES: Victor Pelevin, Arno Schmidt; PORTFOLIOS: Hannah Höch, Kara Walker; POEMS: Vittorio Sereni, Marjorie Welish.

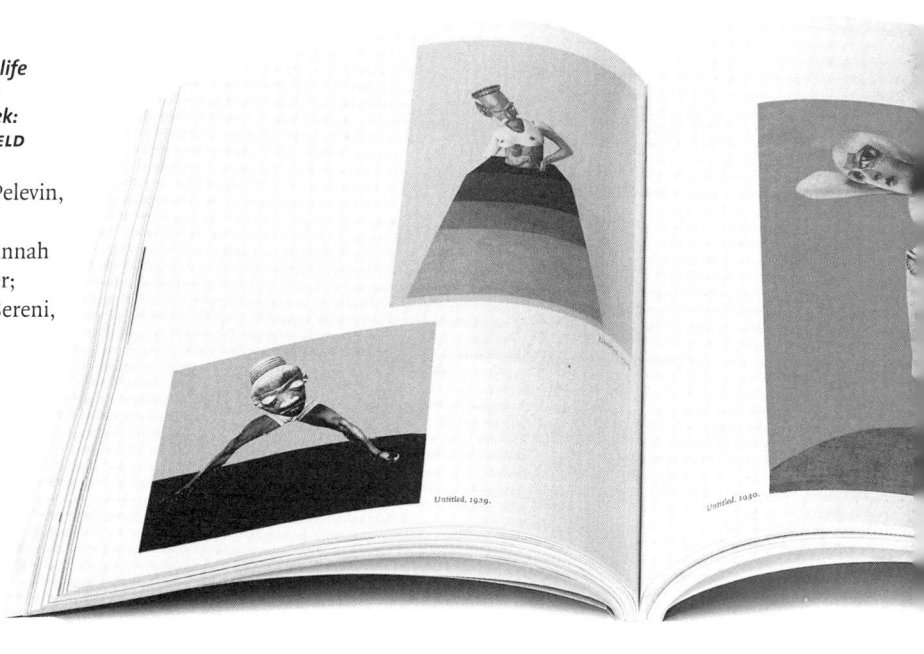

Some of the bookstores where you can find
GRAND STREET

Magpie Magazine Gallery, Vancouver, CANADA

Newsstand, Bellingham, WA
Bailey Coy Books, Seattle, WA
Hideki Ohmori, Seattle, WA

Looking Glass Bookstore, Portland, OR
Powell's Books, Portland, OR
Reading Frenzy, Portland, OR

...On Sundays, Tokyo, JAPAN

Baxter's Books, Minneapolis, MN
Minnesota Book Center, Minneapolis, MN
University of Minnesota Bookstore, Minneapolis, MN
Walker Art Center Bookshop, Minneapolis, MN
Hungry Mind Bookstore, St. Paul, MN
Odegard Books, St. Paul, MN

ASUC Bookstore, Berkeley, CA
Black Oak Books, Berkeley, CA
Cody's Books, Berkeley, CA
Bookstore Fiona, Carson, CA
Huntley Bookstore, Claremont, CA
Book Soup, Hollywood, CA
University Bookstore, Irvine, CA
Museum of Contemporary Art, La Jolla, CA
UCSD Bookstore, La Jolla, CA
A.R.T. Press, Los Angeles, CA
Museum of Contemporary Art, Los Angeles, CA
Occidental College Bookstore, Los Angeles, CA
Sun & Moon Press Bookstore, Los Angeles, CA
UCLA/Armand Hammer Museum, Los Angeles, CA
Stanford Bookstore, Newark, CA
Diesel, A Bookstore, Oakland, CA
Blue Door Bookstore, San Diego, CA
The Booksmith, San Francisco, CA
City Lights, San Francisco, CA
Green Apple Books, San Francisco, CA
Modern Times Bookstore, San Francisco, CA
San Francisco Camerawork, San Francisco, CA
Logos, Santa Cruz, CA
Arcana, Santa Monica, CA
Midnight Special Bookstore, Santa Monica, CA
Reader's Books, Sonoma, CA
Small World Books, Venice, CA
Ventura Bookstore, Ventura, CA

Asun Bookstore, Reno, NV

Sam Weller's Zion Bookstore, Salt Lake City, UT

Bookman's, Tucson, AZ

Chinook Bookshop, Colorado Springs, CO
The Bookies, Denver, CO
Newsstand Cafe, Denver, CO
Tattered Cover Bookstore, Denver, CO
Stone Lion Bookstore, Fort Collins, CO

Nebraska Bookstore, Lincoln, N

Kansas Union Bookstore, Lawrence, KS
Terra Nova Bookstore, Lawrence, KS

Bookworks, Albuquerque, NM
Page One Bookstore, Albuquerque, NM
Salt of the Earth, Albuquerque, NM
Cafe Allegro, Los Alamos, NM
Collected Works, Santa Fe, NM

Honolulu Book Shop, Honolulu, HI

Page One, SINGAPORE

Book People, Austin, TX
Bookstop, Austin, TX
University Co-op Society, Austin, TX
McKinney Avenue Contemporary Gift Shop, Dallas,
Bookstop, Houston, TX
Brazos Bookstore, Houston, TX
Contemporary Arts Museum Shop, Houston, TX
Diversebooks, Houston, TX
Menil Collection Bookstore, Houston, TX
Museum of Fine Arts, Houston, TX
Texas Gallery, Houston, TX
Bookstop, Plano, TX

Bookland of Brunswick, Brunswick, ME
University of Maine Bookstore, Orono, ME
Books Etc., Portland, ME
Raffles Cafe Bookstore, Portland, ME

Pages, Toronto, CANADA

Dartmouth Bookstore, Hanover, NH
Toadstool Bookshop, Peterborough, NH

Northshire Books, Manchester, VT

Wootton's Books, Amherst, MA
Boston University Bookstore, Boston, MA
Harvard Book Store, Cambridge, MA
M.I.T. Press Bookstore, Cambridge, MA
Cisco Harland Books, Marlborough, MA
Broadside Bookshop, Northampton, MA
Provincetown Bookshop, Provincetown, MA
Water Street Books, Williamstown, MA

Main Street News, Ann Arbor, MI
Shaman Drum Bookshop, Ann Arbor, MI
Cranbrook Art Museum Books, Bloomfield Hills, MI
Book Beat, Oak Park, MI

Afterwords, Milwaukee, WI

Accident or Design, Providence, RI
Brown University Bookstore, Providence, RI
College Hill Store, Providence, RI

Farley's Bookshop, New Hope, PA
Faber Books, Philadelphia, PA
Waterstone's Booksellers, Philadelphia, PA
Andy Warhol Museum, Pittsburgh, PA
Encore Books, Mechanicsburg, PA
Encore Books, State College, PA

Yale Cooperative, New Haven, CT
UConn Co-op, Storrs, CT

Rosetta News, Carbondale, IL
Pages for All Ages, Champaign, IL
Mayuba Bookstore, Chicago, IL
Museum of Contemporary Art, Chicago, IL
Seminary Co-op Bookstore, Chicago, IL

Indiana University Bookstore, Bloomington, IN

UC Bookstore, Cincinnati, OH
Bank News, Cleveland, OH
Ohio State University Bookstore, Columbus, OH
Student Book Exchange, Columbus, OH
Books & Co., Dayton, OH
Kenyon College Bookstore, Gambier, OH
Oberlin Consumers Cooperative, Oberlin, OH

Encore Books, Princeton, NJ
Micawber Books, Princeton, NJ

Community Bookstore, Brooklyn, NY
Talking Leaves, Buffalo, NY
Colgate University Bookstore, Hamilton, NY
Book Revue, Huntington, NY
The Bookery, Ithaca, NY
A Different Light, New York, NY
Art Market, New York, NY
B. Dalton, New York, NY
Books & Co., New York, NY
Coliseum Books, New York, NY
Collegiate Booksellers, New York, NY
Doubleday Bookshops, New York, NY
Exit Art/First World Store, New York, NY
Gold Kiosk, New York, NY
Gotham Book Mart, New York, NY
Museum of Modern Art Bookstore, New York, NY
New York University Book Center, New York, NY
Rizzoli Bookstores, New York, NY
St. Mark's Bookshop, New York, NY
Shakespeare & Co., New York, NY
Spring Street Books, New York, NY
Wendell's Books, New York, NY
Whitney Museum of Modern Art, New York, NY
Syracuse University Bookstore, Syracuse, NY

Iowa Book & Supply, Iowa City, IA
Prairie Lights, Iowa City, IA
University Bookstore, Iowa City, IA

Box of Rocks, Bowling Green, KY
Carmichael's, Louisville, KY

Louie's Bookstore Cafe, Baltimore, MD

Xanadu Bookstore, Memphis, TN

Studio Art Shop, Charlottesville, VA
Williams Corner, Charlottesville, VA

Bridge Street Books, Washington, DC
Chapters, Washington, DC
Franz Bader Bookstore, Washington, DC
Olsson's, Washington, DC
Politics & Prose, Washington, DC

Library Ltd., Clayton, MO
Whistler's Books, Kansas City, MO
Left Bank Books, St. Louis, MO

Paper Skyscraper, Charlotte, NC
Regulator Bookshop, Durham, NC

Chapter Two Bookstore, Charleston, SC
Intermezzo, Columbia, SC
Open Book, Greenville, SC

Square Books, Oxford, MS

Oxford Bookstore, Atlanta, GA

Books & Books, Coral Gables, FL
Goerings Book Center, Gainesville, FL
Bookstop, Miami, FL
Rex Art, Miami, FL
Inkwood Books, Tampa, FL

Lenny's News, New Orleans, LA

And at selected Barnes & Noble and Bookstar bookstores nationwide.

$22.95 • 288 pages • ISBN 1-55970-365-2

famine
A NOVEL BY TODD KOMARNICKI

"Todd Komarnicki's powerful, remarkable new novel, *famine*, more than fulfills the promise of his daring first, *Free*." — George Plimpton

"A tough, fast-paced narrative in the greatest tradition of *noir*, with perfect-pitch dialogue, an unerring sense of place, and forensic lyricism." — Jack Womack

"Powerful and pure enough to make you cry for what shouldn't be so true." — Andrew Vachss

$19.95 • 196 pages • ISBN 1-55970-368-7

"One of the most compelling novelists now writing in any language." — *Wall Street Journal*

"Kadare is a supreme fictional interpreter of the psychology and physiognomy of oppression." — *Los Angeles Times Book Review*

"[Kadare's] work...powerfully depicts a bleak world in which life is marked by alienation and dread." — *New York Times Book Review*

ISMAIL KADARE
THE THREE-ARCHED BRIDGE
A NOVEL

ARCADE FICTION 1997

$25.95 • 512 pages • ISBN 1-55970-358-X

The DEATH AND LIFE OF MIGUEL DE CERVANTES

"An exuberant fabulist romp...this exemplary fiction matches incredible fact with ingenious storytelling." — *Publishers Weekly*, starred review

"It takes a certain amount of guts to write a picaresque novel about one of the the creators of the form. But Marlowe does so brilliantly.... A spirited and witty tale for a sophisticated readership." — *Booklist*, starred review

A NOVEL BY STEPHEN MARLOWE

$19.95 • 224 pages • ISBN 1-55970-364-4

Private Confessions
A NOVEL BY INGMAR BERGMAN

PRAISE FOR *SUNDAY'S CHILDREN*
A *New York Times* Notable Book of 1994
Elegant, honest, and emotionally brutal...a perfectly shaped treasure that stands among the finest work of Mr. Bergman's career."
— Caryn James, *New York Times*

ARCADE PUBLISHING NEW YORK
AVAILABLE AT BOOKSTORES EVERYWHERE OR DIRECTLY FROM LITTLE, BROWN & COMPANY
1 800 759 0190 • www.pathfinder.com/twep/bookworks